Terrible Innocence

General William Tecumseh Sherman. He became a legend by leading 60,000 midwestern farmboys on a rampage through Georgia and the Carolinas during the Civil War. A hero to some, a devil to others, he was a complex individual who escaped easy characterization.

Terrible Innocence

General Sherman at War

Mark Coburn

Maps by Page Lindsey

HIPPOCRENE BOOKS
New York

Acknowledgments

I wish I could say that anything good in this book is my doing, while those who helped me are to blame for every flub and infelicity. But it's not true.

My warm thanks to everyone who critiqued part of the manuscript: Jerry Coburn, Pete Peterson, John Sanders, Sylvia Sullivan, Shaila Van Sickle.

No words can express my gratitude to those who read a big chunk, and then re-enlisted to march through the whole thing: Red Bird, Larry Hartsfield, Doreen Mehs, David Petersen.

Very special thanks to Page Lindsey, who not only drew the maps but adjusted her busy schedule to mine.

Lastly, a scritch behind the ears for my dog Matilda, who squandered endless hours under a computer desk when she had better things to do. Matilda could have licked Sherman's whole army, wagging her tail the while.

For information, address
Hippocrene Books, Inc.
171 Madison Ave.
New York, NY 10016

Library of Congress Cataloging-in-Publication Data
Coburn, Mark.
        Terrible innocence : General Sherman at war / Mark Coburn.
            p.   cm.
        Includes bibliographical references and index.
        ISBN 0-7818-0156-7 :
            1. Sherman, William T. (William Tecumseh), 1820-1891.
2.United States—History—Civil War, 1861-1865—Campaigns. I. Title.
E467.1.S55C63 1993   93-18327
973.7'092—dc20   CIP

Printed in the United States of America.

For Doreen,
who put up with it

Contents

Maps

. . . because it was that innocence again, that innocence which believed that the ingredients of morality were like the ingredients of pie or cake and once you had measured them and balanced them and mixed them and put them into the oven it was all finished and nothing but pie or cake could ever come out.

—William Faulkner, *Absalom, Absalom!*

No Horns, No Tail, No Brimstone

General Sherman was like Attila the Hun, but less cuddly. Such is the view imbedded in American folklore. People who can't tell you who won at Gettysburg know what they think of the barbarian who ravaged Atlanta and tormented Vivien Leigh.

Beyond respect for truth and common sense, there's a better reason not to reduce Sherman and his army to cartoon monsters. It's the idea Hannah Arendt termed "the banality of evil": In Eichmann in Jerusalem, Arendt outraged many by suggesting that Adolf Eichmann was less a fiend than a drab businessman who tried to do his job efficiently.

We don't want horror to come that close to home. We need Nazis to be madmen for the same self-protective reason that we need to call so many forms of human nastiness "inhuman."

It's important to see Sherman and his marchers as *people*. It *matters* that Georgia and the Carolinas were devastated not by Lucifer or the Bogeyman, but by an intelligent, often witty general. It matters that those Sherman led were not devils out of the pit, but sixty thousand young fellows out of Wisconsin and Indiana and upstate New York. If you and I had been Illinois farmboys in 1864, we might have been there in Georgia with them—burning barns, stealing a war widow's last cow, carrying off pretty mulatto girls, raising merry hell. And that's why it matters.

Sherman was brilliant and pigheaded, farsighted and foolish, cruel and tender, a friendly soul and a porcupine, prophetic and naive, a lousy politician and a splendid writer. And more. Whittle him down to fit some pet interpretation, and he'll keep squiggling away. I've tried to capture some of that human diversity.

Above all, I've tried to avoid writing a moral pageant. Better to see Sherman for the complex creature he was than to fling rocks or gold stars at his ghost. Though some have yet to hear the news, the Civil War is over; neither damning nor defending Sherman will un-burn a single house in Columbia.

It seems useful to mention a few biases at the start—if only to keep them from sneaking in unannounced. My negative views are self-explanatory and obvious: the burning of cities doesn't charm me. I don't care much for pillaging, terrorizing women and children, or slaughtering horses and dogs. I tire of Sherman's racism, his occasional whining and his frequent ranting. His vindictiveness against the South appalls me. I also loathe his habit of justifying mayhem in pompous Biblical cadences—as if he confused himself with Jeremiah.

While all of that might go unsaid, my pro-Sherman sympathies need to be spelled out.

First, I admire his vitality. Clear down to his corns he was what his era called a "live man." The force and energy of Cump Sherman's personality sparkle through everything he wrote and spill from everyone's reminiscences. Many plod through their existence; Sherman lived.

Second is a notion I first came upon in Lloyd Lewis's biography of Sherman:

> In the later and more spectacular years of the war Grant had

won his victories by steady, remorseless slaughter. Sherman had won by avoiding blood-shed and by destroying property instead. Northerners hated the Confederate raider Morgan, who had only burned their buildings, far more than they hated Lee, who had killed bluecoats by tens of thousands. Both sections came to praise if not revere those enemies who had destroyed human life and to execrate those enemies who had destroyed barns.

Lewis oversimplifies. And yet, the core of truth haunts me. Sherman's men loved him because they knew he would not sacrifice them needlessly. Like his great opponent, Confederate General Joseph Johnston, Sherman had no lust for battle. He tore up railroads. He burned cities. He drove people from their homes. But he spared lives. After all the qualifications have been added, Lewis is still right. The true butcher in Georgia was Confederate General John Bell Hood.

Third, I can't forget that most of the men and women in Sherman's path were overjoyed to see him coming.

Now it's my turn to oversimplify. I do so to highlight a difficulty we face in seeing the past. It's harder than we care to admit to perceive slaves as individual "men and women." Where racism doesn't cloud our vision, a problem of historiography often does—compulsory illiteracy masks each slave's uniqueness. Because Sherman's white victims recorded their outrage and despair so powerfully, we acknowledge them as people. But we see slaves *en masse*, and usually hear them only as a chorus.

When a slave's voice does come down to us, it's through a white person's letters or diary—often the diary of one of Sherman's men. But whether Northern or Southern, pro- or anti-slavery, the recorder generally saw blacks as childish creatures, marginally human and scarcely individuals.

A slave stood by the road as one of Sherman's corps rambled by. Suddenly she threw her arms around a Michigan drummer boy, and cried out, "They tole us this here army was debbils from hell, but praise the Lord, it's the Lord's own babes and sucklings!"

Even there, for all her eloquence, spellings like "debbils" give the speaker a whiff of the minstrel show, and thereby diminish her moral weight.

Sherman's was no army of liberation; many slaves suffered or died because they followed the Yankees. But here again, after all the qualifications have been noted the core idea abides: each slave who helped foragers find buried spoons was as unique a person as each plantation mistress who hid them. For the black majority, Sherman's divisions were the legions of God.

Last, Sherman did not pillage in a vacuum. I won't swallow the folk history that damns him as Supreme Vandal while portraying Lincoln wringing his gentle hands over wartime horrors. The only qualms Lincoln voiced were fears for the vandals' safety. Grant supported the devastation. So did the cabinet. So did Army Chief-of-Staff Henry Halleck. ("Should you capture Charleston," Halleck wrote to Sherman, "I hope that by *some accident* the place may be destroyed, and if a little salt should be sown upon its site, it may prevent the growth of future crops of nullification and secession.") The North greeted the army's safe arrival in Savannah with celebrations and thanks-giving sermons. The song "Marching through Georgia" appeared *after* the march, to cash in on the rejoicing.

Sherman led the army, gave the orders, commanded or condoned the havoc. But he was agent as well as instigator. "The Union" burned Atlanta in the same sense that "Japan" bombed Pearl Harbor.

* * *

In calling this a "personality sketch," I mean a book whose central question is the one we ask about an interesting stranger: What is he like? I've tried to steer my course between the mountain of biography and the bottomless gulf of Civil War history, relying on each for what it has to tell about the man himself. The reader who craves exhaustive coverage of Sherman's campaigns had best seek exhaustion elsewhere.

I focus on one crucial year—May 1864 to April 1865. During those twelve months Sherman fought his way down to Atlanta, chased Hood around northern Georgia, marched to the sea and through the Carolinas. His fame or infamy rests on that busy interval.

Chapter 1 summarizes Sherman's pre-war life, Chapters 2 and 3 overview his wartime activities before the key year, and the Epilogue glances at his post-war days. In all these chapters, I have emphasized what seemed useful for understanding Sherman in 1864 and 1865, and largely ignored everything else.

Chapter 1

Besieged at Lancaster

On his fortieth birthday—February 8, 1860—William Tecumseh Sherman lived three miles outside Alexandria, Louisiana, and commanded fifty-one schoolboys.

The Louisiana State Seminary of Learning and Military Academy had opened that January, with more words in its name than faculty on its staff. Before the month ended Sherman had booted out "five noisy, insubordinate boys"— three of them over an unpleasantness involving knives. Thirty others had threatened to leave.

When not squelching rumbles, President Sherman taught American history and geography, subbed for absent teachers and served as dean, accountant, cashier, fund raiser and admissions staff.

For the nonce, he lodged with his faculty in the only classroom building, but by fall he would have a house. (The president was also construction foreman.) Then his wife would come down from Ohio, bringing their five young children. Sherman brooded over how to persuade her that, with white servants unavailable, they would have to buy slaves.

His lofty position had its drawbacks. The parents of the expelled boys were after his hide. The state legislature was stingy to the budding academy. And in 1860, it did not much help a man in Louisiana to be the brother of John Sherman, that much-quoted abolitionist congressman.

When Sherman wrote to his wife just after his milestone birthday, he sounded resigned and weary—"I have now crossed the line and suppose I must rest satisfied with the title of the 'Old Man,' the 'cross old schoolmaster,' but time won't wait and we must rush on in the race to eternity."

He saw no rich promise for the years ahead. And surely his first four decades had done little enough to delight him. Fate had dealt him good cards—the more reason to regret how badly the game had turned out.

* * *

In 1811, a lawyer named Charles Sherman, with his wife and baby, left Connecticut to join the western migration. Charles and Mary chose Lancaster, a prospering Ohio village. There Charles set up practice, and he and Mary set about filling the Hockhocking Valley with little Shermans.

Four years later, the town gained another young lawyer—a driven, self-educated man named Thomas Ewing. Sherman befriended the new arrival. Charles and Thomas rode the legal circuit together, sharing beds in the dreadful taverns of what had lately been frontier hamlets.

On February 8, 1820, came Tecumseh, the sixth of eleven Sherman babies. John came three years later.

The year after Tecumseh's birth, his father was appointed to the Ohio Supreme Court. Thomas Ewing was also a rising man; by the mid-1820s he had gained national renown in Whig political circles. Ewing's fortunes grew with his fame— he and his wife Maria erected one of Lancaster's finest dwellings. Charles lacked his friend's fiscal talents, and the Shermans continued to live simply, half a block down the hill.

In 1829, Charles Sherman suddenly took ill and died, leaving Mary with nine children still at home.

Gathering Sherman's friends and relatives, Thomas Ewing raised enough cash to cancel the mortgage. Then he and

Maria approached the widow and offered to add one of her boys to their own growing brood. Family lore says it was the oldest daughter who blurted, "Take Cump, the red-haired one. He's the smartest."

For nine-year-old Tecumseh, the change in households apparently came easily. The Ewing and Sherman children had always roamed the town as one tribe, and Phil Ewing was his best friend. But even after Cump moved up the hill, both boys could often still be found with their legs tucked under Mary Sherman's dinner table. All his life—his later strains with the Ewings notwithstanding—Sherman regarded both families as his folks.

Staunchly Catholic, Maria Ewing yearned to have her foster child baptized. Mary, though Protestant, voiced no qualms. But the priest demanded that a proper Christian name be prefaced to the heathen "Tecumseh." By chance, the baptism occurred on St. William's Day. Though he would use the new name for formal purposes, and sign himself "W.T. Sherman," he remained "Cump" to family and friends.

As a brevet Ewing, Cump grew up in a home where politics were served hot at all hours; any stage might bring Webster, Clay or some other Whig titan for a stopover. Almost forgotten now, in the 1830s and '40s Thomas Ewing was nationally prominent.

He served a full term and part of another in the Senate, and held two cabinet posts. In 1851, Ewing nominally retired from politics. Thereafter, in theory, he practiced law and managed his considerable fortune. But in fact he remained a force to reckon with in Columbus and Washington until his death in 1871.

When Cump was fourteen, Senator Ewing told him to prepare for West Point, and when the time came, Ewing sponsored his application. Sherman was enrolled in 1836.

A strong student with a bent for math, Cump took to the academy well. But he was too much the western rowdy to accept military discipline gladly—for four years he minored in demerits. His style was slouchy, his life-long aversion to spit and polish ran deep, and he scorned petty rules. Friends would recall him as always game for sneaking off to buy forbidden treats. William Rosecrans dubbed Sherman the most gifted after-curfew hash maker of their West Point generation.

The class of 1840 began with a hundred members and ended with forty-three. Sherman ranked sixth among the survivors, and would have placed fourth without his demerits.

For officers nurtured in the toy-sized ante-bellum Old Army, the Civil War would be a tiff among cronies. The West Point class lists of the 1830s, '40s and '50s read like an index of generals, Blue and Gray; in the years after graduation, as the army shuffled them from post to post, their friendships and knowledge of one another deepened.

Graduating in 1837, when Cump was a lowly plebe, were Braxton Bragg and Joseph Hooker. The other classes ahead of him included P.G.T. Beauregard, William Hardee, Irvin McDowell, Henry Halleck and E.O.C. Ord. George Thomas was Cump's classmate and intimate friend.

A year or two below Sherman came Don Carlos Buell, William Rosecrans, James Longstreet. In Sherman's last year, Grant was a plebe.

The faculty included Robert Anderson, who taught artillery to Sherman—and to Beauregard, who would later apply his lessons by shelling Anderson out of Fort Sumter.

Following graduation in 1840, Sherman served briefly at three posts in Florida and Alabama. For a time, he was on the fringes of the Seminole War, though he saw no action. In 1842 came promotion to first lieutenant and a move to Fort Moultrie, at Charleston, where the army let him settle down for a while.

At Moultrie, Sherman's duties were light and his leisure plentiful. He had led his class in drawing and in Charleston he taught himself to paint. Long outings took him hunting or riding across the Carolinas. Twenty years later, when he heard the South Carolina swamps declared impassible in winter, Sherman would recall the hunters' wagons splashing their way across the cold, boggy terrain.

Even before Cump won his commission, the Ewings had begun urging him to resign it quickly. For Thomas Ewing, West Point was merely a fine place for a boy to gain a free, prestigious education. But Cump resisted—asserting that he liked being a soldier. From Moultrie his letters to Ellen Ewing, his foster sister and favorite correspondent, at times sounded wistful; as if—at age twenty-four—his training had doomed him to be forever an army man. But more often he wrote like a monk snugly cloistered, viewing the military as a haven of decency in a sordid world. Beneath all the chatter glowed the satisfaction of a man who knew he had picked the right career.

On a long furlough home in 1843, Sherman became engaged to Ellen. Now that Cump was to be both son and son-in-law, family pressure for a resignation grew more intense. Sherman's brother John—a rising young man of miraculous stuffiness—added his voice to the Ewing chorus.

Everyone but Sherman wanted Sherman out of uniform. Neither Ellen nor her parents could picture her as a career officer's wife, cheerily hopping from fort to fort. For years, Sherman would hear (and hear) about the bliss of a civilian job and a fixed Lancastrian abode.

In the spring of 1844, Lieutenant Sherman served as temporary aide to a traveling army inspector. For six weeks they dwelled in Marietta, Georgia, where Cump filled his spare time with horseback treks to nearby sights like Kennesaw Mountain and Allatoona Pass—again learning country he would one day invade.

The southern landscape charmed him, as did most Southerners. Sherman became a lukewarm advocate of slavery, not so much venerating the institution as judging it the only arrangement in which the two races could survive together in the South. Had opportunity—and Ellen—permitted, he would gladly have lived and died in Dixie.

Early in 1846, with the Mexican War looming, Sherman longed for reassignment to Texas. But the duty of leading Moultrie's troops to war went to his friend Braxton Bragg, while Sherman was sent to Pittsburgh as a recruiter.

Bitterly certain he was missing his only chance at combat, Cump tried the ploy of leading a band of recruits to a collection point in Kentucky, rather than shipping them. He was reprimanded for deserting his post and prodded back to Pittsburgh. There new orders awaited: he'd been reassigned to California—not exactly the part of Mexico he had in mind.

Warning Ellen to expect a long engagement, he took ship in July from Brooklyn. His companions included his schoolmates Ord and Halleck. Theirs was a classic 'round-the-Horn voyage; including South American stopovers, they were half a year at sea. When not drilling the hundred soldiers on board, the officers passed the interminable days with interminable card games. Sherman read and reread every book on board. Halleck, later to be nicknamed "Old Brains," devoted his young brains to translating a life of Napoleon from the French.

In January 1847, they docked in Monterey, then both California's capital and army headquarters. Sherman became adjutant to Colonel Richard Mason, commander of American forces in California and de facto governor. By 1847, the war was about over on the Pacific Coast; the young officers endured a quiet year, seething over their inactivity and envying their friends who were down below the Rio Grande, dodging Santa Anna's bullets. Three decades later, in his *Memoirs*, Sherman evoked that quiet old time in pages that glow with poignancy. The men he knew fill California's legends and atlas: General Kearny, Colonel Frémont, Commodore Stockton. San Francisco's Fort Mason would someday honor his commander. He knew Sutter, Vallejo and a nondescript courier named Kit Carson. He befriended the first surveyors of the transcontinental railroad. His hunting trips with Ord took them galloping over today's Fort Ord. He rode the old trail from Puebla de los Angeles to Monterey, leading men of the Mormon Battalion—that improbable force Brigham Young leased to President Polk, to mollify the government while the Mormons fled to Utah.

Sherman saw the old Spanish way of life in its last hours. He visited dons on their ranchos, where luxuries were few but every guest carved his own steak from the hanging carcass. He refused to buy cheap lots in Yerba Buena, the village that became downtown San Francisco. Hunting along the Salinas, he watched Mason bring down eleven birds with one load.

On a Monterey spring day in 1848, two men rode up to the office and asked to see Mason privately. Shortly, Mason called Sherman in. On the desk, he would recall, sat a few tawny lumps: "Mason said to me, 'What is that?' I touched it and examined one or two of the larger pieces, and asked, 'Is it gold?'"

As the rush began, prices exploded. Two-dollar blankets soared to fifty dollars, while army pay couldn't be boosted without approval from distant Washington. Mason let his lieutenants draw extra rations—worth more now than their pay vouchers.

Officers were forced to work on the side. Cump traded real estate, taking lots in payment for surveying jobs. On furlough, he and Ord surveyed in two new towns, Stockton and Sacramento, returning with six thousand dollars. When he had spare cash he loaned it at gold-rush usurious interest. He and Mason set up a store, then sold it profitably.

In June (the same month when they heard the Mexican War was over), Sherman joined Mason on a tour of the new mines, and then wrote a description for Mason to edit and sign. The account was rushed to Washington and printed. Says the *Dictionary of American Biography*, praising the wrong man, "[Mason's] report at Monterey . . . remains today the most authentic and descriptive story of the discovery of the gold deposits in California, especially at Sutter's Fort. It was copied in all parts of the world, published everywhere in the newspapers and distributed in thousands of pamphlets."

The next year, General Persifor Smith replaced Mason and retained Sherman for his staff. Though he dissuaded the bored, frustrated lieutenant from resigning, Smith had no work for him. Cump spent 1849 surveying, watching other men grow rich, and twiddling his thumbs.

Late that year, Smith arranged the only assignment likely to keep Sherman in the army—he sent him to Washington, bearing dispatches. In January of 1850, Sherman departed for the States, this time saving a few months by crossing at Panama.

Upon his arrival, he was delighted to find Thomas Ewing (then secretary of the interior) and the family in residence. When Sherman was granted a half-year leave, he and Ellen decided a six-year betrothal would suffice.

On May 1, 1850, Sherman married Ellen Boyle Ewing; the bride was twenty-six, the groom thirty. Secretary Ewing put on the political dog for the wedding—Ellen was kissed by President Taylor and his whole cabinet. Also in attendance were such senatorial luminaries as Clay, Webster and Stephen A. Douglas; heady company for a lieutenant who despaired of ever winning his captaincy. The ceremony was performed in the Ewings' temporary home, the residence now called Blair House, by Father James Ryder, president of Georgetown College.

Despite his Catholic baptism and upbringing, and his priestly wedding, Sherman would withstand Ellen's lifelong campaign to bring him into the fold. As a young man he had claimed to accept the main Christian tenets, but said he was put off by all the fuss over minor doctrinal points. After their engagement, he spoke of yielding to Ellen's "more pure and holy heart and faith." He let her know when he attended services, and once even summarized for her a sermon on the folly of rejecting Christ.

Sherman was less hypocrite than lover. His nibbles at piety were standard Victorian rah-rah—a gentleman was supposed to be drawn Upward by the purer light of his beloved. After the wedding, it all went the way of male pledges to give up cigars and female vows to continue piano practice.

Justin Kaplan called Sherman a man without a shred of religion. I agree. During the Civil War he enjoyed imagining God's wrath blistering the South. An avid reader, he quoted Scripture as readily as Dickens, Shakespeare and other pet authors. But he was an unbeliever. When children came they were raised in the Church, and in his later days he supported Catholic charities generously. Toward Ellen's many church involvements his attitude was usually tolerant, though satirical—as if he viewed religion as her odd, consuming hobby. Her faith was a cross he could bear, most of the time.

In September 1850 the army moved him to St. Louis. Soon thereafter, thanks to his own efforts and Ewing's, Sherman was finally promoted to captain.

Ellen was pregnant and chose to remain behind at her parents' home in Lancaster, where their first daughter, Minnie, was born in January 1851. Cump returned to Ohio and escorted his wife and their baby to St. Louis . . . or, more accurately, he removed Ellen despite her parents' howls.

From the modern angle—and her husband's—Ellen was chained to the parental hearth. Over the years would come three more daughters and four sons. Save when distance made the journey impossible, Ellen would respond to each pregnancy with a four- or five-month bout of Lancaster sickness. Between pregnancies, she found no lack of other reasons to scurry home. Sherman once informed his father-in-law that "it was full time for her to be weaned." He swore that if Ellen were blindfolded and spun around, she would point toward Lancaster.

Until Sherman became a general, Ellen yearned to glue him

to Ohio. She pictured him happily managing her father's affairs or content in some other lucrative, family-sponsored station. She never became as much Sherman's wife as she remained Thomas Ewing's daughter.

While stationed at St. Louis, Sherman managed his father-in-law's local properties, beginning a pattern of fiscal ties and aid that lasted for years. Ellen expected to live well, and so (more than he confessed) did Cump. A captain's pay never sufficed.

The late summer of 1852 found Sherman alone in New Orleans, where he had lately been reassigned. Ellen was again home on maternity leave. With a second baby coming, he finally admitted the impossibility of getting by on service pay.

Cump sought help from Major Henry Turner, an old army friend who was now a partner in a St. Louis bank. The firm was about to open a San Francisco branch, and Turner invited Sherman to become its manager. He won a six-month leave, early in 1853, and returned to California. Satisfied that the bank was a good risk, Sherman resigned his commission in September. As manager of Lucas, Turner & Co. he would earn at least four times his captain's pay.

While the family's pressure for his resignation had been excessive, their arguments made sense. Throughout the century, "the Volunteer soldier" was a phrase to conjure with. Particularly in the North, the military were not esteemed. Yankees feared a standing army and took pride in not, by God, needing some damn paid force to protect them. Career officers were lazy and useless—teats on the national bull. In the South, with its richer military tradition, officers were more highly regarded. That was another of Sherman's reasons for preferring Dixie; he had enjoyed the yearly round of Charleston parties to which Moultrie's bachelor lieutenants were welcomed.

As professionals without professional status, many West Pointers intended to resign as soon as possible; others, like

Sherman, were driven out by wretched pay. And yet, few officers wholly cut their service ties. The old-boy web was a steel mesh. Typically, Sherman owed his bank job to the former Major Turner.

John approved of his brother's new position. The Ewings were of two minds—delighted to see Cump out of uniform, but distraught over the move to San Francisco. "Do not think of ever going there!" wrote Maria Ewing to her daughter. "I shall never consent to it, nor do I think your father ever would."

In the fall, Sherman returned to Lancaster to reclaim his family. But Ewing first pleaded with him to leave Ellen behind, then urged him to give up California entirely. Finally, Thomas begged him at least to leave Minnie with her doting grandparents. His teeth well clenched, Sherman went back to San Francisco, taking only Ellen and Lizzie, the new baby.

The fortunes of Lucas, Turner & Co. soared and plunged in sync with California's wobbly economy. Sherman proved a good manager—his bank fared better than most in flush times and dropped more gently in bad. But the firm's prosperity mainly depended on the throbbing price of gold.

When he grew famous, observers were struck by Sherman's nervous energy. He seemed always to be prowling, prowling as he more chewed than smoked his way through crates of cigars. His talk was endless, excited, chaotic. Yet Sherman ran a bank, launched a school, and would someday feed, move and deploy a hundred thousand troops. For all his scattered surface, he thrived on detail, organized superbly, and worked happily with numbers. Beneath the fizzy speech and arm flailing, a CPA screamed for release.

No sooner was Sherman established in his bank than he became an informal investment broker. Delighted to know a financier, Cump's army friends deluged him with their savings. Soon he was managing $130,000 for Braxton Bragg and many others.

Banker, broker, gentleman of appointments and social

obligations: The San Francisco years were among the most tranquil of Sherman's boisterous life, and the most prosperous. He was a man of substance.

Willy, the first son, came along in 1854; two years later came Tommy. Both were born in San Francisco. The distance from Lancaster kept Ellen more at home—one of the many reasons Sherman enjoyed California life.

In 1855, he rejected the Democratic nomination for city treasurer, telling a committee that he was ineligible, "Because I have not graduated from the penitentiary." He was alluding to the conflict of interest between the treasury and his bank; but the man who would put "If nominated I will not run . . . " in the quotation dictionaries was already waving his anti-political colors.

The next year, the shooting of a newspaper editor by a politician yanked Sherman out of his ledgers and flung him into the midst of a vigilante uprising. The details are a complicated muddle, and the version in Sherman's *Memoirs* is self-serving. But for our purposes what matters is how the episode festered in his memory.

According to Sherman's account, he yielded unwillingly to the pleas of Governor J. Neely Johnson, and accepted the post of major general of the California militia. He and the governor called on General Wool, the regional army commander, and received Wool's pledge to provide muskets if they should be needed to prevent a lynching. When the editor died, mob retribution seemed imminent. Johnson ordered Sherman to call out the militia.

Sherman rounded up a few hundred volunteers to oppose five thousand vigilantes, while several newspapers slandered and damned him for upholding law and order. But then General Wool dithered, made excuses and finally refused the guns. Sherman's position had become impossible; he resigned his empty title in shame and fury. The vigilantes lynched the killer and ruled San Francisco for months thereafter.

This humiliation destroyed whatever faith Sherman may have had in a free press. When the Civil War came, his memory of how the papers had savaged him would not sweeten his attitude toward journalists and editors.

Moreover, the episode intensified his belief that laws and institutions were all that saved society from the fickle passions of the mob. He scoffed at the notion that "The People" were blessed with collective wisdom or decency—any demagogue could fool most of the people most of the time.

Though anything but hoity-toity in surface ways, Cump was elitist to the bone. He would have chosen monarchy over mob rule, because he found the self-interest of one man a "safer criterion than the wild opinions of ignorant men." During the war, he would be contemptuous of the tributes that were suddenly heaped on him. To Ellen he said, "Long before this war is over, much as you hear me praised now, you may hear me cursed and insulted. Read history, read Coriolanus, and you will see the true measure of popular applause." Sometimes he put it more tersely—"Vox populi, vox humbug!"

Lloyd Lewis conjectured that Sherman's fear of democratic excess stemmed from 1840, when he left the shelter of West Point during the "Log Cabin and Hard Cider" campaign—the era's shoddiest political orgy. But whether or not "Tippecanoe and Tyler Too" had kindled his cynicism, the vigilantes most definitely fueled it.

* * *

Late in 1856, California entered a long economic slump. Like most of its competitors, Lucas, Turner & Co. became a non-profit enterprise. The owners gave up the following March; Sherman was told to refund deposits and close shop. His bosses wished him to go to New York and open business there.

It says more for Sherman's pride and conscience than for his business sense that he took the blame for his army friends' losses. He wiped out his own assets—around a hundred thousand dollars—to repay what he considered debts of honor. He told John Sherman that he was "used up financially."

On May 1, Sherman closed the bank. Then he took his family back to inevitable Lancaster, where they would stay while he launched the New York office.

Cump opened in July, just as the slump struck the East. "I am the Jonah of banking," he lamented to John. "Wherever I go there is a breakdown." In October, the Missouri home office failed. Sherman was told to close the ephemeral New York branch and tote the remaining assets back to St. Louis.

Thanks to the wealth of James Lucas, the senior partner, his banks again paid all depositors. Sherman took what consolation he could: "I may say with confidence, that no man lost a cent by either of the banking firms of Lucas, Turner & Co., of San Francisco or New York; but, as usual, those who owed us were not always as just."

At thirty-seven, Sherman was jobless, broke, and blessed with a wife and four children. Save for his ever-helpful in-laws, he had nothing to fall back on. He sought a new army commission, but without success. In love with the West, he thought of hunting other work in California. Ellen opposed both schemes—"I have wandered enough with my children and I hope and pray that you may be willing to attempt something besides California and the army." For a time, Cump loitered in St. Louis.

There's an old tale, too melodramatic to gulp without salt, yet too good not to repeat. One raw November day (so the story goes) while Sherman was moping down a St. Louis street, he recognized a fellow in a ratty army coat, vending firewood from a wagon. The wood dealer evidently knew him too, and seemed undelighted to meet an old acquaintance. But Sherman halted and they talked awhile. The man confessed that he was struggling for a living on a farm provided by his wife's family. Cump searched the wind-burned face for signs of drinking—army gossip had carried stories.

Supposing the meeting did occur, it's fun to imagine the dialogue—to guess how much frustration each of them revealed or held back. Surely it was the banker, still overtly a man of affairs, who closed the meeting.

"Well, must keep an appointment. It was good to see you, Grant."

"Good seeing you again, Sherman."

To Ellen's dismay, her wandering husband volunteered to return to San Francisco that winter to recover whatever he could of the bank's assets.

From California he wrote to her: "You can easily imagine me here, far away from you, far away from the children, with hope almost gone of ever again being able to regain what little self-respect or composure I ever possessed."

To John, he spoke more openly:

> . . . after I get through here I will be absolutely penniless, and I
> don't know how I shall earn a living. I trust therefore if it be
> possible my friends in Washington would get me a commis-
> sion in a new regiment if one be raised, as that would play into
> my hands at once.
>   Whilst out here I get no salary further than personal expenses,
> so that the longer I stay the worse I am off. I suppose I am
> justly punished for giving up my commission . . .

But though he had lost all perspective, we must not. Sherman was broke and desperate. His rise between 1858 and 1864 (when there would be talk of the White House) would be astounding. But Sherman at his nadir was no Ragged Dick; his resemblance to Ulysses Grant, the Galena tanner and St. Louis woodchopper, was superficial.

From his adoption until his death, Sherman never lacked a wealthy, sustaining family, whether or not he was thrilled about it. And—emphatically—he had connections. In 1854, while Cump was in San Francisco, John Sherman had been elected to Congress from Ohio, the beginning of a stellar Washington career. While a man loved and aided by both Thomas Ewing and John Sherman might have died in rags and tatters, it wouldn't have been easy. All his life Tecumseh Sherman was privy to inside information. When he couldn't pull a string for himself, he knew someone who could and would. In the letter just cited, Sherman interrupts his moans to prod John to find him a regiment. The walls of his pit were lined with handholds.

Ellen responded to his misery with a strong buck-up letter, reminding him that he had done his best, and that his conscience was clean. "As for me, I feel that I have never loved and admired you as much as now. That I believe is natural, where love has the solid foundation of esteem mine has had."

In late winter, still in San Francisco, Sherman accepted an old offer from Ewing to run the family's Hockhocking Valley salt works. "I go back to Lancaster," he wrote to a friend, "to start where I began twenty-two years ago." Well, not quite Lancaster. He insisted on living out by the works, not in town. He could not face that abasement. "At Lancaster," he admitted to Ewing, "I can only be Cump Sherman." In July 1858, he finished his California chores and came home.

But he evaded the salt works. Tom Ewing, Jr., was practicing law in Leavenworth, Kansas, and managing his father's regional properties. Old Thomas (aware that Cump equated Lancaster with defeat) urged him to go out and give Tom a hand.

Sherman went in September. Two months later, Ellen and the children followed. Soon his father-in-law was happily lavishing deeds to Leavenworth town lots on Ellen, and promising more to come if Sherman would settle there. Kansas, it seems, was acceptably close to home.

Until the following July, Sherman raced around Leavenworth and scurried over Kansas for his father-in-law and on his own hook. He handled the Ewing properties, set up and ran a farm, managed Ewing's investments and his own, sold insurance, and became a notary. Most improbably, he got himself admitted to the Kansas bar, "on the ground of general intelligence and reputation," in order to join his brother-in-law's practice.

Through an army friend, Sherman picked up yet another job, repairing a military road near Fort Riley. He told Ellen how much at home he felt with these soldiers, though they were strangers to him, "because I know their feelings and prejudices." He doubted that he could ever understand civilians half so well. Then came the barb: "On the extreme frontier, I feel as much at ease, and far more so than I could in Lancaster."

The Shermans never viewed Leavenworth as The Answer. Despite all his flurrying around, there wasn't enough profitable work; nor did they aspire to end their days in Kansas.

In April 1859, Ellen took the children home for yet another prenatal sojourn. From Kansas, Sherman favored her with one of his most lugubrious outbursts: "I am doomed to be a vagabond, and shall no longer struggle against my fate. I look on myself as a dead cock in the pit . . . ."

In fact, the cock had never stopped crowing around for a real job. The letter that finally did the trick went to Don Carlos Buell, the assistant adjutant general. Buell told Sherman that a new military academy in Louisiana was seeking a president.

Sherman tugged the old-boy net with both hands. His application named three Louisiana gentlemen who would vouch for him—"Col. Braxton Bragg, Major G.T. Beauregard and Richard Taylor, Esq." It did no harm that the last of these Confederate-generals-in-embryo was the son of President Zachary Taylor; nor that one member of the hiring board was the half-brother of Sherman's old California commander, Colonel Mason.

In July, soon after Sherman gave up on Kansas and came back to Lancaster, he received word of his appointment. He loitered only for the birth of Ellie, their fifth child, then headed down to Alexandria.

That fall he worked without pay, sharing a carpenter's room and helping to convert an old mansion into a school building. On January 2, 1860, the Louisiana State Seminary of Learning and Military Academy opened its doors. . . .

And this, sighs the patient reader, is where we came in.

* * *

To hasten on then, Sherman needn't have worried about reconciling Ellen to household slaves. In the autumn of 1860, with Lincoln elected and the Union crumbling, the lonely husband told his wife not to join him unless things blew over. Ellen never came to Louisiana.

David Boyd, the professor who would replace him as the academy's president, never forgot Sherman's response to South Carolina's secession, on December 20, 1860. With tears running into his red beard, he grieved that he might soon be fighting people he loved. Some Southern leaders were pooh-poohing the idea of armed conflict, declaiming that a lady's thimble would hold all the blood to be shed. Nonsense! Secession meant *war*, and the South, Sherman warned Boyd, had a grandiose view of war. To men deluded by romantic claptrap, war was all battle cries and cavalry dashes. No lingering suffering. No thousands dying of camp diseases. Striding back and forth amid the school's Christmas decorations, Sherman rattled on, babbling about the South's agrarian helplessness before Northern gun and locomotive factories. In an hour of flailing arms, he outlined what would befall America before Appomattox.

Around the end of the year—whether out of love, good sense or patriotic fervor—Ellen became reconciled to his returning to uniform: "I have for some time past been convinced that you will never be happy in this world unless you go into the Army again."

On January 10, 1861, Louisiana troops seized the federal

arsenal at Baton Rouge, and Sherman was ordered to accept a shipment of guns. In his eyes, that made him the receiver of stolen goods. He resigned on January 18, saying, "I prefer to maintain my allegiance to the Constitution as long as a fragment of it survives; and my longer stay here would be wrong in every sense of the word." His superiors had been impressed with what he had achieved in launching the school known today as Louisiana State University; his resignation was accepted with sincere regret. To his cadets and faculty, he cut his farewell remarks short—unable to speak without tears.

Sherman brought his accounts up to date, offered advice for the academy's future and journeyed to New Orleans to clean up paperwork. There he lunched with Braxton Bragg, who now wore the uniform of Louisiana. Mrs. Bragg voiced concern over how well her husband would get along with the new president. It took Cump a moment to grasp that she did not mean Abraham Lincoln.

About March 1 he headed home. Two letters awaited him in Lancaster. Major Turner's offered the presidency of the Fifth Street Railroad, a St. Louis tram line. John Sherman's letter urged him to come to Washington. He accepted Turner's offer, but decided to visit his brother anyway.

John had lately become a senator, appointed to finish the term of Salmon Chase, the new secretary of the treasury. Senator Sherman took his brother to meet Lincoln, on the pretext that Cump had just returned from the South.

"Ah," said Lincoln, "how are they getting along down there?"

"They think they are getting along swimmingly—they are preparing for war."

"Oh, well. I guess we'll manage to keep house."

Furious, Sherman quit talking. But when the brothers were alone, he announced that John and all the other damn politicians could God damn well straighten up the mess they had caused without his help. And off he stormed to Ohio.

On March 27 he moved his family from Lancaster to St. Louis. While his friends tried on new uniforms and regiments, while Anderson yielded Fort Sumter to Beauregard, W. T. Sherman devoted his energies to improving a trolley line.

All that spring, John, Thomas Ewing and many others kept urging army and War Department posts on him; but Sherman continued to decline. Throughout April and May, he ran his trolleys and his mouth—barraging everyone with lectures on how the war ought to be managed.

The simplest reason for his perverse coyness was that he craved job security. Considering his family responsibilities and all that he had been through, he wanted no part of any three-month regiment.

He was also appalled by the bumblings of the new administration. The president and his advisors seemed to have no concept of what awaited them. When Lincoln called for 75,000 three-month troops, Sherman said he needed 300,000 three-year men. At least.

Through his private letters that spring, there ran a colossal self-confidence. Sherman told John that the war's early leaders would tumble and new men would rise. When victory came, only those left on top would matter. He intended to be one of them. Months before the first battle, this paragon of unsuccess was aligning himself with the Grants and Sheridans, and disdaining the trash heap of McDowells and McClellans.

By May, Sherman had declined and over-explained himself into an embarrassing corner. He feared, with cause, that he was beginning to strike people as unpatriotic; and he had pushed John's patience very far.

But on June 5 came one more offer—a cable from Tom Ewing, Jr., telling him to come to Washington *now* if he wished to be colonel of a three-year regiment.

And come he did.

Chapter 2

Grant Stood by Me

B_y 1865, Sherman's name would be inseparable from the shaggy armies of the West; few would recall that his war had begun in Washington. He arrived there to see the three-month recruits pouring in as fast as governors could shovel them onto trains. Like most West Pointers, he was appalled by the hapless mob the newspapers called an army.

The papers themselves outraged him. "When we do move," he informed Ellen, "it will be in some force, but we know that Beauregard has long been expecting such an advance, and is as well prepared as he can be . . . that nothing is now secret or sacred from the craving for public news is disgraceful to us as a people."

He had three weeks to drill his men before McDowell moved the army south, toward the stream called Bull Run. Years later, Sherman appraised that first clumsy battle:

> . . . nearly all of us for the first time then heard the sound of cannon and muskets in anger, and saw the bloody scenes common to all battles, with which we were soon to be familiar. . . . Both armies were fairly defeated, and, whichever had stood fast, the other would have run. Though the North was overwhelmed with mortification and shame, the South really had not much to boast of, for in the three or four hours of fighting their organization was so broken up that they did not and

could not follow our army, when it was known to be in a state
of disgraceful and causeless flight.

His own performance was less disgraceful than most. Held
in reserve awhile, Sherman's brigade saw less action than
some. But once engaged, their fight was typical and severe:
First, an advance climaxed by the capture of a hill. Then, as
the Rebels struck back, a defensive stand that crumbled into
a rout. But only some of his troops fled, and those who stood
by him were among the last withdrawn from the field. His
four regiments suffered 609 casualties, including 111 killed.

Cool during his first battle, Sherman lost control later,
during the night-long retreat toward Washington. He threatened and cursed his men, trying to flail them into order.

Two weeks after the army slunk back to camp, Sherman
was one of six colonels promoted to brigadier general of
volunteers. It wasn't Sherman but another of the colonels
who cried, "Promotion? We deserve to be cashiered!" But
Cump agreed.

In August, General Robert Anderson was assigned to
Kentucky, to defend the Middle West. He chose two of his old
students as assistants, Sherman and George Thomas.

Anderson's health was wretched; at fifty-six, the hero of
Fort Sumter was frail and old. Before leaving town, Sherman
met with Lincoln and won a pledge that he would not be
raised to high command—in Kentucky or elsewhere; he may
have been the only man in Washington to beg for less than the
frazzled president might wish to dole out.

Kentucky was pure chaos. The recruits descending on
Louisville were greener, if possible, than those Sherman and
Thomas had struggled with in the East. Supplies were deplor-
able. Half the men had no guns, blankets or canteens. There
was no rational plan for receiving regiments, too few camps
to put them in . . . and so on for a litany of woes.

While Thomas drilled, Sherman (taking a Louisville hotel
room as his headquarters) begged the regional governors for

more men and supplies. He slapped at fifty jobs at once, too overwhelmed to do anything right.

On September 17, the Rebels burned a bridge thirty miles from Louisville. Fearing a major thrust toward the Ohio, Sherman went racing to block them with a rag-tag defensive force. At Muldraugh's Hill he halted, awaiting the onslaught. Several peaceful days later, he admitted that the enemy had stood him up. He returned to Louisville, and to his flurry. That one-sided stand was the closest Sherman ever came to battle in Kentucky.

On October 8, Anderson resigned because of his health. Despite Lincoln's pledge, Sherman was named commanding general in Kentucky.

His flayed nerves were not soothed by the dreaded promotion. He convinced himself that Albert Sydney Johnston or some other Confederate general was about to come rampaging through Louisville, en route to Indianapolis or God knows where. As his premonitions snowballed, he battered the War Department, nearby governors and the president with strident, frantic cables. Sherman had no spies or scouts to verify anything, and Sidney Johnston kept the dire rumors flying his way. Living on whiskey, cigars and catnaps, Cump had trouble separating actual Southern brigades from the legions assailing his dreams.

In truth, Sherman always held the numerical edge. More to his discredit, his fears transformed the Confederates into an army, instead of a rabble much like his own.

* * *

On October 16, Simon Cameron, secretary of war, arrived with an entourage of reporters. He invited Sherman to his hotel in Louisville for a talk. When the general hinted that the press should leave, Cameron replied, "We are all friends here." Sherman staggered Cameron by stating that Kentucky needed 60,000 defenders. To attack, he would require 200,000 men. Years later, Sherman and a witness vowed that he had said 200,000 would be needed to drive the Rebels from the entire Mississippi Valley—if true, a low enough estimate.

En route to Washington, Cameron and the journalists spread the word that the red-haired general had gone round the bend. To Harrisburg reporters, Cameron blurted that Sherman was "absolutely crazy."

When McClellan, then general-in-chief, asked Sherman to assess the Kentucky front, Cump cabled back, "Our forces are too small to do good, and too large to be sacrificed." McClellan requested specifics—where was the enemy and where were they headed? He wanted daily reports. Sherman answered that with Kentucky so unstable, he could not return cogent reports. Then McClellan sent out an advisor, who told him Sherman appeared too unsteady for command, and that Louisville was in no danger.

Ellen came running from Ohio, bringing their two boys and Phil Ewing. John Sherman followed. They found Cump looking like Macbeth, when "Birnam Wood doth come to Dunsinane." He was sleepless, despondent, wild eyed. A servant boy told Ellen that the general often went days without food. By the time the family left, she believed they had calmed him down. A little.

In mid-November, at Sherman's request, Don Carlos Buell relieved him. Sherman was moved to St. Louis, where Henry Halleck commanded the western theater.

Halleck put him to work immediately, sending him on a Missouri inspection trip. But Sherman began telegraphing warnings to headquarters: an army under Sterling Price might soon attack here; more Rebels threatened there. Halleck ordered him back to St. Louis, where the papers were already recounting tales of Sherman's extreme nervousness. By the time he reached headquarters, Ellen had arrived. At Halleck's insistence, he requested a twenty-day leave. Ellen took him back to Lancaster.

Once he left the war, Sherman quickly regained his composure. But not long after he reached home, the *Cincinnati*

Commercial ran a story headlined "General William T. Sherman Insane." The item was reprinted widely.

The Ewings circulated outraged denials. Army friends (though never McClellan nor the War Department) published rebuttals. Ellen sent Lincoln an impassioned plea for fair treatment. Most important, Halleck wrote Sherman a calming letter, underscoring that he expected him to return to duty. His commander's gracious conduct went far to placate Sherman and quell the crisis. By Christmas, his leave was over and he was back in harness. For a few weeks, Halleck kept his high-strung subordinate in St. Louis, training thousands of recruits.

Sherman was profoundly embarrassed. For a while, his letters teemed with apologies for the disgrace and trouble he had brought on the family.

There is no simple explanation for his "Crazy Sherman" phase, nor for the abrupt transformation from the addled Sherman of Kentucky to the warrior who would emerge the following April. One reporter insisted that the general had gone mad from too many cigars—an analysis rich in Freudian implications, and no sillier than the average psychobiography. I offer a few hesitant thoughts:

His determination to emerge later in the war partly explains his dread of taking command—but only partly. Had Sherman's frustrating civilian career left him petrified of failure? If so, why had he kept on seeking positions of responsibility? For me, his terror of military command must remain a puzzle.

Most obviously, Sherman's collapse stemmed from overwork. He had dithered around Kentucky so frantically that he created his own hell. Moreover, he had arrived there exhausted: Sherman had been on the go and overwrought since January, when secession drove him from his academy and renewed his fiscal worries. Spring brought the frets of the railway job combined with pressures to enter the war. Then came the Bull Run campaign, and then Kentucky.

As well, there was the cumulative distress of the anarchy he had witnessed. In the East, Sherman had seen regiments sent home because the War Department didn't know where to put them. He was accustomed to working with professional soldiers—not volunteers who couldn't load their muskets. At Bull Run, Union men were slain by their own side because they had been issued gray uniforms. In Kentucky, the theater least smiled on by the War Department, the confusion was much worse. And there the army forced command on a general who had been a banker—a man who would not forsake his academy until he had balanced his books and done his paperwork.

Whatever had happened to Sherman never recurred. Nor was it ever forgotten. For the rest of the war, his every mistake, questionable decision or outburst would strike someone as proof of madness.

But here a comparison begs to be made: Always outspoken, an enemy of the press, and too agile with his pen for his own good, Sherman had made a flagrant ass of himself. By contrast, the suave, dapper George McClellan charmed reporters and won the deepest fidelity of his army. "The Young Napoleon" was never frenzied, never a babbler. Yet in a few weeks Sherman regained his balance; he stopped imagining Rebel hordes. But McClellan became useless to the country and to himself because he never learned to count his own troops or to accept that his force outnumbered Lee's. No journalist called McClellan "Crazy George"; his delusions ran much quieter than Sherman's, and deeper.

* * *

By February 1862, when Grant gave the North its first joy by capturing forts Henry and Donelson, Sherman was down at Paducah, sent by Halleck to run Grant's supply center. Although Cump then outranked Grant, he urged the field commander to treat him as an aide.

In March, Halleck sent Sherman back to war, to lead a division of Grant's newly titled Army of the Tennessee.

The end of that month found Grant's force—about thirty-nine thousand—camped beside its namesake river, waiting for the roads to dry. Most of them were spread around Pittsburg Landing, near a country church named Shiloh.

Cump's officers could see that in one regard he was nothing like the Crazy Sherman of the newspapers. This Sherman laughed at rumors of enemy movements. Like most of the generals, he *knew* that Sidney Johnston was down at Corinth, twenty-five miles away. On Sunday, April 6, 1862, while blueclads yawned around breakfast campfires, no officer was caught with his pants farther down than W.T. Sherman when Johnston's forty-four thousand men came screaming out of the forest.

During the two-year Mexican War, 1,733 Americans were slain. At Shiloh, in two days, 1,754 Union men died. Total losses (killed, wounded, missing) for both sides came to nearly twenty-seven thousand; higher than American casualties for the War of 1812 and the Mexican War combined. Sherman told Ellen that the carnage would have cured anyone of a taste for war. Grant would remember a field "so covered with dead that it would have been possible to walk across the clearing, in any direction, stepping on dead bodies, without a foot touching the ground."

On Sunday, Grant's achievement was survival. Though pressed far back toward the Tennessee, his army was neither destroyed nor forced into the river.

Sherman was everywhere that day—encouraging, threatening, pulling his division together, radiating competence. Three horses died under him. He took a painful hand wound and a scratch wound. As much as regiments, cannon and wagons could be dragged into order amid the screeching retreat that morning, Sherman made things coherent. While thousands ran away to huddle under the riverside bluffs, the division commanders prevented a rout. By noon, though still pressed back almost everywhere, the Federals were firing from behind recognizable lines.

Too late for Sunday's action, a misdirected division under Lew Wallace arrived in the evening, streaming in on a road that Sherman and General John McClernand had protected. As well, the lead regiments of Buell's thirty-six thousand troops showed up late Sunday afternoon. All night Buell kept coming. Beauregard, who had taken Confederate command when Johnston was killed, would have done well to withdraw by dark.

As the rain poured down that night, Federal gunboats shelled the Rebel camps; between the lines, the dying shrieked. Long after dark, Sherman still hurried around— meeting with Grant, with this general, with that colonel; quizzing prisoners, arranging burial details, looking to what little could be done for the wounded.

On Monday, in fighting nearly as brutal as Sunday's, Grant's now enormous army pushed the Confederates back toward the woods. Late in the afternoon, Beauregard disengaged and withdrew toward Corinth.

In his report on Shiloh, Grant commended Sherman's good judgment and gallantry. Halleck noted that Sherman "saved the fortune of the day" on Sunday and "contributed largely to the glorious victory of the 7th. He was in the thickest of the fighting on both days." By Halleck's request, he was promoted to major general of volunteers.

Whether jealous of Grant's growing fame or alarmed by stories of his drinking, Halleck came down after Shiloh to take charge. He made Grant his second in command—a meaningless post. Halleck then squandered the fine weather and dry roads of May in a mile-a-day advance on Corinth. After the town fell, on May 30, he traded his snail's pace for a halt, finding nothing better to do with his monster army than to break it into chunks and scatter it.

Sherman frittered away part of June rebuilding a bridge over a swamp into which the Rebels had dumped commissary trains. "The weather was hot," he would recall, "and the swamp fairly stunk with the putrid flour and fermenting sugar and molasses." He grew ill and spent two days commanding from an ambulance. Sherman was asthmatic. In San Francisco he had suffered intervals when he could only sleep sitting up. He was also prone to rheumatism or bursitis; camp life aggravated his aching arms and shoulders. But that touch of swamp fever shamed him—the only malady that sent him to bed during four years of war.

Immediately after Shiloh, the press had lauded Grant; but as the casualty figures rolled in, he was renamed The Butcher. Sherman came to his friend's defense, scorching the stay-at-home critics in a widely reprinted letter. "How his wrath swells and grows," said Charles Eliot Norton; "he writes as well as he fights!"

During the June doldrums, Sherman gave support of another kind. Halleck mentioned in passing that Grant was leaving for home. Cump went to investigate and found the general in his tent, wrapping his papers in neatly ribboned packets. Grant said he wouldn't remain where he wasn't wanted.

Sherman begged him to stay, "illustrating his case by my own":

> Before the battle of Shiloh, I had been cast down by a mere newspaper assertion of "crazy"; but that single battle had given me new life, and now I was in high feather; and I argued with him that, if he went away, events would go right along, and he would be left out; whereas, if he remained, some happy accident might restore him to favor and his true place.

As William McFeely observes in his life of Grant, the talk was critical for both men. Grant remained, and would remember Sherman's loyalty, while Sherman would enjoy a support that let him grow at his own pace, even if he sometimes blundered. Sherman cherished their friendship, and often confessed his reliance on Grant. He put it best near the end of the war, when both could smile at their early woes: "Grant stood by me when I was crazy and I stood by him when he was drunk; and now, sir, we stand by each other always."

In mid-July, Lincoln freed Grant by kicking Halleck upstairs; summoned to Washington, he replaced McClellan as head of the armies. Thereafter, Halleck commanded a neat desk. He was little more than the conduit between Edwin M. Stanton, who replaced Cameron as secretary of war, and the generals who fought. Sherman served under Grant from July 1862 until 1877, when Grant left the White House.

On July 21, Grant sent Sherman to Memphis as military governor of western Tennessee. There he built forts and drilled troops for the re-energized army. But mostly he ran the city. The war had numbed Memphis—"no business doing, the stores closed, churches, schools, and every thing shut up," as his *Memoirs* put it. But now Union advances had opened the Mississippi to the north, and so Sherman kicked the town into life: "I caused all the stores to be opened, churches, schools, theaters and places of amusement to be re-established, and very soon Memphis resumed its appearance of an active, busy, prosperous place."

He revived the government, while serving as dictator himself when military and civil law conflicted. Runaway slaves he put to work on the forts—giving them food and clothes, but not yet paying them or otherwise acknowledging their freedom. He had his own way of returning a church to the Union. When an Episcopal clergyman skipped the prayer for the president, Cump stood up tall and added it. Loudly.

Since the war had made cotton scarce in the North, buyers raced to Memphis with the blessing of the secretary of the treasury. Sherman banned the trade, only to be overruled. He then accused Salmon Chase of aiding the enemy: before Union troops arrived, Southerners had destroyed their own cotton to keep it out of Yankee hands. Hence, the army would have been justified in seizing the bales. But instead Chase had allowed brokers to exchange goods or gold for it. Those resources, Sherman insisted, quickly passed through Memphis and were transmuted to food and weapons for Confederate armies.

Once his pen was warm, he added some reflections: "When one nation is at war with another, all the people of the one are enemies of the other. . . . the Government of the United States may now safely proceed on the proper rule that all in the South are enemies of all in the North."

Shortly, as if to illustrate what war against "all the people" might mean, Sherman went after the guerrillas—elusive, quasi-military bands that had begun to fire on commercial steamboats. On September 27, he issued Special Order Number 254, which stated that "for every boat fired on, ten families must be expelled from Memphis." Four boats had been attacked, so forty families must go.

When the public howled, he suspended his order for fifteen days—telling the people of Memphis to demand that Confederate leaders suppress the guerrillas. No families were deported. But when guerrillas near Randolph shot at steamboats, Sherman burned the village and announced that if such incidents recurred, he would load captive partisans onto boats and take some target practice. Peace descended on the Mississippi.

In Kentucky, he claimed later, his warfare had been fastidious: "I, poor innocent, would not let a soldier take a green apple, or a fence rail to make a cup of coffee." Possibly so. Sherman inaugurated his version of "total war" in Memphis, in that he burned villages and threatened civilians; but his officers still punished random arson and looting. On the whole, unsupervised havoc wasn't condoned by generals until later—perhaps the summer of 1863, in Sherman's case.

But what generals permitted and what troops got away with were different matters. By 1862, neither green apples nor spotted hogs were safe from hungry soldiers on either side; many a lieutenant smiled at pillage, or looked the other way while his men roasted a "tame deer" that smelled wonderfully like pork.

* * *

In November 1862, Sherman's gubernatorial stint ended when Grant drew him into the campaign against Vicksburg. That lavishly fortified town sat on high bluffs, its guns dominating the Mississippi. To storm Vicksburg from the river side was impossible; to pass below its batteries in order to land downstream seemed nearly so. Grant had begun moving south through the state of Mississippi, intending to approach Vicksburg through the hills to the northeast. Sherman led three divisions down from Memphis, catching up with Grant near the huge Union supply depot at Holly Springs. From there, the enlarged army headed southwest. But at the Yalabosha River, Confederate General John Pemberton had entrenched in a strong position. On December 8, with his advance halted, Grant called Sherman to his camp at Oxford, where they spent the night plotting strategy.

Grant opted for a double-sided assault. He would continue to press from the northeast. Even if he got nowhere, he would hold Pemberton's army in place. Meanwhile, Sherman would approach from the north, where the Yazoo made its twisty way to the Mississippi. To reach Vicksburg through the delta seemed at least possible.

Sherman moved fast, taking one division and leaving the other two with Grant. By December 12 he was back in Memphis. Fresh troops had lately arrived from the north, and he scooped up two divisions' worth. Down from Cairo rushed Admiral David Porter with a fleet of transports and gunboats. By December 19, the army was afloat. They paused at Helena, Arkansas, to load yet another division on board. Sherman now led about thirty-three thousand men.

> The preparations were necessarily hasty in the extreme, but
> this was the essence of the whole plan, viz., to reach Vicksburg

as it were by surprise, while General Grant held in check Pemberton's army about Grenada, leaving me to contend only with the smaller garrison of Vicksburg and its well-known strong batteries and defenses.

So Sherman reported in his *Memoirs*; but in truth a big chunk of "the essence of the whole plan" remained off the record: Grant did his best fighting that December not against Pemberton, but against U.S. General John McClernand.

An Illinois politician, McClernand was a "War Democrat"—a member of the loyal opposition whose support was crucial to Lincoln. Despite his success at Shiloh, McClernand was not beloved by Grant, who thought him a pompous ass. In turn, McClernand believed himself undervalued by the West Pointers. In September, McClernand had finagled orders from Lincoln sanctioning him to raise an army for opening the Mississippi. The president didn't trouble himself about where McClernand would stand in the hierarchy. In effect, he now stood outside the normal flow—no longer clearly Grant's subordinate. That fall, Grant prodded Halleck for confirmation that he, Ulysses Grant, was still top dog in the West. He received his assurance; but McClernand still outranked Grant's pet generals, including Sherman.

It was McClernand who had stashed the troops in Memphis, to await his coming. By rushing Sherman toward the Yazoo, Grant snitched McClernand's army out from under him. By the time McClernand wafted into town, Sherman had put Memphis well behind him.

On December 26, the armada entered the mouth of the Yazoo. That night, they camped ten miles upstream, in the heart of the delta; to their east ran a long ridge called Chickasaw Bluffs. Once aloft, Sherman would be on the same elevation as Vicksburg, ten miles to the south.

The fighting started the next day; heavy Confederate shelling killed one of Porter's commanders and damaged a boat. Then it turned nightmarish. The soil was boggy. Rivers and bayous, some almost without current, twined every which way. Even at Christmas, the bugs were thick enough to keep the men from fretting overmuch about the alligators. Dead trees choked the waters; live ones scraped Porter's smokestacks. Sherman's commanders hardly knew where to point their troops. They built a bridge over the wrong bayou. Regiments got lost. Companies were severed from their regiments.

The heaviest assault came on December 29. That day's worst fighting befell General Frank Blair, whose brigade sloshed across a bayou and reached the base of a hill, only to be slaughtered by Confederate muskets. One regiment climbed high enough to come literally under enemy fire— trapped below a slick precipice as unseen Rebels blasted down at them. Blair suffered five hundred casualties.

During lulls, the Federals could hear trains arriving in Vicksburg. Though the defenders were doing nicely on their own, help was coming.

Sherman stuck it out three more days—getting nowhere, yet unsure of what to try next. The train whistles preyed on his nerves. Worse, he saw no sign that he was part of a two-pronged operation. Why wasn't Grant keeping the Rebs off his back? On New Year's Day 1863, a thick fog saved many lives. Sherman had planned a final all-out attack with a naval diversion, but the pilots couldn't see to steer, and he gave up. The maimed army piled onto Porter's battered transports and steamed back down the Yazoo.

In the first full-scale battle under his sole direction, Sherman lost 1,776 men. Confederate casualties came to 207. To add more bile to his New Year's cup, he learned that McClernand was waiting downstream. At the Yazoo's mouth, Sherman reported his defeat and surrendered his command.

McClernand had some news too: Grant had given no aid because he had been forced to retreat. On December 20, Van Dorn's gray cavalry had swept around Grant and into Holly Springs, where the raiders destroyed a million dollars worth of Yankee supplies. Farther north, Nathan Bedford Forrest's cavalry had spent Christmas merrily uprooting the railroad Grant needed for resupplying himself.

Itching to make up for his defeat, Sherman persuaded McClernand to let him sail up the Arkansas and attack a bastion called Arkansas Post. Charmed by the scheme, McClernand elected to lead the whole army, rather than sending only Sherman's divisions. The venture was deftly managed, and caught the Confederates off guard. On the assault's second day the garrison surrendered. McClernand took five thousand prisoners.

Grant had been furious when he first heard of the intended foray. It struck him as a dangerous sidetrack from the mission against Vicksburg. But after Arkansas Post fell, and after he learned that Sherman had been the instigator and field commander, he voiced warm approval. Generals like McClernand, appointed for political reasons, were not always paranoid in their view of West Pointers.

In mid-January 1863, Grant came to the Mississippi to take personal command. He reorganized the army, putting McClernand, Sherman and the brilliant young James B. McPherson (another of his favorites) each in charge of a corps.

For three months, from a base opposite and above the town, Grant assailed Vicksburg with complicated schemes of varying absurdity and uniform futility. Sherman and McPherson thought the best course would be to return to Memphis, and then fight their way over much the same route Grant had attempted in the autumn. To Cump's supreme disgust, Grant rejected that approach; to head north, even temporarily, would strike the correspondents as a retreat. And Grant would not be seen as a retreater.

In April, against Sherman's objections but with his energetic aid, Grant ventured a more direct approach. He built an inland road on the west side of the river, beyond the range of Pemberton's artillery, then marched the bulk of the army down to a good crossing point below Vicksburg. He asked

Porter to take his ships past the deadly batteries. The admiral consented, and on the moonless night of April 16, the navy made its famous run. Porter's gunboats and supply-laden transports floated without lights, covered with water-soaked hay bales to cushion them against shells. While Grant's generals watched from ashore, the fleet started down, drifting in silence.

They might better have risked it at high noon under steam. The boats were spotted at once, and Pemberton's men ignited wood piles along both banks. Each craft was a silhouetted target. Yet the fleet spun past successfully, losing only one transport and no lives. By the next day, the sailors were hard at it, patching the boats in preparation for the crossing.

On April 30, after half a year of false starts, Grant stormed the east bank against surprisingly light opposition. Sherman led the most important of the diversions that kept Pemberton's troops scattered.

In requesting his aid for this venture, Grant showed how well he knew his man. Alluding to the bad press Sherman had endured after Chickasaw Bluffs, Grant said that he would never *order* Cump to undertake a mission that could strike the reporters as another failed assault, but . . .

Back came the predictable reply: Did General Grant think Sherman gave a bloody damn what the press said? Of course he would help. The reporters "are as much enemies to good government as the secesh, and between the two I like the secesh best, because they are a brave, open enemy and not a set of sneaking, croaking scoundrels."

While Grant made his crossing, at Bruinsburg, Sherman headed up the Yazoo one last time. He spread his soldiers all over the decks, instructing every man to "look as numerous as possible." At Haines Bluff, they marched ashore and tromped around, with bands playing. Meanwhile, the gunboats provided the heavy shelling that preceded major assaults. All day, while Rebel pleas for reinforcements sped to Pemberton, infantry and navy kept it up. In order to hold the enemy in place a while longer, they camped out that night and gave a farewell performance on May Day. Late that afternoon—in happy spirits—they steamed away to catch up with Grant.

Once he had finally placed his army where he wanted it, Grant staged the finest campaign of his career. Between Pemberton in Vicksburg and another Rebel force to the east, under Joseph Johnston, he was outnumbered. Moving swiftly, Grant kept the odds and initiative on his side.

He sent McClernand's corps north toward Vicksburg, to hold Pemberton on the defensive. Soon, McClernand was astride the Southern Mississippi Railroad—the east/west tracks that linked Vicksburg to the Confederacy and brought in food. Meanwhile Sherman and McPherson headed inland, toward Johnston. On May 14, they swept into Jackson, Mississippi, shoving Johnston's force out of town toward the east—farther away from Pemberton. "So quick was the Confederate withdrawal and Union occupation," wrote Basil Liddell Hart, "that Grant and Sherman, walking into a factory, found the looms still at work weaving tent-cloth marked 'C.S.A.' and their presence hardly noticed, until Grant suggested that work might stop, as he wished to set fire to the factory."

With Johnston temporarily removed, Grant rushed McPherson's corps west to aid McClernand. He ordered Sherman to stay in Jackson for a day or two, tearing up railroad, public buildings and whatever might comfort the enemy.

Meanwhile, Pemberton—tardily grasping that he faced only one corps and that perhaps his railroad was worth a fight—at last moved out of his lines to attack. But McPherson arrived in time to support McClernand in the battle of Champion Hill on May 16, the campaign's heaviest engagement. Badly whipped, Pemberton retreated toward Vicksburg, with McClernand and McPherson on his heels.

The next day, he barely escaped over the Big Black River,

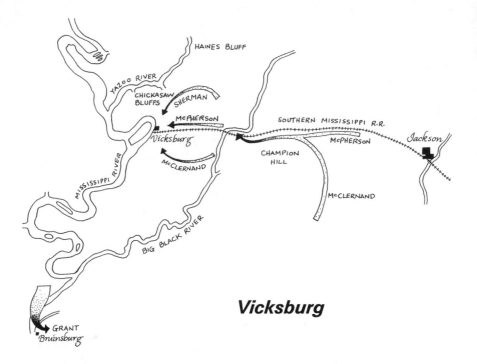

Vicksburg

destroying the bridges behind him. Seventeen hundred of his men were captured. Within a day or so, Grant's engineers had strung their own bridges; the Union army (including Sherman's lately returned corps) poured across the Big Black and began to spread out around Vicksburg.

Only eighteen days had passed since Grant crossed the Mississippi.

Hoping to catch the Rebels in disorder, Grant ventured two direct attacks on Pemberton's lines. Both were bloody failures; the Federals suffered heavy losses and got nowhere. From Grant's view, the only good that ensued was McClernand's statement that he could have taken Vicksburg had McPherson and Sherman not bungled. He then issued a self-congratulatory press release. The impolitic political general had finally self-destructed. Relieved of his command by

Grant, McClernand went off to join the many others who ended their war at home, "awaiting further orders."

Opening a new supply line by way of the Yazoo, Grant brought in enough reinforcements to invest the city, enough siege guns to batter it, and enough rations to keep his army fat while the Rebels starved.

Sherman's corps saw only part of the six-week siege before they were moved to the Big Black to defend against Johnston. Until the end, Grant feared being sandwiched—besieged by Johnston while he himself surrounded Pemberton. But Johnston's attack never came.

When Pemberton surrendered, on the same Fourth of July that saw Lee in retreat from Gettysburg, Grant at once sent Sherman onto the offensive. In five days, he flung Johnston's army back into Jackson and, after a brief siege, pushed the Rebels east once again. For the second time in two months, Sherman's men ravaged Mississippi's capital. This time he permitted heavy foraging and destruction of private property.

That ended the campaign. Sherman returned to his camps along the Big Black, as Grant's whole army settled down to rest awhile and savor their conquests.

* * *

For Sherman, Vicksburg had been a graduate seminar in warfare. He lavished praise on his commander, making a point of announcing that Grant had been right and he had been wrong about strategy. He had learned what an army of invasion could achieve by pressing relentlessly.

In Grant's two disastrous assaults on Pemberton's lines, Sherman confronted another truth—one that he would master slowly and many generals never learned at all: even with long odds on your side, to attack an entrenched position was suicidal.

But the most far-reaching lesson had come in a simple exchange of notes. As they pushed inland after crossing the

Mississippi, Sherman had grown alarmed. The farther from the river they advanced, the more strung out and vulnerable became Grant's sparse collection of supply wagons. On May 9, 1863, Sherman suggested that Grant might halt until he could forge an adequate supply line. Back came a few words that marked a turning point in Sherman's life, and in the history of war: "I do not calculate upon the possibility of supplying the army with full rations," wrote Grant. "What I do expect, however, is to get up what rations of hard bread, coffee, and salt we can, and make the country furnish the balance."

In June, writing to Ellen from his camp on the Big Black, Sherman described the look of things where armies had passed, and where the people had been made to "furnish the balance." Both the horror and his way of justifying it fore-shadow the coming hell:

> I doubt if history affords a parallel to the deep and bitter en-
> mity of the women of the South. No one who sees them and
> hears them but must feel the intensity of their hate. Not a man
> is seen; nothing but women with houses plundered, fields
> open to the cattle and horses, pickets lounging on every porch,
> and desolation sown broadcast, servants all gone and women
> and children bred in luxury, beautiful and accomplished, beg-
> ging with one breath for the soldiers' rations and in another
> praying that the Almighty or Joe Johnston will come and kill
> us, the despoilers of their homes and all that is sacred. Why
> cannot they look back to the day and the hour when I, a
> stranger in Louisiana, begged and implored them to pause in
> their career, that secession was death, was everything fatal . . .

Chapter 3

The Road to Meridian

At Cump's urging, Ellen came to Mississippi for a visit, bringing the older children. As Sherman played host that August, he watched his nine-year-old Willy fall in love with the army. A battalion made the boy a sergeant, and his doting father beamed to see how seriously he took his duties.

Another source of pleasure for Sherman was his new commission as a brigadier general in the regulars. Once the war ended, volunteer ranks would be meaningless. But regular-army rankings were permanent. At age forty-three, Cump finally had a secure job.

In late September, he was ordered to lead two divisions toward Chattanooga. After sailing to Memphis they would work their way east, repairing a railroad as they crossed Tennessee.

Sherman decided to accompany his family as far as Memphis. Soon after they took ship, he noticed that Willy looked flushed. Within hours, his malady was diagnosed as typhoid fever. The steamer arrived too late for the Memphis doctors to be of any help; on October 3, 1863, Willy died.

The next evening, at midnight, Sherman poured out his

grief in a letter to the captain of the battalion that had adopted the boy, and provided the escort at his military funeral:

> Willy was, or thought he was, a sergeant in the Thirteenth. I have seen his eye brighten, his heart beat, as he beheld the battalion under arms, and asked me if they were not *real* soldiers. Child as he was, he had the enthusiasm, the pure love of truth, honor, and love of country, which should animate all soldiers. God only knows why he should die thus young. . . .

The boy's death was Sherman's heaviest loss of the war, perhaps of his life. For weeks he was despondent; for months, amid all the carnage around him, he berated his own selfish folly in bringing the family south during the fever season. It was well for him that his duties kept him so busy. In letters to Ellen as sentimental as he ever penned, he envisioned Willy's soul hovering above the Mississippi, or inspiring him to improve his own flawed character.

* * *

In the next few months Sherman fought his last battle under Grant's eyes and led his first marching campaign. Though an over-simplification, the old remark that Sherman never won a battle or lost a campaign bears a fat nub of truth. Both Chattanooga and the raid on Meridian merit a close look for what they reveal of his powers and limits as a general.

The main fighting in late summer occurred in the middle theater, where William Rosecrans (he who had been so respectful of Sherman's West-Point hash-making) pushed Braxton Bragg's Army of Tennessee down through Chattanooga and into Georgia. In the South's most complex troop movement of the war, James Longstreet's corps of Lee's army came by rail from Virginia to aid Bragg.

At Chickamauga Creek, in September, Bragg's expanded force defeated Rosecrans's Army of the Cumberland. Rosecrans fled toward Chattanooga, but George Thomas stood firm until dark, covering the Union retreat before withdrawing his own survivors. Thereafter lauded as "The Rock of Chickamauga," Sherman's old friend had saved thousands of lives.

Bragg's failure to destroy the enemy in flight or to storm Chattanooga led Bedford Forrest to curse him as a coward and fool. The cavalry chief then detached himself from Bragg's command.

Bragg was soon entrenched on the hills above Chattanooga. His troops or guns controlled all major roads and the Tennessee River, leaving the bluecoats in danger of starvation.

In October, Lincoln appointed Grant head of the newly created Military Division of the Mississippi, which included most forces west of the Alleghenies. Grant immediately sacked Rosecrans, replaced him with Thomas, and came himself to Chattanooga. At Grant's request, Sherman replaced him in command of the Army of the Tennessee.

In aid of Chattanooga, two divisions under Major General Joseph Hooker had already been shifted west from Meade's Army of the Potomac. Hooker was camped near Bridgeport, the closest town beyond the siege where he could feed his men.

Grant reached Chattanooga on October 23. A few days later the besieged army forced open what the men called "the Cracker Line"—a land-and-water route that trickled food into town. On November 3, Grant ordered Sherman to give up his railroad repair and hurry forward.

Ahead of his army, Sherman reached Bridgeport and rode the Cracker Line into Chattanooga. Gazing at the trenches and guns looming over the city in a seven-mile arc, he voiced one of his least dazzling judgments—"Why, General Grant, you are besieged." "It's too true," said his commander.

But with an opponent like Bragg, things were less dire than they seemed. General Ambrose Burnside had established a Federal garrison in Knoxville, 110 miles northeast of Chattanooga. Heeding Jefferson Davis's advice, Bragg dispatched

Longstreet to conquer Burnside. He augmented Longstreet's twelve thousand foot soldiers with five thousand cavalry.

Joseph Johnston once remarked that not even God could make a soldier of Bragg. He was thinking of strokes like this, whereby Bragg injured himself at least five different ways: First, he reduced his army to forty-three thousand, against what would soon be a Hooker-Thomas-Sherman force of seventy-five thousand. Next, he retained only a few hundred cavalry—his best resource for keeping tabs on a fast-moving enemy. Third, he chose the wrong crusader. As a newcomer from Virginia, Longstreet was unfamiliar with eastern Tennessee, and (having come west by train) he was short of mules and wagons. Fourth, Bragg again drove away a general more competent than himself. Last, the bold stroke assured not one but two defeats—while Bragg would be badly outnumbered at Chattanooga, Longstreet's seventeen thousand attackers would have no prayer against Burnside's twenty thousand fortified men at Knoxville.

The center of Bragg's position was Missionary Ridge, which stretched above Chattanooga, six hundred feet high. Once Sherman's men were moved into place, they would make the main attack—against Tunnel Hill, the far left end of the ridge. Grant counted on surprise. He pictured Sherman sweeping up Missionary Ridge and piercing the end of Bragg's army.

But surprise comes hard against an enemy aloft. Cupped by hills, Chattanooga was truly a *theater* of war—Gray in the gallery and Blue on stage. Men on both sides watched the unfolding action with cheers and groans: tactics, for once, were as clear to the private on the line as to his generals.

When his army reached Bridgeport, well behind the Union right, Sherman led them on a thirty-five-mile march to their post on the far left. To keep out of view, they circled through the hills, far from Chattanooga, on the side of town opposite Bragg. They marched on miserable paths, sometimes by night, impeded by their artillery and supply wagons. To

Sherman's mortification, Grant had to keep postponing the battle because they slogged so slowly.

On November 23, Sherman's transit set off a series of preliminaries. When his outposts spotted the moving columns, Bragg deduced that Sherman was crossing to take the road to *Knoxville*. He decided to reinforce Longstreet. Two divisions began preparing to leave, one of them under the fine Irish-born general Patrick Cleburne.

Noting signs of the departure, and not wanting Burnside to face heavier opposition, Grant ordered Thomas to try to hold the enemy in place.

In the curtain-raiser fight called Orchard Knob, Thomas sent his men forward—stage front—with a flourish of drums and trumpets. For a while they held a review, going through all sorts of parade-ground rigmarole while the Rebels cheered. In the Confederate line around Orchard Knob, in front of the base of Missionary Ridge, men called their friends out from behind the embankment to enjoy the pageant.

And then the paraders charged.

There were light casualties on both sides as the defenders woke up; but in a few minutes there were only shamefaced Rebel prisoners and escapees fleeing up the ridge. Thomas had advanced one mile. His men now sat just beyond the range of Bragg's guns. From another viewpoint, the battle had failed. Confident that Missionary Ridge itself was impregnable, Bragg let his orders stand—the two divisions continued to pack for Knoxville.

On the night after Orchard Knob, Sherman finally moved into place, hidden near the banks of the Tennessee, opposite Tunnel Hill.

Grant planned a three-pronged attack. Early on November 24, while Sherman took the base of Tunnel Hill and began to climb, Hooker would assault on the right, at Lookout Mountain, seven miles away. Lookout was cut off from the right end of Missionary Ridge by the valley of Chattanooga Creek. Thus, Hooker's attack would be a large-scale diversion: Even if he took the summit, he could not assail Bragg's center without climbing down the mountain and up the ridge.

Grant had less faith in Thomas's army than in Sherman's (so recently his own men), or even in Hooker's relocated Easterners. Perhaps the demoralized Army of the Cumberland would fight well after Sherman set the example. Or so Grant hinted. I suspect that his bad-mouthing was calculated—a ploy for igniting the troops who had fled from Chickamauga.

Grant intended to hold Thomas back until Bragg had rushed brigades left and right to oppose Hooker and Sherman. Then Thomas would assault the weakened center, storming the face of Missionary Ridge.

Sherman's first men crossed the Tennessee well before daylight and quietly seized the handful of Rebel pickets. The foggy dawn found his advance regiments dug in well at the base of the hill. Engineers then strung pontoon bridges; by mid-morning, four divisions were crossing—unopposed.

It wasn't until noon, when his men ascended, that Sherman found out he had invaded the wrong hill.

Idiotic as it sounds, it's a flub anyone who knows high country can appreciate. Days earlier, Sherman had scrutinized the landscape—crawling within musket range of the enemy to do so. From his observation point, the spot chosen *was* Tunnel Hill. But in truth it was a separate elevation, a foothill severed from the ridge by a narrow, steep valley he couldn't see.

So much for Grant's co-ordinated attack. Early that foggy morning, Hooker had done his share. Climbing and firing toward half-seen, astonished Rebels, his men began the so-called "Battle Above the Clouds." By dusk, they controlled half of Lookout Mountain.

Sherman's culpable error on the 24th was his failure to change plans. He might still have assaulted the real Tunnel Hill before dark. Instead, he wasted the afternoon preparing

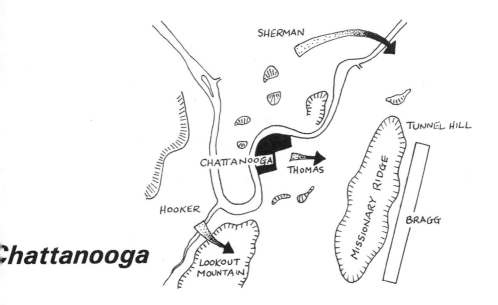

Chattanooga

to attack a day late. A day late and against far heavier opposition than he would have faced at twilight.

Finally grasping what was going on, Bragg reacted in time to halt Cleburne and call him back. That afternoon, Sherman would have faced only a few of Cleburne's disordered regiments as they scrambled in; but by morning, Cleburne's whole division were superbly entrenched.

More concerned now about his right, Bragg withdrew the division on Lookout Mountain after dark. The men hastened through the night, all the way to Cleburne's end of the ridge, where they would stand as reserves. On the clear morning of the 25th, Hooker found himself king of the mountain.

While Hooker basked in glory, Sherman got thrashed. So cramped was his position that he could deploy only a fraction of his army. From dawn until mid-afternoon, the Rebels fired down on hapless bluecoats who could not claw their way up. When Cleburne's men grew bored with shooting, they rolled down boulders.

Grant sent two more divisions around to help. Later, he offered to send yet another, but Sherman refused it. He already had far more men than he could send into action—or wanted to. Early in the afternoon he told Grant that his situation was hopeless. Grant replied, "Attack again." Sherman did so, but with as few troops as he could justify wasting.

The plan had called for the Army of the Tennessee to show the Cumberlanders how it was done. But long before noon, Sherman was praying for Thomas to take the pressure off him. Years later, he would console himself for those slaughtered men by recalling how much Bragg had thinned his center to kill them. But in fact Cleburne received little aid. His lone division mangled six Union divisions all day long, until Sherman quit.

About 3:30, Grant reluctantly sent Thomas forward, seeing for himself that most of Bragg's force still waited above. Grant wished Thomas to take only the first line of trenches, at the base of the ridge.

But after the Cumberlanders overwhelmed that line, they were in a dilemma. Squatting where infantry shot down on them and gunners rolled down shells with lit fuses, Thomas's men had marched themselves into something very like Sherman's plight. But the critical difference was that Thomas was spread along a mile-wide front. His men had room to move.

And move they did. The charge began without command, without leaders, against orders. Veterans—tired of insults, tired of watching for two days while Hooker won glory and Sherman's troops were decimated—the Army of the Cumberland started up. They crept, they marched, they marched double-quick. Then many started running, as fast as men with muskets could run uphill into bullets. It took less than an hour—thirty or forty minutes that stretched like the long end of eternity.

Had Longstreet's corps been there, the result might have been different. But the gray lines, formidable as they appeared from below, were too skimpy to hold.

Grant stared up astounded as the first bluecoats reached the crest and the Confederate flight began. Men climbed over the top screaming "Chickamauga! Chickamauga!" They grabbed or shot stampeding Rebels. Soldiers hugged each other, panted, danced, cried. General Phil Sheridan rode a captured gun, waving his hat like a child playing horsey. Another officer tried the same trick and scorched his butt. General Granger screamed and cackled, warning his men over and over that he would court martial them all for disobeying orders.

Down at their end of the ridge, Cleburne's division was celebrating when General Hardee rode up to announce that the Confederate center had collapsed. Their victory turned to ashes, the exhausted men pulled themselves into line; they would cover the flight of the Army of Tennessee out of its namesake state and back once more into Georgia.

Hooker's corps pursued. Two days later, the Confederate rear guard lingered to face them at Ringgold Gap, where Cleburne's force—four thousand against sixteen thousand—paved the hillside with Hooker's dead. Hooker limped back to Chattanooga while Cleburne rejoined Bragg, who continued his retreat unmolested.

The Confederate Army settled into camp around Dalton, Georgia. Their fighting for the year was over. To no one's dismay, Braxton Bragg resigned. Davis placed General Joseph Johnston in command.

For Sherman's men there would be no snuggling into winter quarters just yet. Lincoln's congratulatory cable to Grant had ended "Remember Burnside." Still Grant's pet, Sherman hurried off to relieve Knoxville.

Since Burnside was said to have little food, Sherman moved his weary soldiers fast. Some had no shoes, few had tents, and the late fall nights were icy. As he rushed them along, Sherman sent messages ahead urging Burnside to hold on.

At Sherman's approach, Longstreet ended his siege and

withdrew. His men would winter in the Tennessee hills, then cross into Virginia to rejoin Lee.

On December 6, Sherman and his cavalry guard dashed into Knoxville . . . to espy a herd of fat cattle on the outskirts of town. Burnside greeted him with an invitation to dinner—a fine turkey dinner, with fixin's spread across a more elegant table than Cump had seen in months.

Fighting in a Unionist region whose citizens aided his army, Burnside was well supplied. He seemed puzzled that Grant ever thought otherwise.

Disgusted, furious and guilty over every bruise and empty stomach in his ranks, Sherman turned around. As steam poured from his ears, he marched slowly back to Chattanooga and on into northern Alabama, where he made winter camp.

* * *

Sherman spent Christmas week in Lancaster. He would not see his family again until the close of the war.

In early January 1864, he persuaded Grant to let him try a large-scale raid through northern Mississippi. Intentionally or not, it would be a trial run for his March to the Sea and Carolina march.

Confederate forces in Mississippi were led by Lieutenant General Leonidas Polk, in peacetime the Episcopal bishop of Louisiana. Polk was no Stonewall Jackson, but his cavalry commander, General Stephen D. Lee, was a young soldier to reckon with. Sherman also knew that somewhere in northern Mississippi lurked Forrest, said to be collecting more riders to replace the cavalry he'd given up when he told Bragg where to stick his stars.

On January 10, Sherman arrived in Memphis, where he ordered General Stephen Hurlbut to prepare two infantry divisions for departure and told General William Sooy Smith, the regional cavalry commander, to gather a huge mounted force. Then Sherman was off to Vicksburg where he instructed McPherson to prepare two more infantry divisions.

McPherson was also to erect a second bridge over the Big Black.

Returning to Memphis, Sherman gave Sooy Smith detailed written and verbal orders. Probably, he was forced to work with Smith, just then Grant's highest-ranking cavalry man; the unusually finicky detail of Sherman's orders hints that he felt queasy.

Smith was to ride southeast from Memphis until he struck the Mobile & Ohio, then follow the tracks south to Meridian, a railroad junction and key Rebel supply center. His cavalry would rip up the railroad as they advanced.

While Smith's riders covered 250 miles, Sherman's four infantry divisions would march about 150, following and wrecking the east/west railroad from Vicksburg to Meridian. After cavalry and infantry met, they might head east to destroy a foundry at Selma, Alabama. When they had raided as far as they dared, they would find an escape route to the Union lines.

One of Smith's tasks was to keep Forrest off Sherman's back. Cump dwelled on the problems Smith should expect in dealing with the man Sherman himself titled "That Devil Forrest." But Sooy's seven thousand troopers would be the largest cavalry force yet assembled in the western war—far larger than whatever Forrest could muster. Smith vowed that he would not be halted.

Late in January, Hurlbut shipped his divisions down to Vicksburg, with Sherman close behind. Sherman made sure no reporters took ship. On *his* campaign, the press would give the enemy no comfort.

Because he was determined to keep Polk off balance, his field orders emphasized speed:

> The expedition is one of celerity, and all things must tend to that. Corps commanders and staff officers will see that our movements are not embarrassed by wheeled vehicles improperly loaded. Not a tent will be carried, from the commander-in-

chief down. The sick must be left behind, and the surgeons can find houses and sheds for all hospital purposes.

Each of his few big guns was hauled on a light wagon and pulled with a double team of horses—"Artillery carriages must not be loaded down with men and packs, nor must imperfect ammunition be carried along, nor shots wasted at imaginary objects. Chiefs of artillery will see that each box is inspected . . . "

Still, when twenty-three thousand fighting men go walking, they require more than knapsacks and canteens. In Sherman's frugal, stripped-down train moved a thousand wagons; behind it came a large herd of cattle.

Smith was to depart on February 1, two days before the infantry left Vicksburg. On the 2nd, Sherman wrote to the local commander in Columbus, Kentucky. He had heard that cavalry had not gotten through from Columbus to Memphis because of a flood. "If," said Sherman delicately, "knowing that the movements of the armies . . . depended on a simultaneous movement of cavalry, the officer commanding that cavalry has turned back from any cause, he should be double-ironed and put under guard. Death would be a mild punishment."

That same day (too late to reach Sherman), Smith wrote to explain why he was still in Memphis. The horsemen from Columbus had indeed not arrived. Without them he would have only five thousand troopers. He would be off as soon as possible, and was "exceedingly chagrined" that he hadn't left yet.

On February 3, McPherson and Hurlbut swept out of Vicksburg. Each corps took a separate road (hence the second bridge over the Big Black). Sherman traveled a few days with one corps, then switched to the other. As far as Jackson, they followed the same railroad along which most of them had fought last May in the Vicksburg campaign.

From the start, Stephen Lee's gray riders bit at the army's

flanks—dashing in for a skirmish, pulling away, then darting in to attack elsewhere. For the Federals it was like brushing away gnats. Depending on their place in the line of march, which rotated daily, a regiment might fight several times in a morning, then stroll in peace for a week. There were no full-scale battles, and neither side lost many men. Sherman avoided combat because he could not tend his wounded properly. Polk, to the annoyance of his generals, never pulled his infantry together sufficiently to risk a big fight.

The troops ignited whatever they could contrive to call "public," but men caught damaging private property were punished. Foraging was another story. Mississippi's pigs and cattle vanished into the army's bellies. The men appropriated every gristmill they passed—Southern granaries became Yankee cornbread.

Borrowing as many regiments of helpers as they needed, Sherman's engineers built bridges, repaired bridges the Rebels had burned, and demolished their own bridges behind them. Gigantic crews flung aside whatever obstructions Polk's men put on the roads.

In early February, fine weather meant dry walking. Later, the rains came and deep mud glued itself to boots and wagon wheels; then the engineers felled trees and dismantled barns to lay down corduroy—supportive wood stretched across roads like railroad ties. When the wagons pressed the corduroy into the goo, a fresh layer was dropped above it.

Despite it all, Sherman's horde averaged sixteen miles a day. Most astonishing was the day when Hurlbut's corps bridged a big river and two small ones, and still advanced thirteen miles.

For many a marcher, the expedition was only a jolly, strenuous break from the dull winter camp routine. Rain, sodden gear, and occasional hungry days caused most regiments more woe than the enemy. A signal officer's report conveys the army's spirit. That day he had led a detachment—

off on the flank of Lake Station for the purpose of destroying the public property, consisting of machine-shops, cars, locomotives, &c. While the cavalry were fighting the rebels, the Signal Corps went through the town like a dose of salts, and just as we were leaving I noticed a man hunting around to get some one to make an affidavit that there had been a town there. Property destroyed valued at $1,000,000.

On February 6, the Federals were in Jackson, where—on this third visit—Sherman's arsonists must have seemed like old acquaintances, if not quite friends. That day Cump sent a message out to Vicksburg by courier: Things were going well. He guessed they had killed twenty of the enemy and wounded at least fifty. His own losses so far were ten killed and twenty-five wounded. "The delay of William Sooy Smith at Memphis may compel me to modify my plans a little, but not much."

On February 8, Sherman reached Brandon, riding with McPherson's corps. It was his forty-fourth birthday, four years since he had declared himself doomed to plod toward eternity as a schoolmaster.

On a rainy Valentine's Day, the blue army drove Polk out of Meridian. Once he found a haven, the good bishop wrote to tell Jefferson Davis how things stood:

> The enemy entered Meridian the 14th. . . . His movement was so compact as to make it difficult to do more than annoy him. Since he has been in Meridian he has been breaking up the Mobile and Ohio and the Meridian and Demopolis Railroads . . . What his intentions are has not yet been determined. He may still go to Mobile or return to Jackson. . . . All stores from the Mobile and Ohio Railroad of special value removed, and rolling-stock placed beyond his reach. Am increasing stores of garrison at Mobile.

All month long, Polk persuaded himself that Sherman's

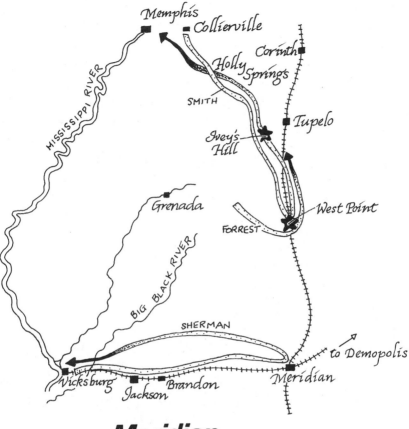

Meridian

major target was Mobile, far to the south. Though Cump had spread rumors that he might amble down that way, he did very little feinting toward the Gulf. He simply kept moving, while Polk defended his district like a man who guards his rear end while someone batters his face.

The devastation around Meridian was fierce—the hardest work of the campaign. Regiments tore track in four directions, 115 miles of it. Explained a captain of engineers: "[Destruction] was effected by taking up the rails and piling the ties together 5 or 6 feet wide and 4 feet high, balancing the rails on their sides with weights on each end, and setting fire to the piles. The rails would invariably bend from 30 to 40 degrees."

Sherman later recorded that "Meridian, with its depots, store-houses, arsenals, hospitals, offices, hotels and cantonments no longer exists." He also bragged that he had put the tracks out of use for the year. But Polk had his engineers hard at it immediately, and some roads were running in two months. Throughout the war, officers on both sides over-estimated the permanence of their railroad deconstruction.

Smith should have reached Meridian on February 10, ahead of the marchers. Sherman sent out search parties to no avail. Without the cavalry, he dared not venture farther. On the 20th, the infantry started back toward Vicksburg, taking a more northerly route because they had exhausted the forage in their path.

As they marched, the expedition grew larger. Their herds increased because they seized more livestock than they ate. The human multitude grew as well, as slaves flocked to join them. Sherman would later tell Halleck that he had brought out "about 10 miles of Negroes." In his less flamboyant official report he estimated that he had gathered five thousand slaves, plus one thousand white refugees.

The march west was uneventful. There was less skirmishing, and the hiking and camping had become routine. The commander later asserted that Hurlbut and McPherson had overseen all the real work of the campaign, while for him the trek had "more the character of a pleasure excursion than of hard military service."

Aside from Smith's seven thousand vanished riders, everything had gone even better than Sherman anticipated. The troops returned healthy and his pack animals were stronger than when they started.

In Vicksburg, to which he returned on February 28, he pieced together the Smith mystery. What with the delayed

Kentucky cavalry, and this and that, Smith had not departed until February 11, the day after he should have reached Meridian. But while Sooy was a bit tardy getting off, it must be acknowledged that once he finally hit the trail he proved to be slow, bumbling and cowardly.

The venture went badly from the start: too much raiding of crops and too little hard riding. When Smith reached the railroad, he busied himself tearing it up—deeming that task more important than hastening to join Sherman. He too gathered refugees. But Sooy couldn't seem to control his followers; he needed two thousand troopers to guard three thousand blacks. That left five thousand to confront what Smith had by then inflated into Forrest's mighty host.

On February 21, in swampy land near West Point, Mississippi, Forrest hid his men along the rails. Sensing the trap, Smith could find no better response than to skedaddle for home. Much less averse to violence, Forrest pursued for days, fighting whenever he could. At Ivey's Hill he managed to hold Smith long enough to whip him; otherwise, the combat was mostly a running skirmish.

Eventually, Smith found sanctuary in Memphis. His losses were about seven hundred—perhaps three times what Forrest had suffered. And his frantic flight had left most of his horses unfit for service.

Among Forrest's many gifts was a knack for what Sherman termed "looking as numerous as possible." Long after the debacle, Smith still swore that he had been outnumbered. In fact, Forrest may have led as few as twenty-five hundred men. Moreover (as Shelby Foote observes), most of the Rebels were green recruits—newcomers Forrest had gathered since he forsook Bragg. For Forrest, the humiliation of Sooy Smith was merely basic training.

* * *

Some historians have belittled Meridian, viewing it as a foray in which Sherman—virtually unopposed—burned sixty-plus bridges, destroyed much track and a few locomotives, raised hell, and marched out again. But as Margie Bearss underscores in her study of the expedition, Polk's scattered command included about twenty-two thousand men. He could also, as he did much too late, call on Johnston for aid. Had Polk reacted promptly, Sherman could have found himself, somewhere along the road to Meridian, facing eight or ten thousand well-protected infantry.

Clausewitz observed that "Everything is very simple in war, but the simplest thing is difficult." Meridian looked easy because Sherman made it so. He marched the population of a small city in and back out with negligible losses; elegant planning kept the army hustling, even on days when four divisions and a thousand wagons were forced to share one road. Despite the army's mass, a compact line of march kept them safe. There were few stragglers for Stephen Lee's horsemen to pick off. Moreover, while Sherman had counted on seven thousand cavalry, he did not let their absence fluster him or do more than limit the scope of his campaign. Though he did less permanent railroad damage than he supposed, he still destroyed millions of dollars worth of goods and captured a vast wealth in slave "property."

Above all, he gave Polk no time to think straight. For Sherman, that was the most important idea the campaign verified: "I think the time has come now," he wrote later that year, "when we should attempt the boldest moves, and my experience is that they are easier of execution than more timid ones, because the enemy is disconcerted by them."

Soon after Meridian, Grant was made lieutenant general and head of all U.S. forces. On March 18, 1864—thirty months after his nervous breakdown in Kentucky—General W. T. Sherman assumed command of the Military Division of the Mississippi. He would be responsible for tens of thousands of men scattered through the western states. His main force, assembling around Chattanooga, would soon number a hundred thousand.

Chapter 4

The Delicate Point of My Game

*A*fter receiving his third star from Lincoln, Grant returned to Tennessee and closed shop. For the rest of the war, he would remain with Meade's Army of the Potomac as it faced Lee.

Because the two generals had no chance to talk privately in Tennessee, Sherman accompanied Grant as far as Cincinnati. There Grant and Sherman settled into a hotel and sketched the destruction of the Confederacy.

For those who could see, the end was visible. Vicksburg's fall had cut off the western Confederacy. The blockade squeezed Southern ports ever harder. Northern factories were pouring out supplies, while blue armies ravaged Southern factories, mills and railroads. The North had more than twice the men under arms. Thanks to immigration, Northern states still grew, and many a newcomer fought—two of Sherman's regiments took their orders in German. After the Emancipation Proclamation, Gettysburg and Vicksburg, there was no chance that Britain or France would aid a failing, slave-holding power.

Though the Deep South had scarcely been touched, the Meridian raid had shown its vulnerability; defenders were spread too thin to guard every entrance. With Chattanooga's fall, the Southeast stood open. Atlanta was only 120 miles away, down the Western & Atlantic tracks. The Confederacy's last slim hope had fled down the back of Missionary Ridge.

Grant's broad strategy was simple. As Sherman put it, "He was to go for Lee and I was to go for Joe Johnston. That was his plan." In early May the two great armies would attack simultaneously, with smaller Union forces linked to the same timetable. Grant wanted pressure on Johnston and Lee to be so steady that neither could spare men to re-inforce the other. As for particulars, Sherman could run his armies as he liked. He returned to Tennessee and rolled up his sleeves.

Officially, his Chattanooga force was three "armies," each under its own major general. The biggest was George Thomas's Army of the Cumberland. Thomas led sixty thousand men, about as many as Joseph Johnston's whole force. In the push for Atlanta, he would usually be in the center, taking the straightest route as the two smaller armies and four divisions of cavalry flared and feinted on his wings.

One smaller force—twenty-five thousand—was Sherman's old Army of the Tennessee, now under McPherson. The other, General John M. Schofield's Army of the Ohio, contained only one corps—it was an "army" by courtesy. Yet in the Atlanta offensive Sherman would treat it as an army—as often speeding Schofield ahead of Thomas on one side as he pushed McPherson on the other.

Called "Pap" or "Old Slow Trot," the graying Thomas was forty-seven, four years older than Sherman. Stolid and imperturbable, Thomas seemed more like sixty. His pokiness drew howls from Cump throughout the campaign—howls that were partly real concern over keeping a gigantic army rushing, and partly just talk. As he told Grant in mid-campaign:

> My chief source of trouble is with the Army of the Cumberland, which is dreadfully slow. A fresh furrow in a plowed

field will stop the whole column, and all begin to intrench. I have again and again tried to impress on Thomas that we must assail and not defend; we are the offensive, and yet it seems the whole Army of the Cumberland is so habituated to be on the defensive that, from its commander down to the lowest private, I cannot get it out of their heads. I came out without tents and ordered all to do likewise, yet Thomas has a headquarters camp on the style of Halleck at Corinth; every aide and orderly with a wall tent . . .

Delighted with his own fetish for roughing it, Sherman was baffled by Thomas's affection for soft cots and fine dinners. He vented his spleen by riding up to the Cumberland headquarters, gazing around in mock wonder, and asking sentries if this was the famous "Tom Town." He then went into raptures over how well the community flourished.

Nonetheless, Sherman worked snugly with Thomas, grousing the while. They understood each other, and their strengths and failings were compatible. Later on, when their commands were separated, Sherman would say, "I wish old Tom was here."

Young, dashing, handsome, James Birdseye McPherson was everything Pap Thomas was not. Sherman treated him as a protege. Half convinced that the government or newspaper rascals would destroy both Grant and himself if the Rebs didn't, he viewed McPherson as the man likeliest to finish their work and end the war.

John Schofield's gleaming pate, reserved manner and professorial air belied his youth and energy. At thirty-two, he was actually three years younger than McPherson, his close friend and West Point classmate. Schofield was a newcomer from the Missouri theater; Sherman didn't know him well at the start of the campaign and seems to have warmed to him gradually.

* * *

If ever a victory was gained in advance, it was Atlanta. "The great question of the campaign was one of supplies," Sherman later wrote. His main depots were at Nashville, where the Louisville & Nashville rolled in from the North. There he sat through March and April, nailing himself to the center of his logistical concerns. Considering his restlessness, not the least of Sherman's achievements that spring was that he sat still, rejecting every temptation to scurry around the region where his forces were gathering.

That winter and spring, Nashville's facilities multiplied. Warehouses covered city blocks; ten-acre stables and twenty-acre corrals sprawled around the outskirts. Twelve thousand army clerks, mechanics and laborers toiled away. Barraged with Sherman's orders, the quartermasters, purchasing agents and trainmen who served as his viceroys hauled in goods from all over the Northwest. Grain, saddles, hay and food poured into town.

From Nashville, the tracks ran down to Chattanooga, just behind the front. Sherman's immediate goal was to stockpile a month's supplies there, while still keeping his armies fed. His longer-range job was to devise a campaign around the single-track railroad to Atlanta.

As Federal divisions thrust deeper into the South, they paid for their success with lengthening supply lines. By 1864, tens of thousands of troops guarded tracks and warehouses behind the front. Sherman knew well that every step he advanced would increase that problem. He would have more and more rails, bridges and telegraph lines to protect, while each foot the Rebels yielded would tighten Johnston's supply route.

That spring, Sherman made himself the first great railroad strategist—learning to view and handle engines and cars as something very different from a string of animal-powered

supply wagons. In his memos and jottings began the fall of
Atlanta:

> Locomotives don't eat corn and hay like mules; but a single lo-
> comotive will haul 160,000 pounds. A man eats 3 pounds a
> day, and therefore one train will feed 50,000 men. Animals eat
> about 15 pounds. I estimate 65 cars a day necessary to maintain
> an army of 100,000 men and 30,000 animals.

Cump erected blockhouses to guard every bridge along the
360 miles of track from the Ohio to Chattanooga. He ordered
Colonel William Wright's Construction Corps—five thousand men—to put in spring training, practicing track repair.
As the armies advanced, Wright would split his men into six
divisions lodged in huge camps along the track, each poised
to hasten to the scene of a problem.

Sherman accepted beforehand that no multitude of garrisons
and blockhouses could prevent Rebel cavalry from riding in,
time and again, to smash things up. (He guessed that he would
lose two trains a week. Later, when the enemy proved him too
optimistic, he raised the figure.) He was gambling that strong
defense would minimize the damage and that Wright could
mend track and slap down new bridges about as fast as the
enemy could ravage. If that meant repair crews in the thousands, then thousands would be there.

The general commandeered every locomotive he could
seize from the Louisville & Nashville, urging its president to
replenish his line (and keep the cars moving South) by
grabbing whatever entered Louisville from the North. Soon
rolling stock from throughout the Union was dropping into
Nashville and Chattanooga. With train space precious, Sherman coddled no one. New recruits and veterans returning
from leave reached the front afoot. Cattle were driven up,
cowboy fashion. He canceled civilian train use and made the
order stick until Atlanta fell. Nearly all pleas for exceptions
were rebuffed, especially those of the Christian Commission

and other do-gooders—"There is more need of gunpowder and oats than any moral or religious instruction."

All winter, the army had fed destitute residents of the war zone. Sherman squelched that waste of cars; and when Lincoln asked him to do whatever he could "for those suffering people," the president got his answer:

> [It] is demonstrated that the railroad cannot supply the army and the people too. One or the other must quit, and the army don't intend to, unless Joe Johnston makes us. The issues to citizens have been enormous, and the same weight of corn or oats would have saved thousands of the mules, whose carcasses now corduroy the roads, and which we need so much. . . . I will not change my order, and I beg of you to be satisfied that the clamor is partly humbug . . .

* * *

It speaks less for Joseph Johnston's talent than for his luck that Sherman got off to a poor start. Johnston's Army of Tennessee was lodged behind Rocky Face Ridge, an elongated crest whose most approachable point was a vertical horror called the Buzzard's Roost. Sherman called it "the terrible door of death," and did not intend to stick his toes far into it.

With all winter to prepare, Johnston had not only made Rocky Face Ridge impregnable, he had also started defensive lines throughout northern Georgia. Clear back to Atlanta, his fall-back positions were readied. And yet, somehow, he neglected to fortify a side road on the Union right of the ridge, an opening called Snake Creek Gap.

On May 7, 1864 (three days after Grant got moving in Virginia), Sherman launched his attack by advancing part of Thomas's and Schofield's armies toward Buzzard's Roost. Their unenviable chore was to probe and threaten, without risking an assault. Meanwhile, McPherson moved swiftly on the right. Coming forward from behind the front, he jumped

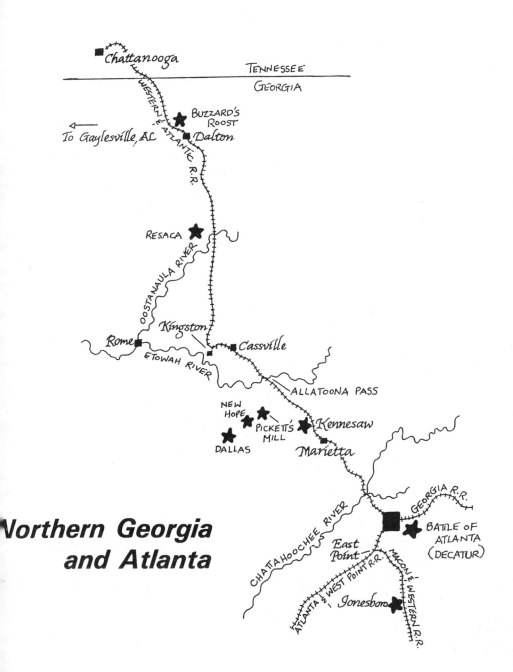

Chattanooga

TENNESSEE
GEORGIA

WESTERN ATLANTIC R.R.

BUZZARD'S
ROOST
Dalton

To Gaylesville, AL

RESACA

OOSTANAULA RIVER

Kingston

Rome

Cassville

ETOWAH RIVER

ALLATOONA PASS

NEW
HOPE
PICKETT'S
MILL
Kennesaw

DALLAS

Marietta

Northern Georgia
and Atlanta

CHATTAHOOCHEE RIVER

GEORGIA R.R.

BATTLE OF
ATLANTA
(DECATUR)

East
Point

MACON & WESTERN R.R.

ATLANTA & WEST POINT R.R.

Jonesboro

off without attracting much enemy notice. By May 9, his twenty-five thousand men were hastening through Snake Creek Gap. McPherson sent word that he would soon descend onto the railroad at Resaca, behind the Confederate rear. With the Rebels' supply line about to be cut and their army squeezed from two directions, Sherman exulted, "I've got Joe Johnston dead!"

Johnston's luck stemmed from an earlier plea for help. With the campaign pending, he had asked General Polk to spare him a division. The bishop himself came from Mississippi and brought most of his army—nineteen thousand men. By chance, four thousand of them had reached Resaca and stopped for a rest when McPherson swept out of Snake Creek Gap. Surprised and flustered, McPherson withdrew back into the gap's shelter and informed Sherman that he had done so. Anything but pleased with McPherson's caution, Sherman began to march nearly his whole command through Snake Creek Gap.

("Well, Mac, you missed the opportunity of your life!" said Sherman when they next met. But to Grant and the War Department he played down the flub. Most of Sherman's officers liked him; high among their reasons was that, as army slang put it, he didn't "throw off" on subordinates. Even when he called an officer a blithering fool to his face, he was likelier to take blame himself than to discuss the blithering with higher-ups.)

One corps remained behind to hold the old lines temporarily, to discourage Johnston from taking the offensive and storming Chattanooga.

Never one to assault rashly, Johnston did not consider moving north. Instead, he at once gave up his splendid fortifications and pulled back to Resaca by night. General O.O. Howard, one of Thomas's corps commanders, would still be marveling over that "handsome" withdrawal many decades later—"No man could make retreats from the front of an active enemy like Johnston." Dalton, Johnston's winter headquarters, fell to Sherman without a fight as both armies slid around it on their move south.

The first battle came on May 14, at Resaca, where the Rebel force, thanks to Polk, numbered at least seventy thousand. For all its havoc, Resaca was a limited battle—two days of see-saw action in which neither commander risked a massive attack. But the field was bloody enough without that, and if there was a winner at Resaca, it was Johnston. Southern losses came to five thousand; Northern, to six thousand. On the second day, Sherman sent a division over the Oostanaula River, well below the left end of the Rebel lines. With Sherman again threatening to grab his railroad or hook around behind him, Johnston once more pulled back, crossing the Oostanaula on a pontoon bridge. The Federals pursued—Thomas and McPherson crossing on their own pontoons; Schofield's corps stripping to wade a ford.

* * *

Three big rivers flowed between Rocky Face Ridge and Atlanta, serving as natural barriers against the Union incursion: the Oostanaula, Etowah and Chattahoochee. In eight days, Johnston had given up one of them, as well as his formidable initial lines.

Those opening moves set the pattern for the whole campaign: The armies confronted; Sherman flanked or threatened to do so, usually by moving right; Johnston, to protect his trains and avoid being pinched, retreated; Sherman pursued; then the armies faced off once more, closer to Atlanta, and the dance began anew.

Johnston's dilemma was that he was outnumbered—when the armies stretched, Sherman's always stretched wider. Johnston's best hope was that Sherman would blunder by leaving part of his force isolated long enough to be snared. Old Joe bemoaned Sherman's "caution"; meaning that his opponent rarely made hasty moves that left divisions exposed. Where a more daring man—a Forrest or a Stonewall

Jackson—might have made his own opportunities, Johnston kept awaiting the glorious chance that never came.

* * *

By June 4, three weeks after Resaca, Johnston had surrendered about eighty miles of railroad. He now sat atop three peaks—Brush, Pine and Lost Mountains. Behind those crests loomed the rugged summit of Kennesaw Mountain; close behind Kennesaw sat the town of Marietta.

What had brought Johnston there was more of the same dance of flank-and-retreat. Foiled in an attempt to cut off and destroy Schofield near Cassville, Johnston had been compelled to pull back across the Etowah, his second river. He then dug in atop Allatoona Pass—an even more menacing height than Rocky Face Ridge. Occasionally, Old Joe was too clever for his own good in choosing defensive positions. He yearned for opponents to attack his lines, yet chose bastions so threatening that Federal generals were scarcely tempted.

Remembering Allatoona from his rambles in the 1840s, and not tempted in the slightest, Sherman made a daring move: he forsook his precious railroad and launched a huge sweep to the right. If unopposed, he would have circled far around through the hills and dropped onto Johnston's railroad near Marietta—far behind the front and dangerously near Atlanta. But Johnston swiftly descended from Allatoona to block the Federal path.

On an extended, crescent-shaped line, the armies tangled for several bloody days in fighting that recalled Grant and Lee's recent horror in Virginia's Wilderness. Even to name the battles gives a shape to things that belies the actuality. Two immense armies groped in land so wooded that the antagonists could scarcely see each other.

The fighting began at New Hope on May 25, where one of Hooker's divisions bumped into unexpected resistance and was flung back in a welter of casualties. Hooker lost at least sixteen hundred; Rebel losses were less than half that.

Two days later, at Pickett's Mill, Howard tried to circle the right end of the Confederate line. While his men stumbled through nearly impenetrable thickets, the one-armed general sent the message that best captures the combat along the crescent: "I am turning the enemy's right flank, I think."

Howard thought wrong. In the woods ahead rested Pat Cleburne's division—well dug in as they watched him coming. That afternoon Cleburne treated Howard as he had treated Sherman at Chattanooga: sheets of fire from the Rebels' best riflemen tore into the leading blue division. In three hours, Howard lost nearly fifteen hundred against Cleburne's 448 casualties.

On a rainy June 1, Sherman's cavalry galloped left to capture Allatoona Pass, which Johnston had left nearly undefended. As willing as Sherman to disengage around New Hope, Johnston had no recourse but to fall back. He did so on June 4, and thus it was that he came to be entrenched atop the three peaks in front of Kennesaw. In following Johnston, Sherman returned to his railroad, a big step closer to Atlanta than where he had left it.

* * *

The June rains poured down for three weeks. Roads became impassable, then got worse. Wrote Federal General Alpheus Williams to his daughter, "All of us have to take to the deeply saturated ground and as our bedding consists of blankets with now and then a buffalo robe you can fancy we sleep rather moist."

While the two armies soaked and sat, Wright's railroad builders kept splashing along to catch up with the front.

Throughout the campaign, Colonel Wright's supermen astonished everyone, including Sherman. The Rebels had hardly abandoned Resaca before trains bearing food and ammunition were steaming in from Chattanooga, tearing along at ten miles an hour. Returning trains conveyed the wounded to Tennessee hospitals. At Resaca, the engineers rebuilt the train bridge over the Oostanaula in three days.

Admitted Sherman to his brother, "My long and single line of railroad to my rear, of limited capacity, is the delicate point of my game."

Nor would he call the roads along which his thousands of wagons slogged invulnerable:

> ... all of Georgia, except the cleared bottoms, is densely wooded, with few roads, and at any point an enterprising enemy can, in a few hours with axes and spades, make across our path formidable works, whilst his sharp-shooters, spies, and scouts, in the guise of peaceable farmers, can hang around us and kill our wagonmen, messengers and couriers. It is a big Indian war ...

But it was the guerrilla threat to his railroad that roused Cump's fury. Anyone caught harming trains or the telegraph should be "shot without mercy"; and perhaps even those who looked suspicious should be exiled. He suggested shipping guerrillas and their friends to Honduras or Santa Domingo; if those places objected, then "Madagascar or Southern California would do."

As in Memphis two years earlier, Sherman had no time to divide the innocent from the guilty; he aimed to halt damage *now*: "Notify the people that if our road is let alone we will feed ourselves, but if it be interrupted we will of necessity strip the country and destroy all things within reach." Later in the year, when guerrillas attacked a train, he ordered a general to "burn ten or twelve houses of known secessionists, kill a few at random, and let them know that it will be repeated every time a train is fired on."

Sherman's decision to marry his army to the Western & Atlantic and its telegraph poles made the Atlanta campaign something new in warfare. Save for enemy disruptions, he stayed in close touch with Washington. Cables sent in the morning reached the War Department that day and were usually forwarded to Grant a day later. Decisions needing Stanton's or Lincoln's approval might be settled overnight.

With wires fanning out behind every corps, messages passed from one officer to another in minutes. Atlanta campaign records sometimes read like transcribed phone calls as questions and orders flashed back and forth.

Similarly, that fragile railroad changed war for every man in the army. The private returning to his tent might find a letter from Sis, mailed that week in Indiana. Should he draw escort duty, he would spend the night in peaceful Nashville before returning to face Johnston's artillery. Papers and magazines were peddled at the front; everyone followed the war in Virginia and cursed the draft dodgers up North. Monitoring the coverage of their own doings, the fastidious urged their families to subscribe to *Harper's Weekly*—it had the most accurate woodcuts. Major James Connolly of Illinois (whose letters and diary give a fine account of the campaign) shared thoughts with his wife on everything from politics to poetry. They were reading the same fat new novel, *David Copperfield*, and joked about who would finish first.

On June 9, General Frank Blair reached camp leading ten thousand men—veterans who had returned from re-enlistment furloughs too late to start the campaign. Blair *more than replaced* all of Sherman's casualties so far. To celebrate his own arrival, he brought down a load of champagne, properly iced.

During a lull in the rain, on June 14, Johnston, Hardee and Polk went up Pine Mountain for reconnaissance. Half a mile away, passing through Howard's lines, Sherman glimpsed three observers. "How saucy they are," he said to Howard; "make 'em take cover." The best of Howard's artillerymen, an officer trained in the Prussian army, had been peppering the summit all morning and knew the range. When the first shell dropped, Hardee and Johnston ran. Overweight and never inclined to forget his dignity, Leonidas Polk was still walking away when the second shell took his life. For decades, Southern lore would insist that Sherman had sighted the gun, intentionally aiming at Bishop Polk.

Shortly after, Johnston tightened his lines, pulling back to occupy the double summit—seven-hundred-foot Big Kennesaw and four-hundred-foot Little Kennesaw.

For once, Sherman hesitated over his next move. Marietta sat four miles away and his obvious choice was another flanking march, around the mountain. But he was wary. He fretted that he had tried that move too often, like a boxer too fond of his favorite punch. He cabled Halleck, "We cannot risk the heavy losses of an assault at this distance from our base." Yet even while finding reasons not to launch an attack, he was planning one.

But first he pushed Schofield and Hooker right, as if to give flanking another chance. To block their march, Johnston dispatched John Bell Hood, the most fiery of his corps leaders. Hood bumped into a blue advance party that turned and fled; he pursued, without scouting ahead to see what was down the road. What was there, dug in at Kolb's Farm, was most of Schofield's and Hooker's forces. Hood went reeling back with heavy losses. Not convinced, he ordered another charge—and once again saw his men destroyed. In an hour, Hood had trashed a thousand of his soldiers.

After the defeat, Hood finally did as Johnston had ordered, digging in across Schofield's path to end the attempted circumvention of Kennesaw.

During the battle, Hooker sent Sherman word that he and Schofield were facing three Rebel corps—unlikely, since Johnston led only three in all. The next day, Sherman rode down to Kolb's Farm and spoke his mind to Fighting Joe, who (as Sherman viewed it) went into a sulk. Amid the constant errors of war, Hooker's exaggeration seems trivial. Probably Sherman had grabbed the chance to bully a man he disliked. He sometimes framed orders to Hooker in curt terms he would not have used to one of his pets, as if to rub it in that the former head of the Army of the Potomac was now merely a corps commander.

By the time the rains eased and the roads dried, on the morning of June 27, Sherman had persuaded himself to attack. He gave the troops scant notice—wanting no suggestive bustling around the camps. Nor was there any artillery softening until just before the charge. Schofield again headed around the right, in hope of keeping Rebel attention divided, and there were several minor diversions.

The whole operation was carefully prepared, elegantly co-ordinated, and doomed. When all was said, Sherman was sending troops up a steep hill against the man he himself called the South's finest defensive general.

When Sherman's banks of cannon finally opened, they were answered thunderously—Old Joe had not been caught by surprise. Then came the charge.

"They had along the fronting slopes abundant 'slashings,'" recalled General Howard:

> that is, trees felled toward us with limbs embracing each other, trimmed or untrimmed, according to whichever condition would be worse for our approach. Batteries were so placed as to give against us both direct and cross fires.
>
> To my eye, Kennesaw there, at the middle bend of Johnston's long line, was more difficult than any portion of Gettysburg's Cemetery Ridge, or Little Round Top, and quite as impossible to take. . . .

Massed artillery and muskets tore into the blue lines. There were spots, a few, where regiments scrambled up to the first Rebel entrenchments and held them momentarily. But they were thrown back, as the charge everywhere was thrown back. In an hour Sherman lost fifteen hundred men—one in four of those who charged. Survivors said the rule was "lift your head and win a furlough." Rebel soldiers joked that there was no need to aim; just load, shoot, and kill your Yank.

The retreat left hundreds trapped on the slopes, where they remained the whole steaming day, until they could crawl down by dark.

When Sherman asked Thomas if he should venture a second attack, Pap said, "One or two more such assaults would use up this army."

Three broiling days later, decency compelled a truce. The opposing sides labored together on the mountain, hauling the reeking corpses into mass graves.

The disaster preyed on Sherman like no other in the war. At first, he tried to make small of it. "Had we broken the line today," he wrote Thomas, "it would have been most decisive, but as it is our loss is small, compared with some of those East. It should not in the least discourage us. At times assaults are necessary and inevitable. At Arkansas Post we succeeded; at Vicksburg we failed." To Ellen he said, "I begin to regard the death and mangling of a couple thousand men as a small affair, a kind of morning dash—and it may be well that we become so hardened."

But he had no flair for playing the insouciant killer. Good Shakespearean that he was, it may have struck Sherman that he was sounding too much like Falstaff whistling off the demise of his ragged soldiers—"Tut, tut; good enough to toss; food for power, food for powder." His comments soon lost their glibness and grew apologetic.

Cump's superiors neither criticized nor failed to notice that his losses were indeed small next to those in Virginia. So staggered was the public by the carnage in the East that nothing in far off Georgia seemed very bad by comparison. It had not yet been a month since Grant had lost seven thousand in an hour at Cold Harbor.

But Sherman had seen quite enough of charging. That would suffice. In a year of action—the four campaigns that took him from Buzzard's Roost to the surrender—Kennesaw would be his only major assault.

Schofield had made progress on the right ever since the day

of the charge, and now Sherman sent McPherson to join him. On July 2, a swift lunge carried them so far around the Rebel left that Johnston had to make another of his celebrated nighttime withdrawals. In the small hours, Sherman ordered a few troops to edge cautiously up Kennesaw. Watching through field glasses at dawn, he was elated but not surprised to see the stars and stripes flying from the crest.

With his smaller armies racing, Sherman thought that finally he had a chance to catch Johnston in the open, somewhere along the road between Kennesaw and the Chattahoochee, ten miles away. Failing that, he itched to assail the Rebels while they crossed. He came galloping through Marietta, still early on the 3rd, urging his commanders forward. Kenner Garrard, a cavalry general, took a tongue lashing for not getting the hell after Johnston fast.

But to Sherman's surprise, Johnston entrenched on the *near* bank of the Chattahoochee, where his men flung back their pursuers. By now, Johnston and Sherman thought they knew each other's quirks like an old married couple. But this time Johnston coquettishly failed to perform as expected.

To digress a moment, Sherman's flub at the Chattahoochee highlights his growth as a soldier. In a book delightfully titled *On the Psychology of Military Incompetence*, Norman Dixon argues that bad generals are the slaves of their preconceptions. Never mind how many scouts report enemy on the hill; once General Fuddle decides that the enemy must attack him through the valley, Fuddle will guard that valley to the moment when they descend the hill to swallow him.

By contrast, Liddell Hart called Sherman a "realist"—a man blessed with the precious gift of seeing what was before his nose. In that light, his Kentucky panic, when he saw Sidney Johnston's legions everywhere, and his later certainty that Sidney Johnston would not attack at Shiloh were kindred errors—the head and tail of the same bad penny. In both cases, Sherman had reacted to his notion of the enemy.

But by 1864, such lapses were rare and minor. Almost always, Sherman fought the Joe Johnston before his eyes.

* * *

Though Sherman's armies had not yet crossed the last river, at least they had reached it. "Mine eyes have beheld the promised land!" joked Major Connolly. "The 'domes and minarets and spires' of Atlanta are glittering in the sunlight before us, and only 8 miles distant."

Said Sherman—"We had advanced into the enemy's country 120 miles, with a single-track railroad, which had to bring clothing, food, ammunition, everything requisite for 100,000 men and 23,000 animals." That was the achievement he cared about. Toward the end of the campaign, when boasting to old Thomas Ewing, his theme would again be logistics:

> For one hundred days not a man or horse has been without ample food, or a musket or gun without adequate ammunition. I esteem this a triumph greater than any success that has attended me in battle or in strategy, but it has not been the result of blind chance. . . . I could not have done this without forethought beginning with the hour I reached Nashville.

With his army still entrenched in front of Sherman's, Johnston destroyed the bridges on his left, downstream, and covered the fords with artillery. When Sherman sent General George Stoneman's cavalry to seek a crossing, they found nothing. Along the bank in the other direction he sent both Garrard's riders and part of Schofield's infantry. Garrard had no luck, but Schofield found a shallow ford at the mouth of Soap Creek.

Though his men could see only one Rebel gun on the other side of the river, Schofield took no chances. He executed an elaborate amphibious assault that was no less splendid for being needless. The Rebel gun's crew fired one shot, then skedaddled. There was no other resistance. So positive had

Johnston been that Sherman would as usual flank right that his upstream defenses were rudimentary. He too had taken his mate for granted. On pontoons, Schofield's divisions rushed over the Chattahoochee.

Meanwhile, Garrard's futile attempt to find a crossing had carried him clear up to Roswell, twenty miles beyond the armies. Roswell was a factory town, producing cloth and rope for the Confederate forces. Garrard rescued what cloth he could for Federal hospitals, then destroyed the buildings. He thought it best to notify Sherman that "Over the woolen factory the French flag was flying, but seeing no Federal flag above it, I had the building burnt."

Sensing that Garrard might be feeling squeamish, and knowing that the cavalry general still hurt from the rebuke he had received for dawdling at Marietta, Cump returned an answer that was Shermanesque to the point of self-parody:

> [The factories'] utter destruction is right and meets my entire approval, and to make the matter complete you will arrest the owners and employees and send them, under guard, charged with treason to Marietta, and I will see as to any man in America hoisting the French flag and then devoting his labor and capital in supplying armies in open hostility to our Government and claiming the benefit of his neutral flag. Should you, under the impulse of anger, natural at contemplating such perfidy, hang the wretch, I approve the act beforehand. . . .
>
> I assure you, spite of any little disappointment I may have expressed, I feel for you personally not only respect but affection and wish for your unmeasured success and reputation, but I do wish to inspire all cavalry with my conviction that caution and prudence should be but a very small element in their characters.

No Frenchman swung and no international crisis ensued; but Sherman did send hundreds of Roswell women and girls to work in Indiana for the duration of the war, thereby outraging the South.

After Schofield crossed the Chattahoochee, Johnston was compelled to retreat once more. On July 9, he put his last river behind him, then destroyed the railroad bridge. The blue-coats came hurrying behind him. As a Wisconsin soldier explained to his girlfriend:

> Sherman is our guide, like Moses of old was guide for the children of Israel, but he did not smite the waters of the Chattahoochee River as Moses did the Red Sea, but we had to wade, swim or roll through it, any way to get through, and when we got out of meat he called for chickens, turkey, geese, pigs, sheep and anything that we could take, from the rebs in place of the Egyptians.

As for the railroad bridge, Johnston might as well have saved his matches. In their most impressive achievement, Sherman's indefatigable builders crafted a new bridge in under five days—nine hundred feet long and ninety high.

By July 10 Johnston was ensconced in new lines along Peachtree Creek. The war had reached Atlanta. Confederate defenses were within five miles of downtown.

With Schofield already far to the left after his crossing, Sherman risked a "right wheel" for his approach to the city—an elaborate movement intended to bring his armies arcing down on Atlanta like a giant hinge. Thomas, the inner part of the hinge, would move straight down on Peachtree Creek; Schofield would join him on the left. To McPherson went the serious marching. His army, the hinge's outer edge, would go clear around behind Thomas and Schofield on a fifty-mile hike that would bring them down well east of Atlanta, near Decatur.

The danger of the wheel was that the three armies might become widely separated, handing Johnston his long-sought chance to tackle just one of them. Each army would be extra vulnerable as it crossed Peachtree Creek.

But on July 19, while the complex maneuver was in

progress, Sherman and his staff learned that their peril was greater than they realized. Jefferson Davis, never a friend to Joseph Johnston and driven past endurance by two months of steady retreats, had changed generals. The new commander of the Army of Tennessee was John Bell Hood.

Lieutenant General John Bell Hood, Sherman's adversary during the battles around Atlanta. Hood took control of the Army of Tennessee and wasted his men in ineffective heavy assaults against his numerically superior foe.

A triumphant Sherman in the entrenchments at Atlanta. Sherman began his Atlanta campaign in May of 1864 and took the city on September 2. His victories restored flagging Union morale and invigorated President Abraham Lincoln's attempt at re-election.

Chapter 5

Broken, Bleeding Battalions

*B*eside its symbolic value as a city deep within Dixie, Atlanta was a factory center—Sherman had tired of picking up shells marked "Made in Atlanta." More important, it was the South's premier railroad junction. Including the line down which the armies had fought, four tracks converged. Once Sherman held or severed them all, the South's already weakened railroad system would be decimated.

Heading northeast, by way of suburban Decatur, the Georgia Railroad tied Atlanta to the Carolinas and Virginia. The Georgia conveyed supplies from the Deep South to Lee.

Heading southwest, two railroads shared track for a few miles to East Point. There the Macon line split off to the south, running through nearby Jonesboro, and on toward its namesake city. The other line through East Point, the Atlanta & West Point headed toward Alabama and Mississippi. This track and its connections brought food from the Confederacy's breadbasket to Atlanta.

Before he reached Atlanta, Sherman had stretched a distant finger to disable the west-bound line. He cabled General Lovell Rousseau in Tennessee, asking for cavalry to shred the tracks near Montgomery, Alabama, "doing as much mischief as possible."

Though not a cavalry officer, Rousseau opted to lead the raid himself. He reached Alabama in mid-July and mangled thirty miles of track. His raiders grabbed twenty-one tons of bacon, plus freight cars laden with other goods; they then rode east to join Sherman. The four-hundred mile outing crippled the railroad for months.

Sherman might have said that Rousseau's raid succeeded *because* he was an infantry officer. As the war continued, his contempt for cavalry grew. Garrard was not the only cavalry general to face his scorn; nor did Sherman keep his insults and wisecracks quiet. The only cavalry general he respected was Forrest, whose "mounted infantry" dismounted to fight like real soldiers. And the others? As Sherman saw it, most cavalry officers and troopers, both Blue and Gray, seemed more entranced with dashing around and waving their sabers than with winning. Their war was fuss and feathers; his was work.

It especially disgusted Sherman that cavalry wouldn't destroy track properly. By now he knew that rails merely bent over a fire (as at Meridian) could be straightened and re-used. But when red hot rails were twisted, they were worthless unless passed through a rolling mill. Sherman deluged his officers with lengthy, joyous directions on how to "break up track good." But twisting rail was tedious; horsemen, unless commanded by a Rousseau, would not do it.

* * *

Although each was a separate and major battle, many prefer to view the three fights that doomed Atlanta as a single multi-phased action—"Hood's Sorties." Hood tried similar strategy in each, and failed for similar reasons.

Robert E. Lee observed that Hood was "all lion and no fox." A century later, Bruce Catton maintained that the switch from Johnston to Hood was the most grievous error made by either government in the war. At Antietem, one of Hood's regiments had suffered eighty-two percent casualties; more recently, there had been the debacle at Kolb's Farm. Even Hood's own wounds seemed emblematic: At Gettysburg, he had lost the use of an arm that now lay helpless in a sling; he rode strapped to the saddle because of a leg amputated at Chickamauga.

In the West Point class of 1853, McPherson graduated first, Schofield seventh. Thanks to Schofield's tutoring, Hood avoided dismissal and pulled himself up to forty-fourth. Schofield still recalled Hood's go-for-broke style of poker playing. He told Sherman, "He will hit you like hell."

Hood's first sortie, the Battle of Peachtree Creek, came about because a two-mile gap did open between Thomas and Schofield during the right wheel. Then came a second split within the Army of the Cumberland as Thomas crossed the creek. Hood's plan called for Generals A.P. Stewart and Hardee to crush the divisions that had already crossed, while General Cheatham, on the Confederate right, would hold Schofield and McPherson at bay.

The attack was scheduled for early afternoon, July 20. As the hour neared, McPherson was just finishing his long march and moving down on Decatur. Cheatham, alarmed to see McPherson approaching so far to the Rebel right, feared a flank attack and gained Hood's permission to move farther right. That blocked McPherson, but Cheatham's shift compelled Hardee in turn to slide to the right to avoid a gap in the Rebel lines. And once Hardee had moved, Stewart was forced to follow for the same reason.

All this sashaying took three precious hours—long enough for Thomas to finish crossing Peachtree. In an area strewn with thickets and threaded with ravines, the Cumberlanders began to throw up a few breastworks.

The Rebel charge caught Thomas by surprise. Blue divisions near the front were thrown back with heavy losses. But the assault was as poorly co-ordinated as it was tardy;

Cleburne, for example, was withdrawn at the last minute—his division sent over to buttress Cheatham. Because of the terrain, Thomas's lines faced every which way; Rebels who stampeded one blue division sometimes ran straight into the line of fire of another. Between ravines and mismanagement, the Gray charge broke into a jumble of scattered attacks.

Well before sunset, Thomas's men were driving the enemy back everywhere—and in some parts of the field, there weren't many left to drive. Thomas suffered about eighteen hundred casualties; Hardee and Stewart, about forty-eight hundred.

In May and June, the Federal army had lamented that it was impossible to lure Johnston out of his trenches; from Sherman on down, the refrain was the same—you couldn't catch a glimpse of Old Joe in an open field. In turn, Rebs had snarled all the way from Snake Creek Gap that Sherman's three rules of warfare were flank, flank and flank. (Why bother to damn Old Sherman to hell, asked a gray soldier. He would just flank his way back out.)

In one bloody afternoon, however, Hood reversed the campaign's pattern, transposing the meanings of "offense" and "defense." Sherman now confronted an aggressive defender. He himself would be out of the flanking business for a while—too busy protecting his own men and lines.

In savage fighting the next day, McPherson eventually pushed Cleburne off a rise called Bald Hill. Between that lesser victory and Peachtree Creek, Sherman awoke on July 22 suspecting that Hood might be ready to call it quits and abandon Atlanta. Which is to say that Sherman did not yet know Hood.

Toward noon, McPherson dropped by Cump's headquarters for a talk. While the friends chatted, unexpected shooting broke out on the left and McPherson rode off to investigate. An hour or two later, his fought-over corpse was returned to Sherman's camp. Still shy of his thirty-sixth birthday, James

B. McPherson was the only head of a Federal army to fall in the war.

Barking orders every which way, Sherman wept over his friend's body. McPherson had been engaged to a young woman from Baltimore. During the winter, amid the frenzy of campaign preparation, Sherman had denied Mac a wedding leave—a decision he now rued. After the battle he wrote tenderly to McPherson's fianceé, calling her lover a gallant knight and depicting the young commander as Cump last saw him—"so handsome, so smiling, on his fine black horse, booted and spurred."

The day before, Confederate scouts had noted that McPherson's army seemed to be "in the air"—its far end unprotected. The scouts' report led to Hood's second sortie, the Battle of Atlanta (or Decatur).

Hood told Hardee to withdraw his corps from the lines after dark and march quietly out to Decatur. Hardee was to charge after sunrise, smashing through the exposed end of the Army of the Tennessee.

By the time he had passed behind the rest of the Confederate army and found his roads, Hardee's march stretched to nearly fifteen miles. The notion of such a nocturnal stroll leaving troops zesty for battle would be absurd if the men had begun fresh; but they were tired at the start. Many had fought the day before at Peachtree Creek; the rest, that very day at Bald Hill. To add to their joys, the July night was a steambath.

Because it was hard to disengage without alerting the enemy, the march began late. Dawn found Hardee's men still walking; it was blistering noon before they assaulted.

When they did, they struck solid blue lines. As at Peachtree, Hood had seen a weakness but attacked it too late. The purported "air" on McPherson's left was a temporary gap caused by the absence of Grenville Dodge's division, sent to tear up the Georgia's tracks. By noon, thanks to one of McPherson's last orders, Dodge's vandals were back in the line.

The killing of his school friend was all that Hood could boast of after Decatur. Sherman gave Major General John Logan temporary command of the Army of the Tennessee after McPherson's death. "Black Jack" Logan was adept at drawing the best from men in combat, and that day he was supreme—calming and rallying the surprised blueclads, inspiring them to seek revenge for McPherson.

Too much enthralled with the revenge battle, and always too indulgent of rivalries among his forces, Sherman let McPherson's men (his own old army) face Hardee alone. At the cost of soldiers' blood, he indulged himself in the kind of grandiose foo-foo that he usually ridiculed. Logan's force struggled to a victory that would have come easier had Sherman permitted Schofield to help.

For another lapse, both Sherman and Thomas were to blame. Inferring that Hardee's move must have left a hole in the Rebel line, Sherman urged Thomas forward. But Thomas was Thomas—loath to plunge without testing the waters. Reporting *some* enemy before him, he dilly-dallied. Sherman did not force the issue. Almost certainly, Thomas could have knifed through Hood's lines and stormed Atlanta.

But even so, the Union wreaked terrible destruction that afternoon. For hours, gray divisions murdered themselves against Logan's lines before Hardee finally withdrew his survivors. This time, Confederate losses ran so high that neither side at once understood them. With Sherman still barred from Atlanta, thousands of Yankee prisoners being led through the streets, and the glad news of McPherson's death, there were many in town who saw Peachtree and Atlanta as victories. On the other side, Sherman kept raising enemy losses as his officers slowly gauged their triumph. The final tally came to thirty-seven hundred casualties for the victors, against eight thousand for Hood.

Or rather, for William Hardee, who toiled to execute Hood's labyrinthine plans and was blamed by Hood for both defeats. Among the many ironies of "Hood's sorties" was that

Hood, for all his bellicose reputation, never came near the battlefields. Sherman, who viewed himself as a behind-the-scenes commander, stayed far closer to danger.

With Thomas's strong encouragement, Sherman brought O.O. Howard from the Army of the Cumberland to take permanent command of the Army of the Tennessee. Howard's career had been a mixed bag. He had fought well at Seven Pines (where he lost his right arm) and at Gettysburg. But in between, he had been badly fooled—and thrashed—by Stonewall Jackson at Chancellorsville. Intensely devout, Howard was lauded by the press as "the Christian soldier"—a title that endeared him more to the public than to his brother officers.

Still, Thomas found Howard's professional, self-effacing manner far more to his liking than the flashy style of Logan, a two-term Illinois congressman and emphatically a political general. Thomas was disgusted by what he viewed as Logan's noisy, self-serving flamboyance.

The decision displeased many in the ranks. For John Logan, his demotion was a supreme instance of West-Point bias. But he swallowed his pride, resumed his corps command and soldiered on.

Less docile was General Hooker. Though he had not been considered for the post, Hooker knew himself superior to Howard, Thomas and Sherman too. Outraged by the decision, he demanded reassignment. With Sherman's hearty approval, Fighting Joe left the war. Sherman brought in Major General John Slocum from Vicksburg to replace him.

With the Georgia Railroad lost and Rousseau's damage to the western line not yet mended, Hood was down to one railroad—the Macon. Because that target was now so obvious, Sherman tried an elaborate approach: a two-pronged cavalry swoop combined with an infantry advance. At General Stoneman's urging, the cavalry effort was expanded to include an attempt on the Confederate prison camp at Andersonville.

For the horsemen, all that resulted was a thrashing inflicted by Joseph Wheeler, a young Rebel general; Wheeler's horsemen split and re-split the blue riders, then whipped them piecemeal. For days, survivors dribbled back to the Union lines. Stoneman was surrounded and captured. Held in Macon, he watched his men being led off to the very prison he had dreamed of storming.

On July 27th, while the cavalry sped to their destruction, Howard's infantry set off toward the railroad fork at East Point. To stop Howard, Hood sent Stephen Lee, who had just arrived to take over a corps. Hood instructed Lee to hasten down a parallel road, get ahead of Howard, and entrench to block the Union advance. Behind Lee's corps marched Stewart's. Once Lee had obstructed Howard, Stewart was supposed to circle Lee's rear and then come tearing in to hit Howard's outer flank, where danger would be unexpected.

Read that again—it will sound even more insane. The worse the odds grew, the more rococo became Hood's stratagems.

The next day Logan was leading the march when heavy skirmishing made him suspect an imminent attack. Logan halted at a crossroads called Ezra Church; Howard ordered the men to cover their front with timber from a half-cleared field.

When Lee neared the crossroads where he planned to entrench, he found Logan in residence. Stephen Lee was the youngest of Davis's lieutenant generals—brand new in his rank as well as in corps command. A seasoned leader might have withdrawn. Instead, and without waiting for his whole corp to come up, Lee threw his divisions forward.

Howard, only a day or two older in *his* command, and aware that his promotion had left raw spots, let Logan garner the glory. Six times at Ezra Church Lee's men charged Logan's barricades. During respites, the bluecoats dashed into the fields for logs to enhance their defenses.

Ezra Church—"Hood's third sortie"—was less battle than

massacre. "This pays for Kennesaw," said a Northern soldier. All their lives, Logan's men would recall the dead stretched before them like windrows—two and three lines of corpses resting side by side. Wrote Major Connolly, "We slaughter them by the thousands but Hood continues to hurl his broken, bleeding battalions against our immovable lines with all the fury of a maniac." General Hardee sadly agreed: "No action of the campaign probably did so much to demoralize and dishearten the troops engaged in it." Logan lost 562 men. Lee's casualties probably exceeded five thousand.

That night, two pickets conversed across the lines: "Well, Johnny, how many of you are left?" "Oh, 'bout enough for another killin'."

At the end of June, just before he was relieved, Johnston's campaign losses came to fourteen thousand. For the invading general, in a war in which one man entrenched was said to be worth three attackers, Sherman's casualties were impressively low: about seventeen thousand.

But in July Hood devastated an army for which there could be no Frank Blair wafting in with fresh men and chilled champagne. After Peachtree Creek, Atlanta and Ezra Church, Confederate casualties stood at 27,500, against twenty-five thousand Union losses. In a month, Hood had bled the South of over thirteen thousand men. While Hood had not yet destroyed the Army of Tennessee, he had made a significant start.

Sherman told Ellen, "I am glad I beat Johnston, for he had the most exalted reputation with our old army as a strategist. Hood is a new man and a fighter and must be watched closer, as he is reckless of the lives of his men."

Ezra Church quashed Sherman's hopes for a fast move down to the Macon line; Confederate defenses now stretched left to block his way. In August, the armies went nowhere. Sherman saw no profit in sliding right if the enemy would match him step for step. Nor would he attack the Rebel lines—fierce entrenchments begun by Johnston and greatly strengthened by Hood.

Instead, he brought in long-range siege guns from Tennessee, asking Thomas to let him know when they arrived—"I want to come over and watch the effect of a few of the first shots."

Atlanta had suffered death and damage from artillery in July, but the August shelling was systematic. It began on the 10th and lasted all month—over two hundred guns flinging iron into the city with such regularity that blueclads called the shells from certain guns "the Atlanta Express." Hood's cannon replied in kind.

The noisy stalemate was no siege. The Rebels were free to withdraw, the Macon stayed open, and wagon roads also brought in supplies. But it was more siege than anyone within Atlanta desired. Though Sherman once claimed that few civilians remained, he knew better. Many had departed, but the war-swollen population may still have approached ten thousand.

In the beleaguered city, survival became, literally, a hit-or-miss affair. Some buildings were struck repeatedly; others escaped harm. Throughout the bombardment, a semblance of normal life went on. Churches held services and stores held sales. Newspapers came out until almost the end—one of them, the former *Memphis Appeal*, had fled the Yankees so often that Southerners called it "The Moving Appeal."

Sherman had his own troubles. In late July he had requested that none of his top officers be promoted until the campaign was done. After the squabble regarding McPherson's successor, he needed no more quarrels over rank. But shortly after his request came word that two of his brigadiers, both currently inactive, had been raised to major general. Cump rampaged: "It is an act of injustice to officers who stand by their posts in the day of danger to neglect them," he informed the War Department. "If the rear be the post of honor, then we had all better change front on Washington."

To his embarrassment, his tirade reached Lincoln, who returned a placating note to say that Sherman's list of promotions would be approved whenever submitted.

In August, Sherman himself was promoted to major general of regulars. He accepted with tepid grace, asking Stanton to convey his thanks to Lincoln, but adding, "I would have preferred a delay to the close of the campaign."

By far his biggest worry was the stalemate itself. With Grant holding Lee down before Richmond, there was all the more reason for Sherman to be moving. As Lincoln later put it, Grant could hold the bear's leg while Sherman skinned it. But in August he wasn't doing any skinning. He was sufficiently concerned over his lack of progress to seek War Department approval; he needed confirmation that his delay was acceptable.

Lincoln accepted it, but without bliss. For him, August of 1864 was among the war's darkest months; it had been over a year since Gettysburg and Vicksburg, yet the South held on. With both of his great armies stalled, the president despaired of re-election.

On August 10, Hood sent Joe Wheeler and half the cavalry, forty-five hundred men, to wreck Sherman's railroad. Hood wanted the cavalry to ride clear to Tennessee, shredding both the Western & Atlantic and the lines around Chattanooga before returning.

Throughout northern Georgia, Wheeler struck and struck again—tearing track, upturning trains, grabbing Yankee cattle. And yet, the whole thing was more disruption than devastation, more a nasty headache than a dire wound. Messages were delayed and rerouted; supplies came in trickles. But the army was never grievously short of food.

Viewed broadly, Wheeler's raid was another of Hood's self-destructive stratagems. Like Bragg at Chattanooga, he had injured himself by dispatching so many riders. Though Sherman scorned the cavalry, he knew they were an army's eyes. While cursing the damage, he had his fingers crossed that Wheeler would keep right on galloping. And to his joy, Wheeler rode himself clear out of the campaign into East Tennessee. There Sherman's commanders kept him entertained as long as they could, until his bedraggled force at last escaped to Alabama. Wheeler would be out of Sherman's red hair until October.

Late in August, with the gray cavalry vanished beyond recall, Sherman got moving again. This time it was a left wheel—a wide, counter-clockwise sweep toward the tracks below Atlanta. The armies moved in concentric arcs, with Schofield inside Thomas and Howard on the outside. There was a thin chance, Sherman thought, that Hood's remaining cavalry might not discover that he was moving *en masse*. He risked leaving only Slocum's corps to hold the old lines and guard his railroad.

On August 28, Howard and Thomas, a few miles apart, reached the Atlanta & West Point. Their men put in a hard Sunday melting and twisting rails to supplement Rousseau's old damage in Alabama.

Sherman's commanders were surprised to move with so little hindrance. On the flank closest to Atlanta, Schofield fought, but not much; farther from Hood, Howard and Thomas were scarcely molested.

By the 30th, the three armies were circling more east than south as they neared the Macon. Howard would strike at Jonesboro; Thomas and Schofield, a few miles up the line. That afternoon they hit strong Rebel cavalry; scouts reported the enemy in force ahead, particularly around Jonesboro. But by then the blue armies were very near their goal, bearing toward the tracks in overwhelming numbers. Riding beside Thomas, Sherman announced, "I have Atlanta as certainly as if it were in my hand!"

Indeed he did, though he couldn't have said why the end was coming so easily. Nor can hindsight wholly explain Hood's last blunder.

He had been badly fooled by Sherman's move. It may be

that the cattle and spoils Wheeler had sent back to town encouraged Hood in the fantasy that his cavalry were starving Sherman out—there had been rumors of severe Yankee food shortages. Then the siege guns grew silent, and the Federal lines were found empty—further proof that Sherman had taken his army and gone home, perhaps leaving Slocum as a rear guard.

But what self-delusion must have gone into interpreting such evidence! Snake Creek Gap, Resaca, New Hope, Kennesaw, the triple slaughter at Atlanta . . . all that and then retreat?

Many civilians were fooled. People went roaming for souvenirs in the Union lines. Visitors came from Macon to share the rejoicing. How much the high command were duped remains a mystery. "I let my opponent make a flaring ass of me" is not a line often found in military memoirs. Still, one wonders what Hood might have done had Sherman left behind a huge wooden horse.

Shelby Foote speculates that Hood was misled for three days. This, despite warnings from Red Jackson, the leader of his remaining cavalry, who had pierced far enough beyond Schofield to guess what was happening.

Once he finally grasped that Howard was aiming for Jonesboro, Hood apparently decided that the move was a feint to draw him south of town. Sherman must be hidden somewhere, ready to pounce on Atlanta. When Hood shook off *that* delusion and sent troops south, it was too late.

The final engagement, on September 1, was far smaller than the July sorties. Hardee and Stephen Lee intended to launch an early-morning attack at Jonesboro. But on their way down, the gray troops had to dodge so many Union detachments that it was past noon before they were more or less in place. When it finally came, the attack was weak and poorly structured. Howard repulsed the chargers quickly— as much throwing the Rebels aside as defeating them.

Sherman had his fourth railroad. It seemed an apt finale for a campaign so dependent on the trains: Without invading Atlanta, he had amputated the city.

Sherman's only lapse occurred after the battle. Hood, from Atlanta, shrewdly ordered Lee's corps to withdraw, thus leaving Hardee to face the whole Union army. But Sherman couldn't shift his forces quickly enough to surround Hardee and compel surrender. No thanks to his commanding general, Hardee saved a third of the Confederate army. By night, his corps slipped away to the south.

Late that same evening, as they settled down along miles of the Macon tracks, weary Federal soldiers heard explosions to the north. Sherman feared that Hood had turned on Slocum in a night attack. Yet the concussions didn't sound quite like battle. The next day, September 2, rumors trickled in. But it wasn't until the 3rd that Sherman and his army knew anything for certain. By then, the whole North was rejoicing, thanks to a cable from Slocum—"General Sherman has taken Atlanta."

On the night after Jonesboro, Hood had blown up his ammunition dumps and abandoned the city. The next morning the mayor surrendered to Slocum.

Hood circled Sherman and rejoined Hardee. But for now, Cump didn't care. His men needed a rest. Ignoring the Rebel army, he went to take a look at his prize.

Chapter 6

Scope

*D*uring the Civil War, life came fast. Survivors stared over an abyss at the lost world before Fort Sumter. "In the war," said a Southerner to Mark Twain, "each of us, in his own person, seems to have sampled all the different varieties of human experience."

Few packed more life into those years than Tecumseh Sherman. In the quiet days after Atlanta, he paused to take stock. It's time that we paused as well; this chapter and the next consider the man himself rather than his eventful year.

On the way from Jonesboro to Atlanta, he wrote Halleck an overdue thank you:

> I confess I owe you all I now enjoy of fame, for I had allowed myself in 1861 to sink into a perfect "slough of despond," and do believe if I could I would have run away and hid from the dangers and complications that surrounded us. You alone seemed to be confident, and opened to us the first avenue of success and hope, and you gradually put me in the way of recovering from what might have proved an ignoble end. . . .

Such overt reflections weren't common for Sherman. Mostly he seemed to take his rise for granted, as if it had been a commonplace progression. But now and then a tinge of wonder crept in. He sounded no more boastful than astonished when confiding to Ellen that, "The soldiers think I know everything," or when he told Thomas Ewing, "They will march to certain death if I order it, because they know and feel that night and day I labor to the end that not a life shall be lost in vain."

It can be startling to view Sherman in 1864 through contemporary eyes. Suddenly, his utterances were portentous. His message to Washington—"Atlanta is ours, and fairly won"—seemed a line destined for the history books. Writing home the day they first glimpsed Atlanta, the sensible Major Connolly sounded like a mortal beholding demigods:

> . . . In a very few moments Generals Sherman and Thomas (who are always with the extreme front when a sudden movement is taking place) were with us on the hill top, and the two veterans, for a moment, gazed at the glittering prize in silence. I watched the two noble soldiers—Sherman stepping nervously about, his eyes sparkling and his face aglow—casting a single glance at Atlanta, another at the River, and a dozen at the surrounding valley to see where he could best cross the River, how he best could flank them. Thomas stood there like a noble old Roman, calm, soldierly, dignified . . .

Late in August, Farragut's "damn-the-torpedoes" victory at Mobile Bay had brought the North a breath of hope. And then came Slocum's message: "General Sherman has taken Atlanta." The hater of politics had returned Lincoln to the White House. Sherman himself began to be mentioned for the presidency.

His army had long since begun to dote on Sherman stories—to make a legend of him. Everyone knew how he paced his camp at two and three in the morning, plotting his next move, poking about the fire in an old nightgown, red flannel drawers and slippers. "When Old Sherman can't get all the marching he wants by day, he marches by night," said his men.

A joke swept the nation—about the Johnny Reb who wasn't impressed when he heard that a Yankee railroad tunnel had been dynamited—"Hell, don't you know Old Sherman carries a duplicate tunnel?"

Cump had always chattered with soldiers, but now each exchange became some veteran's treasure to bore his grandchildren with. When Sherman jumped into a creek to bathe with his troops, the men loved his easy nakedness—the antithesis of some stuck-up Potomac general. All the quirks that had once hinted of madness were now eccentricities of genius. "Crazy Bill" and "Crazy Sherman" were nicknames, fond reminders of the Old Man's audacity. But more and more his hardened veterans called him "Uncle Billy."

Of those who now itched to depict him, the least successful were the photographers. "All his features express determination, particularly the mouth," said one observer. The pictures caught that, and caught his expressions in repose. But there lay the trouble—few faces were so mobile, and thus so slandered by the long exposure time early cameras required.

He overflowed with vitality. "Nothing was more exciting than having Sherman enter a room," said an officer, "and nothing was more relaxing than having him leave." Added a war correspondent: "He walked, talked or laughed all over. He perspired thought at every pore."

One of the best verbal portraits appears in a letter by a Federal major, John Chipman Gray, who met Cump in Savannah, after the March to the Sea:

> . . . If I were to write a dozen pages I could not tell you a tenth part of what he said, for he talked incessantly and more rapidly than any man I ever saw.
> General Sherman is the most American looking man I ever saw, tall and lank, not very erect, with hair like thatch, which he rubs up with his hands, a rusty beard trimmed close, a wrin-

kled face, sharp prominent red nose, small bright eyes, coarse red hands; black felt hat slouched over the eyes (he says when he wears anything else the soldiers cry out, as he rides along, "Hallo, the old man has got a new hat"), dirty dickey with points wilted down, . . . brown field officer's coat with high collar and no shoulder stripes, muddy trousers and one spur. He carries his hands in his pockets, is very awkward in his gait and motions, talks continually and with immense rapidity. . . . It would be easier to say what he did not talk about than what he did. . . . At his departure I felt it a relief and experienced almost an exhaustion after the excitement of his vigorous presence.

Like all of us, Major Gray saw as he had been taught to see. His fine portrait is mainly eccentricities and mannerisms. Victorians knew each other by such touches, much as we know each other by post-Freudian labels like "he's insecure." Major Gray's Sherman might have stepped out of *The Pickwick Papers*. The same is true of most contemporary descriptions: Sherman comes across as some standard type out of Victorian popular fiction or melodrama; often, as a Dickensian grotesque.

The quirks most frequently mentioned involved his energy, cigars and speech. Everyone marked his restless pacing and abrupt gestures. Most of the cigar anecdotes also emphasized his energy—insisting that he more chewed than smoked his stogies and never had the patience to finish one. (He once borrowed a cigar from a soldier to light his own, then absentmindedly smoked it.) The *rows* of Sherman's chewed cigars leap from old descriptions like some insistent tic. So too, his rattling talk: Cump splattered people with bursts of words. He also repeated phrases—warning a poky quartermaster that "we'll eat your mules up, Sir, eat your mules up," or telling a general that an assault was "Fine! Just what I wanted. Just what I wanted." Again, it's all suspiciously

Dickensian, like Scrooge repeating "Bah, humbug!" Perhaps Sherman didn't reiterate quite as often as he was heard to do.

At times he cultivated his own quirks, as someone today might strive to live up to a psychobabble label like "self-actualized." When he cabled an unfortunate general, "Saw your proclamation; don't believe in proclamations," he was trying too hard to sound Shermanesque.

Similarly cultivated was his way of covering kindness with gruffness. Victorians adored that style of prickly-lollipop behavior, and Sherman could play it to the hilt. When he dealt with Mother Bickerdyke, for example, their encounters could have been written by Bret Harte.

Mary Anne Bickerdyke was a backwoods Florence Nightingale who attached herself to Sherman's armies. Throughout the Atlanta campaign, she and her helpers ran kitchens and laundries for the wounded, begging supplies from the North and foraging them from the South. In her spare time, the "Cyclone in Calico" and her clean-up crews assailed the ghastly field hospitals.

What Mother Bickerdyke needed, she took; and when she couldn't steal it from lower officers, she went to the top, barging into Sherman's office. He would growl something suitably fierce, or tell her he was too busy to talk, too busy to talk. When that didn't work, he would shout at her awhile about why he would not change an order, or why she could not possibly have those train cars. Without a flinch, Mary Anne let him rant. Then she would tell him to show a little common sense; and (of course) would depart triumphant. They both had a good time.

As a nurse recalled, "She had a great admiration for several of our great generals, but most of all for Sherman. She loved him . . . and considered herself a part of his force." When surgeons complained that Mother Bickerdyke was cluttering the hospitals with her soups and jellies, Cump just shrugged—"I can't do a thing in the world. She outranks me."

Besides playing the bear, Sherman was often a whiner and

occasionally mean-spirited. More than once he threatened to resign, complaining that the press or politicians were making it impossible for him to continue. He shot from the hip so much that it's hard to know when to take him literally. Were his threats to quit serious? I think not, just as I think that his griping over Thomas's slow ways was largely shop talk. Sherman was one of those men who can growl the livelong day while staying happy—like a driver who offers damnation and odd sexual advice to his fellow motorists, then enters his front door whistling.

"My opinions are very strong," he needlessly explained. So assertive was he, and so intense his personality, that his every failing trumpeted itself. Sherman's noisy smallness—all that fizzle and frazzle—made his bigness harder to see. And yet, to focus too much on his flaring, rambunctious surface was like viewing a Van Gogh from six inches away.

His pettiness and cantankerousness need no belaboring, but his scope does. His mental stretch was enormous—Sherman was far bigger than he was small.

For starters, he was a gifted writer. He could not have displayed his failings half so clearly had he not written so well.

If style is personality translated into words, Sherman was an outstanding stylist. His voice is unmistakable. Skim the war's *Official Records* and his words jump off the page—there's no need to check the signature. A century after his death, the voice still lives.

Like Grant and Lincoln, Sherman anticipated the new, undecorated prose that matured in the hands of Twain and Howells. There were those (Henry Adams for one) who spotted him early as a splendid writer. To the public, he seemed only a man who said his two-cents' worth unusually clearly. How could anything so much like plain talk be "writing"? Which is what the genteel would soon be saying about *Roughing It*. Today, his style seems so modern that occasional old-fashioned phrases look out of place: Sherman says "a million of dollars," "a storm of rain"; he prefers "whilst" to "while."

Cump was appalled by how easily orders could be misconstrued and, like Grant, determined to make his own commands unambiguous. Thus, his prose became workmanlike in the highest sense. By 1864, only a fool could read a Sherman order and come away confused about whether something *has been* done or *should be* done or *will soon* be done—verb tenses are crystalline. He also shuns gobbledygook and all the sleazy tricks we call Orwellian. The more important the message, the more often his sentences begin with "I" followed by a blunt active verb. Sherman rarely says "a factory caught fire" or "a factory was ordered destroyed." He says "I burned the factory."

Faulkner once explained why he loved Sarah Gamp, a repulsive old bitch in *Martin Chuzzlewit*: "Most of her character was bad, but at least it was character." Even at his most ruthless, Sherman leaves a similar impression. He wrote as a man who took responsibility for his deeds, said what he wanted to say, and refused to be mealy-mouthed. He had character.

He also had a mind that he enjoyed using. Again, his unlovely surface traits hid larger matters. Sherman's language was blunt and salty. He enjoyed coarse humor. He encouraged other officers to tell dirty jokes in front of General Howard, for the fun of watching "the Christian soldier" squirm. Many described him as coarse or unpolished.

Coarse? In spades. Unpolished? By no means.

He was well read in the literature of his era (Dickens and Burns were particular favorites) and sprinkled his writings with allusions to the Bible, Shakespeare, and classic English and French authors. He enjoyed opera and concerts and was avidly devoted to the stage.

Sherman also read history of many kinds, and his knowledge of military history was unusually rich. In later years, when he wrote of Civil War battles or strategy it was often in the context of modern European warfare. A cosmopolitan in spirit, his mind moved comfortably among nations and eras.

"War's over—occupation's gone," he wrote after the surrender. For me, the line captures the ambiguity of Sherman's roughness—a rattle of brusque words enclosing a deft Shakespearean allusion.

At his most tedious, Sherman was far less philistine than pedant. There had always been a fat dollop of the schoolmaster in him, and age did not wither his fondness for lecturing. Throughout the war, he lavished unsought advice on Lincoln, Stanton, Grant and anyone else handy. Now and then he mentioned (to Grant, among others) how much more knowledgeable he was than Grant. He could never stick to his own business; nor could he ravage the South without pontificating, in nauseating detail, on why he was doing it. Even when the fighting ended, the lectures did not. He titled the last chapter of his *Memoirs* "Military Lessons of the War." That is pure Sherman.

But (and in Sherman's case, there is so often a "but") he shared the pedant's virtue as well his flaws—Cump was a voracious student, a glutton for knowledge and information. That youthful half-year voyage to Monterey, when he gobbled every book on the ship, anticipated a life-long addiction. In the 1870s, when he made a long tour abroad, Sherman was the model tourist—reading copiously on the places he was seeing, asking questions, taking notes.

Decades after the war, Charles Dana (a distinguished editor who had served as Stanton's assistant) recalled his first encounter with Grant's generals—"One or two of them I found were very rare men. Sherman especially impressed me as a man of genius and of the widest intellectual acquisitions." Grant put it simply: "Sherman bones all the time."

He loved to stretch his mind—through books, travel, conversation—and to the end of his days he kept on boning.

* * *

It's a commonplace of military history that Sherman was one of the first campaign generals. He handled the movements of whole armies far better than the minute-by-minute particulars of a battle. He was a great strategist; a mediocre tactician.

Grant, Forrest, Stonewall Jackson and Sherman were soldiers of a new breed. They did not view war as traditional generals (and most of the public) still saw it: set-piece engagements with long pauses between. After a battle, a McClellan or a Burnside stopped to think things over and lick his wounds. In the East, that pattern predominated from First Bull Run until Grant took charge.

But for the campaign general, a battle was only a tremendous incident within a larger whole. Sherman contended that the supreme moment of Grant's life was the evening when he moved left after taking his beating in the Wilderness. By heading at once toward Richmond, Grant compelled Lee to follow, thus turning Lee's victory into an episode in the campaign that eventually pinned Lee where Grant wanted him. Until Hood took over, the Atlanta campaign broadly resembled Grant's: Johnston might win battles, but when Sherman flanked, both armies drew closer to Atlanta.

We still lack words for Sherman's kind of war. Unavoidably, all accounts of the Atlanta campaign suggest a fight-by-fight, staccato rhythm that distorts reality. Sherman called the campaign "one immense skirmish with small battles interspersed." Thousands of casualties came not at New Hope or Peachtree Creek, but in skirmishes too small to be named. Even during the rainy weeks before Kennesaw the fighting continued. Recalled Private Robert Hale Strong: "We were under fire every day for about a month from Buzzards' Roost to Atlanta. . . . I don't mean that we were in a big fight every day, but we were in at least a skirmish on the picket line. We were always firing at one another. All the way to Atlanta was a series of fights."

But by 1864, Sherman was waging war on a scale that even "campaign general" won't cover. Decisions involving thousands of men had become his routine chores. Quandaries that once would have prostrated him he now disposed of with a few snarling memos and a handful of curses. But mainly he did his job with a casual competence that made enormous difficulties seem minor. Three examples should suffice.

—Through most of 1864, Sherman faced a frustrating reminder of how long the war had dragged on: His three-year men were going home. In March and April, some divisions were so depleted that their actual strength was not half of their paper strength. (It was not a problem Johnston shared; Confederate troops were enrolled for the duration.) Re-enlistment ran gratifyingly high in the western armies—around fifty percent returned for a second hitch. But re-enlistment leaves caused their own ample problems, as witness General Blair's ten thousand late arrivals. Throughout the year, Sherman's regiments and officers kept coming and going. He faced Johnston and Hood with amorphous armies.

—Nathan B. Forrest did not vanish. All year long, the cavalry wizard kept finding new and interesting ways to trounce and fluster Sherman's generals. For Sherman, he was an unsolvable problem. But what Cump couldn't stop he had learned to contain. Until Atlanta fell, he goaded and wheedled his distant generals into keeping Forrest preoccupied— far away from North Georgia, where he would have done damage that mattered. Sherman wanted Forrest in hell, but settled for northern Mississippi.

—As a last instance, there was the little difficulty of Major General Nathaniel Banks and the ten thousand missing soldiers.

Shortly after returning from Meridian, in early March, Sherman had journeyed to New Orleans to consult with Banks, who was about to start up the Red River on a gigantic raid. Banks persuaded Sherman to loan him ten thousand of his lately returned troops. Cump consented reluctantly, with the proviso that Banks would repay the loan in one month.

Red River should have been another Meridian, but Banks was no Sherman. He was not even a Sooy Smith. His foray became a riverine nightmare that ended with Banks fleeing in panic from a greatly outnumbered Rebel force. By the time he escaped, it was too late for those men still able to fight to rejoin Sherman.

In May, the mishap proved doubly vexing in that Grant's strategy had called for Banks to attempt a Gulf invasion, through Mobile, to keep Confederate forces divided. But with Banks still wallowing in the Red River, there was little doing that month in Mississippi and Alabama. And that is why Polk was able to come to Johnston's aid, bringing nearly his whole army.

By late April, as he prepared to launch the spring offensive, Sherman knew only that Red River had been a disaster. Banker-like, he shrugged his shoulders, added ten thousand lost men plus one canceled diversion at Mobile to his debit column, and kept right on calculating how to go for Joe Johnston.

* * *

In Sherman's day, they spoke of how the war brought forth men whose talents might otherwise have stayed hidden. In his own case, the most impressive and useful of those talents was a gift without a common name. Call it geographic sense or a feeling for terrain. When Sherman climbed a hill, his mind's eye placed it within a mountain chain. He dipped his toe in a creek, and saw a river system. His vision was both detailed and continental—like a satellite's.

In California, years earlier than most men, he had advocated a transcontinental railroad, foreseeing how it would bond and stretch the nation. He also foresaw (and with no regret) how it would destroy the Indians. All his life he was entranced with the Mississippi and its net of tributaries. He spoke of the river as his hobby, swearing that he would gladly be buried within its waters, like DeSoto. But "hobby" is too weak, for the vast river stirred his heart and thrilled his imagination. This he wrote when Grant went to Washington for his third star:

> Now as to the future. . . . Come out West; take to yourself the whole Mississippi Valley; let us make it dead-sure, and I tell you the Atlantic slope and Pacific shores will follow its destiny as sure as the limbs of a tree live or die with the main trunk! We have done much, still more remains to be done. . . .
>
> I now exhort you to come out West. Here lies the seat of the coming empire; and from the West, when our task is done, we will make short work of Charleston and Richmond, and the impoverished coast of the Atlantic.

Sherman had a passion for landscape. His early travel letters abounded with detailed descriptions of terrain, and often included his own careful maps. With Ellen, he treated as a family joke "my old rule never to return by the road I had come." As both traveler and Civil War fighter, Cump assumed that Ellen and the children would read his letters with an atlas handy, eagerly tracing his routes.

As early as Chickasaw Bluffs, each of his divisions included a topographical officer; new maps were duplicated regularly. To minimize confusion, he sometimes gave orders like "camp near the 'o' in 'Mountain.'" Before the Atlanta campaign, he pored over Georgia census figures, plotting resources county by county. (That study may have inspired the March to the Sea. In April he informed Grant, "Georgia has a million of inhabitants. If they can live, we should not starve.")

Roaming the Far West after the war, he often had his face in a map—absorbing information on creeks and hamlets, pestering riverboat crews with his topographical questions.

It's common Civil War knowledge that Sherman had ridden northern Georgia and the Carolinas as a young officer. But what matters is that he *remembered* vast swatches of terrain as some people memorize limericks. Two decades after those horseback rides to Kennesaw, he informed McPherson that about halfway up the north side Mac would find a peach orchard where he could rest his men.

Cump bragged that he knew Georgia better than the enemy did; in Howard's opinion, the boasts were understatements:

> Sherman had remarkable topographical ability. A country that he once saw he could not forget. The cities, the villages, the streams, the mountains, hills, and divides—these were as easily seen by him as human faces, and the features were always on hand for use. It made him ever playing at draughts with his adversary. Let the enemy move and Sherman's move was instant and well chosen.

Sherman understood the value and rarity of his own kind of scope. In the 1880s, he wrote an essay called "The Grand Strategy of the Last Year of the War," in which he presented his campaigns as merely one element of Grant's master plan. In another late essay, he challenged a writer for over-praising Lee. Sherman felt that Lee, for all his greatness, was a regional general:

> He never rose to the grand problem which involved a continent and future generations. His Virginia was to him the world. . . . He stood at the front porch battling with the flames whilst the kitchen and house were burning, sure in the end to consume the whole. . . . Grant's "strategy" embraced a continent, Lee's a small State; Grant's "logistics" were to supply and transport armies thousands of miles, where Lee was limited to hundreds.

* * *

In his later years, Senator Sherman often recalled a June evening in '61, a few weeks before Bull Run. He had sat in a tavern, watching his brother and another colonel, George Thomas, spread a map on the floor. It had amused John to see the budding Napoleons sketching imaginary campaigns, guessing how the war would develop. Most people were saying that one big Virginia battle would settle everything; but apparently Cump and his friend didn't think so. Looking back, John Sherman could see those busy pencils circling the names of western cities—Nashville, Chattanooga. He could remember his brother's arm stretching over the map, as he emphatically circled a remote town called Vicksburg.

Sherman with his commanders who accompanied him on the March to the Sea. From left to right: Oliver O. Howard, John A. Logan, William B. Hazen, W. T. Sherman, Jefferson C. Davis, Henry W. Slocum and J. A. Mower.

Chapter 7

Terrible Innocence

Sherman neither invented total war nor reverted to the warfare of the Huns. As a glance at *Candide* will suggest, combat between Attila and Atlanta was not a spectator sport with civilians barred from the playing field. Gentlemanly warfare had been practiced sporadically for a few eighteenth- and nineteenth-century decades, and only among the self-proclaimed "civilized" nations. Our Revolutionary War was dainty; our Indian wars of the same era were not.

If "total war" means Auschwitz, Hiroshima or My Lai, then no Civil War general waged it. Well over ninety percent of the casualties were men in uniform; on Sherman's two big marches there were at most a few dozen deaths among non-combatants. What Sherman waged might better be called "terror war."

The spread of Civil War violence and destruction beyond the battlefield is murky; each side proved that the other began it and did more of it. For troops who needed an excuse for savagery, "They started it" always made a handy pretext. Some of Sherman's regiments were from Missouri, where pro-Southern guerrillas had rampaged. Not long before the Atlanta campaign came Fort Pillow, where Forrest's men were said to have killed black soldiers who had surrendered.

Later in 1864, Rebel troops burned Chambersburg, Pennsylvania.

Looting and pillage probably began with common soldiers on both sides. Many accounts of First Bull Run (Sherman's among them) depict harried officers trying to keep their men from stealing cows and harassing farm girls. Gerald E. Linderman argues that war against civilians gradually "percolated upward through the ranks." In the later years, says Linderman, things worked the other way around, when commanders began to employ terror warfare as a deliberate weapon.

Sherman's thoughts on extending war to the civilian population had likely solidified by the summer of 1862, as shown by his threats and actions against the guerrillas who attacked steamboats near Memphis. His letter to Salmon Chase, stating that "all in the South are enemies of all in the North" implied everything he would later say, do, or condone.

The crux of Sherman's Memphis Doctrine was his conviction that any Southern civilian or town might justly be punished for whatever sin he was currently punishing because the whole South was in rebellion and thus responsible for the war. That belief was implicit whenever he told some ravaged farmer that "you" shouldn't have seceded.

The second raid on Jackson (July 1863) was probably the first time he allowed unsupervised destruction. That same foray was also Sherman's first chance to practice independently what Grant had taught him about foraging. As a letter to Grant revealed, he proved a quick learner:

> We are absolutely stripping the country of corn, cattle, hogs, sheep, poultry, everything, and the new-growing corn is being thrown open as pasture fields or hauled for the use of our animals. The wholesale destruction to which this country is now being subjected is terrible to contemplate . . .

"The inhabitants are subjugated," he added. "They cry for mercy. The land is devastated for 30 miles around."

From the time of that raid, Sherman was recognizably "Sherman" in all his dark majesty. But again: For terror warfare, all dates and distinctions must remain fuzzy, for Sherman or any officer. In general, what occurred was a gradual loss of scruples and a coarsening of values. In 1861, officers did not openly encourage mayhem—Sherman may really have forbidden his men to snitch green apples in Kentucky. By 1864, Phil Sheridan was boasting that when he finished with the Shenandoah Valley, a buzzard flying over would need to carry his lunch; Sherman was tranquilly admitting that his men were "a little loose in the foraging" on the March to the Sea. But on paper, unsupervised destruction continued to be forbidden; and to the end of the war there were times when officers enforced the rules, even in Sherman's armies.

* * *

Two days after Jonesboro, before he had set foot in Atlanta, Sherman told Halleck his plans:

> I propose to remove all the inhabitants of Atlanta, sending those committed to our cause to the rear, and the rebel families to the front. I will allow no trade, manufactories, nor any citizens there at all, so that we will have the entire use of railroad back, as also such corn and forage as may be reached by our troops. If the people raise a howl against my barbarity and cruelty I will answer that war is war, and not popularity-seeking. If they want peace they and their relatives must stop the war.

From Atlanta, he wrote to General Hood, suggesting a brief truce. Sherman would transport refugees who wished to go south, along with their baggage and all slaves who would go willingly. Once the exiles reached the end of Sherman's part of the Macon line, they would be Hood's problem.

Hood replied that he accepted because he had no choice. After sketching truce terms, he added:

> And now, sir, permit to say that the unprecedented measure
> you propose transcends, in studied and ingenious cruelty, all
> acts ever before brought to my attention in the dark history of
> war.
>   In the name of God and humanity, I protest, believing that you
> will find that you are expelling from their homes and firesides
> the wives and children of a brave people.

That barb led to an exchange of long letters in which the commanders haggled over the causes and conduct of the war. Their "remarkable, pungent, incisive correspondence" (as Howard termed it) was published both North and South, leaving readers everywhere smug that their man won the argument.

Amid these literary fireworks, a committee led by the mayor of Atlanta begged Sherman to cancel the removal because of "the horrors and the suffering" it would cause, especially for invalids and pregnant women.

His volleys with Hood had stirred him up, and Mayor Calhoun got the dubious benefit—receiving one of Sherman's fullest defenses of harsh war. It too was reprinted, and met with approval in the North.

Sherman agreed that the removal would cause grave hardships. Still, he would not revoke his orders "because they were not designed to meet the humanities of the case." The issue was not the peace of Atlanta, but of America—a peace that required the defeat of Rebel armies, "which are arrayed against the laws and Constitution." For now, Atlanta was no place for families; military needs came first. With business settled, Sherman warmed to his theme:

> You cannot qualify war in harsher terms than I will. War is cru-
> elty, and you cannot refine it; and those who brought war into

our country deserve all the curses and maledictions a people
can pour out. I know I had no hand in making this war, and I
know I will make more sacrifices to-day than any of you to secure peace. But you cannot have peace and a division of our
country. . . . The United States does and must assert its authority, wherever it once had power, for if it relaxes one bit to pressure, it is gone, and I believe that such is the national feeling.
This feeling assumes various shapes, but always comes back to
that of Union. Once admit the Union, once more acknowledge
the authority of the national Government, and instead of devot-
ing your houses and streets and roads to the dread use of war,
I and this army become at once your protectors and supporters, shielding you from danger, let it come from what quarter it
may. . . .

Then will I share with you the last cracker, and watch with you
to shield your homes and families against danger from every
quarter.

Now you must go, and take with you the old and feeble . . .

Sherman did not believe in natural law. Adherence to
man-made law was all that made decent life possible. That
idea he repeated many times, once even saying that "This war
will instill in our people the conviction that we must obey the
Law, not because we like & approve it, but blindly because it
is Law." Secession and rebellion were synonymous with
treason. The federal government had whatever rights it
wished to enforce against rebels, including taking their lives;
because war was power unrestrained by compact.

Those who insist on analyzing Sherman's logic in detail are
trying too hard. Often, the most difficult chore in grasping
him is accepting his terrifying simplicity. Any child could
understand the gist of Cump's defense of terror warfare, for
children use the same reasoning: Sammy is quietly eating
lunch when Johnny pokes him with a stick. Sammy at once
smears peanut butter and jelly over Johnny's face and clothes.

Johnny shouts, "Hey! That's my new shirt!!"

"Yeah? Well you started it!"

"Yeah, but you didn't have to do THAT! My momma's gonna KILL me!"

If Sammy answers again, he will likely repeat himself. He knows what he's thinking, but can't phrase it. Sherman, however, could: If you break the rules, don't holler for fair treatment under the rules. He once put it nearly as Sammy might: "I regarded the Constitution as a bargain."

At his most sententious, Sherman was no improvement on the Georgians who called down divine wrath on him. But his reasoning never changed:

> To those who submit to the rightful law and authority all gentleness and forbearance; but to the petulant and persistent secessionist, why, death is mercy, and the quicker he or she is disposed of the better. Satan and the rebellious saints of Heaven were allowed a continuous existence in hell merely to swell their just punishment. To such as would rebel against a Government so mild and just as our was in peace, a punishment equal would not be unjust.

"I never saw a man more utterly possessed with the conviction of the infinite wrong and crime of [the rebellion's] very existence," said one of Sherman's aides.

Most of Sherman's army understood and shared his view. When they reached Columbia, South Carolina, one of his soldiers set fire to a church and ran down the street shouting, "Did you think about *this* when you hurrahed for secession?" Sherman had said little more.

To damn Sherman because there was "no military necessity" for his deeds begs the question. From his angle, it *was* necessary to steal hogs and terrorize women. He wanted the hogs in Union, not Rebel, bellies. He hoped that a destitute, frightened woman would urge her husband to leave the front and come home.

His methods were as pragmatic and simplistic as his justification. But while his excuse for cruel war was one a child would use, his methods were parental: If Daddy gets riled enough, he doesn't care whether it was Bobby, Billy or Betsy who poured glue on the gerbil—he spanks the first one he catches. So much for what has been ponderously called Sherman's "Theory of Collective Responsibility." Further, if the misbehavior gets bad enough, Daddy will keep spanking everyone, harder and harder, until all the children decide that it's easier to be good than to have stinging fannies. That was Sherman's "philosophy" of how to fight a civil war.

He put it plainly to Grant's adjutant, General John Rawlins:

> I am supposed vindictive. You remember what *Polonius* said to
> his son *Laertes*: "Beware of entrance to a quarrel; but, being in,
> bear it, that the opposed may beware of thee." What is true of a
> single man is equally true of a nation. . . . I would make this
> war as severe as possible, and show no symptoms of tiring till
> the South begs for mercy; indeed, I know, and you know, that
> the end would be reached quicker by such a course than by
> any seeming yielding on our part.

In carrying the war to civilians, Sherman had at least three goals beyond wishing to take or destroy whatever might be useful to Confederate armies. All these goals were matters of psychological warfare. He called it "statesmanship," or spoke of the "moral effect" of his marches.

Most important, he wished to show the South its helplessness. Starting with Meridian, his marches dramatized that Federal armies could raid where they pleased. To George Thomas he said: "I propose to demonstrate the vulnerability of the South, and make its inhabitants feel that war and individual ruin are synonymous terms."

After the March to the Sea, he elaborated:

> We must make old and young, rich and poor, feel the hard
> hand of war. I know that this recent movement of mine
> through Georgia has had a wonderful effect in this respect.

Thousands who have been deceived by their lying newspapers
to believe that we were being whipped all the time now realize
the truth, and have no appetite for repetition of the same experience.

When a Carolina gentleman asked Sherman where he
thought of marching next, he explained that with sixty
thousand men behind him he intended to go pretty much
where he pleased.

Second, he wished to tempt Confederate soldiers to desert.
This goal became central in the war's final months. A man
whose farm was in Sherman's path might find his own affairs
more pressing than Robert E. Lee's. Before invading the
Carolinas, Sherman declared that "every step I take from this
point northward is as much a direct attack upon Lee's army
as though we were operating within the sound of his artillery." By the end, that army was vanishing fast, as Lee's men
went A.W.O.L. or surrendered by the thousands. Sherman
was convinced that his marchers deserved much of the credit.

Lastly, he thought that terror had its own value in under-
mining the will to resist. As Southerners turned him and his
forces into demons, Sherman was more pleased and amused
than hurt. As early as 1862, he had said it would be useful if
the approach of Union armies were dreaded. Fine with him if
Southern papers portrayed him as a crazy general leading a
barbarous horde. During the Atlanta campaign, tales spread
that Sherman had ordered his men to fire bullets modified to
"poison the flesh." That sort of blather was just what he
wanted; just what he wanted.

* * *

Winning was all that mattered, and Cump defined "winning" in the simplest, most obvious sense. He didn't worry
about fighting fair, he had few romantic illusions about
glory—*he came to win*. That blunt notion neither "explains"

Sherman nor disposes of his every inconsistency. But it underlies his way of war.

His contempt for cavalry, for instance. At heart, Sherman's was the universal infantryman's gripe, heard throughout the war from foot soldiers on both sides: Troopers were stuck up, cowardly, lazy bastards. ("You never see a dead cavalryman" may have been the war's most overworked joke.) Cavalry pranced; infantry fought. By the end, Sherman's men would be calling Confederate riders "the chivalry," with sarcasm laid on with a trowel. Nor did they regard their own horsemen with much more respect.

Knowing the South well, Sherman understood the lure of the Man on Horseback—all the historical and romantic implications of "cavalier." But to understand was not to sympathize. There were those (North as well as South) who were profoundly stirred when "Jeb" Stuart's gray horsemen rode clear around the Army of the Potomac in the war's most dazzling cavalry escapade. But there were also those like Cump who asked, "What good did it do?"

Sherman once acknowledged that the "Southrons" were better fighters—the South had a far richer military heritage. But the North would win, he said, by working harder. And he saw damn few cavalry who would work.

Sherman's focus on winning was also crucial in his friendship with Grant—the most important working relationship in the war. Both generals cared more about getting the job done than anything else (though Grant's determination to win never became the narrow fetish that Sherman's did). The shared goal made every difference between the quiet, stolid commander and his frothy subordinate seem trivial.

Appropriately, their friendship had begun when Sherman waived rank to help Grant. Throughout the war—episodes like the McClernand affair notwithstanding—both Grant and Sherman remained far less rank-ridden than many West Pointers. They played their rank games, they kept close track of who "ranked" whom among their subordinates; but with them rank never became a preoccupation that ruined careers and crippled battle plans. Both, for example, co-operated well with the navy, establishing unusually smooth relationships with admirals. Grant *and Porter* assaulted Vicksburg. Sherman *and Dahlgren* made Savannah a safe port after the March to the Sea.

His utter concentration on winning also made Sherman one of the generals Lincoln had sought so long. The president too came to win. Lincoln endured it when Sherman said he would not feed civilians because he cherished the drive for victory behind Sherman's tantrums and tirades. Again, a shared focus on the goal neutralized differences in temperament. But Lincoln and Sherman were not as different as they might appear. Both knew how to be bulldogs. In order to gain his ends, Lincoln could make himself simple; Sherman, simplistic. When Sherman spoke of preserving the Union at all costs, it brought to mind Lincoln telling Horace Greeley that he would preserve the Union whether that meant freeing all, none or some of the slaves.

In his own quieter fashion, Lincoln seemed most Shermanesque when he responded to McClellan's gauche behavior by saying "I would hold General McClellan's horse, if he would bring us victory"; and more so when he refused to dismiss Grant because of alcohol—"No. I can't spare this man. He fights."

* * *

Winning was everything. But what about later? What did Sherman envision for America when the last corpse was buried and the last Rebel house stopped smoldering? Well, that too was simple:

> War is the remedy our enemies have chosen . . . and I say let us give them all they want; not a word of argument, not a sign of let-up, no cave in till we are whipped or they are. . . . The only principle in this war is, which party can whip. It is as simple as

a schoolboy's fight and when one or the other party gives in,
we will be the better friends.

We will be the better friends. It was the same thing he said
to Mayor Calhoun: All that the foolish Southerners had to do
was behave themselves. The minute they did that, Sherman
would be their pal again, guarding their homes "against
danger from every quarter." And he would share his last
cracker. In December, after ripping the guts out of Georgia,
he said it once more, to the Savannah Chamber of Commerce:
"The sooner all the cotton in the South is burned up, the
sooner will the people of the South come to their senses. . . .
When war is done we can soon bring order out of chaos and
prosperity out of misery and destruction."

Here again, Cump's attitude was shared by thousands of
his troops. Writing after the surrender, a Wisconsin private
explained that his regiment had been visiting with the
Johnnies: "We get along very well, have no trouble at all.
They are willing to admit that we have whipped them, and
that is all that we want of them, is to acknowledge that we are
too much for them, and we will always get along very finely."

But what is bearable in young soldiers seems appalling in
a mature, thoughtful man who had seen the horrors Sherman
had seen, caused the hell he had caused. Was four years of
carnage—half a million slain men—merely a flesh wound on
the national skin? Apparently so. All the South had to do was
holler "'Nuff! We give!" Then everybody would shake hands,
dust off their clothes and get back to business.

The word is *innocence*. Despite his intelligence, his formidable knowledge, his rare zest and capacity for experience,
Sherman's innocence was so reductive that it blinded him
morally and emotionally. His naiveté diminished human
complexities and the maelstrom of human feelings to little
burps: Secession is treason. If you break the rules, don't holler
if we break you. Winning is everything. After we've pounded

you, we'll be friends again. We'll soon bring prosperity out of misery. Here—take a bite of my hardtack.

Moreover, Sherman's was largely a deliberate innocence, a self-willed blindness. This imaginative nervous man chose to put his sensitivity and compassion on the shelf until he had battered the Confederacy. Riveted on the task at hand, Sherman made himself a Terrible Innocent. The fox commanded himself to be a hedgehog.

Camped by the smoking remains of a factory, early on the March to the Sea, an aide jotted notes:

> Yesterday as we passed one house, the yard full of soldiers, pigs, chickens, cattle rapidly disappearing, an elderly lady seeing Gen. S. pass ran out to gate and begged for a guard. General answered, not roughly but firmly, couldn't do it, army was marching and couldn't stop men . . . At night as he sat by camp fire, I only near him, he said, "I'll have to harden my heart to these things. That poor woman today—how could I help her? There's no help for it. The soldiers will take all she has. Jeff Davis is responsible for all this:" etc., etc.

It's tempting to call Sherman's innocence "unfathomable." But in truth we can fathom it easily; because his Terrible Innocence was terribly American.

It's the naiveté that crops up so often in our attitudes toward the rest of the world, dividing nations into Good Guys and Bad Guys. It lurks in the common American assumption that most foreigners would really rather be just like us if they had the chance, living in Des Moines and shopping at K-Mart. It's the innocence that wishes Jesus had been born somewhere near Kansas City.

At its most Shermanesque, it's the innocence that has never known why other Europeans were a trifle hesitant about sharing their last cracker with the Germans after two world wars. Why not forget the past and be better friends than ever?

Innocence like Sherman's has fascinated our novelists.

Cump recalls the boy-men who march through our literature, blithely certain that they can change anything by the strength of willpower. They treat life as a winnable game and other humans as checkers, never understanding why the checkers keep spoiling things by wriggling off their assigned squares. It's the innocence of Ahab, reducing cosmic evil to a single white whale, then sailing forth to slay it; and it's the deadly naiveté of the Connecticut Yankee, turning Arthurian England into America—and then electrocuting her when she won't behave. Sherman's is the murderous innocence of the Great Gatsby, and of Thomas Sutpen.

Terror warfare is an unusual trade—one where the border between vindictiveness and satisfaction in good craftsmanship gets hazy. Sherman delighted to watch his men "break up rails good"; he savored the skill with which they did "infinite mischief." But it's needless to uncover a personal motive behind his devastation of the South: Sherman was no more adamant against the rebellion than tens of thousands of his own troops. I agree with Liddell Hart's insistence that he was motivated by a "logical ruthlessness" rather than malice. His fury against secession was no less impersonal than implacable.

To call Sherman unmalicious is no compliment. Hot-blooded rage would be far easier to stomach. My quarrel with all who demonize Uncle Billy is that when we make him a vindictive monster we deny the Sherman in ourselves. In *The Thirteen Clocks*, Thurber's villain says, "We all have flaws, and mine is being wicked." A bogeyman Sherman is just another wicked duke in a fairytale.

A Sherman without fangs is more horrifying by a long shot because he reveals our own dark potentialities—the whiff of terrible innocence in you and me. When I write of Cump Sherman pounding on people until they do what he wants done, I am appalled. But (much as it hurts to admit it) I am also just a bit enraptured. Something very nasty within us—something that wearies of the real world's complexities and wants everything to be nice and simple—is stirred by the cowboy as he gallops through his two-dimensional reality, shooting everyone who won't behave. Something in us cheers when a man says, "I will make war terrible! I can make Georgia howl!"

* * *

Sherman's attitudes toward the press and politics reflect that same willful innocence—his determination to be simple-minded.

He began to rage over the villainy of reporters before Bull Run, increased the volume when the papers declared him insane, and did not cease ranting until the surrender. The Constitution that he so fiercely defended did not include a First Amendment.

John E. Marszalek aptly titled his study of Cump and the press *Sherman's Other War*. For Sherman, editors were potential tyrants "who presume to dictate to generals, presidents, and cabinets." He informed a newspaper artist that "you fellows make the best paid spies that can be bought. Jeff Davis owes more to you newspaper men than to his army." Reporters were cowards as well as spies. Refusing to fight, they "follow an army to pick up news for sale, speculating upon a species of information dangerous to the army and to our cause." He told John Sherman that "Napoleon himself would have been defeated by a free press."

One good thing about raids, he thought, was that they carried him away from the telegraph. He could keep most reporters from coming along and temporarily stifle the others. Before Chickasaw Bluffs, he tried to bar correspondents from his ships, and announced that he would treat anyone who wrote up the expedition as a spy. One reporter, Thomas Knox of the *New York Herald*, filed his unflattering article anyway. When Sherman brought him in for a tongue-lashing, Knox explained that, "Of course, General Sherman, I had no feeling against you personally; but you are regarded as the enemy of our set, and we must in self-defense write you down."

Sherman then had Knox court-martialed. Knox was found innocent of criminal intent, though guilty of violating Sherman's orders. Banished from the theater of war, the correspondent appealed to Grant, who sent him right back to Sherman. More brash than judicious, Knox entered the bear's lair again, and got what he might have expected . . .

> Come with sword or musket in your hand, prepared to share with us our fate, in sunshine and storm, in prosperity and adversity, in plenty and scarcity and I will welcome you as brother and associate. But come as you now do expecting me to ally the honor and reputation of my country and my fellow soldiers with you, as representative of the press, which you yourself say makes so slight a difference between truth and falsehood and my answer is, Never.

For Sherman, the choice between one soldier's safety and the freedom of the press was no choice at all. As Marszalek says, he "made himself the sole definer of responsible journalism and the First Amendment." He never attempted to censor his men's letters home, contending that those letters and War Department releases were all the public required.

Cump grew rabid when anything reached the press that might conceivably be of use to the enemy. And to him that sometimes meant whatever pertained to the military. This subtle hint went to a general at Cairo:

> I observe an article in an Evansville paper that looks as though you had communicated my instructions to private parties for publication. If this be so, it is a high military offense for which you must account. You are an officer of the United States and in no manner of ways accountable to an irresponsible press. . . .
> If my dispatches to you reach the public and the enemy again you will regret it all the days of your life.

A correspondent once suggested that "A cat in hell without claws is nothing to a reporter in Gen. Sherman's army." Gen. Sherman had his own thoughts regarding the afterlife. During the March to the Sea, a few reporters were captured, and it was rumored that the Rebels had shot them. "Good," said Cump. "Now we'll have news from hell before breakfast."

* * *

Sherman's loathing of "Washington"—under which rubric he merged politics, government, bureaucracy, and many species of corruption—was, if possible, more simplistic than his hatred of the press. In another man this antipathy would have been less odd—Americans seem born leery of some malevolent "They" that broods upon the Potomac.

But this American was the son of a state supreme court judge, the foster son of a great statesman, a senator's brother, and the friend of many legislators. Yet Sherman was as quick as the most paranoid man in the street to roll all office holders and appointees into one repulsive lump. Even his brother often merged into the villainous pack that Cump called "you politicians."

When the general began to hear talk of himself as a future president, he pronounced it "cruel and unkind," reminding Ellen of his refusal to run for city treasurer in San Francisco. To John he insisted that he "would rather be an engineer of a railroad, than President of the United States."

In 1864, it incensed him that state governors were bent on creating posts for their supporters in new regiments, rather than encouraging veteran officers to stay in harness. He found the very existence of new regiments abominable—the sensible plan was to add green troops to old regiments, where veterans could train and protect them.

Sherman's points were often well taken—much of what outraged him was outrageous. But both the simplicity of his positions and the uncompromising righteousness with which he thundered them were incompatible with political realities.

So too for his refusal to permit regiments to go home to vote. ("Why, Congress itself is not half as important now as this army," he confided to John.) Again, within his own terms Sherman was "right"—the men belonged at the front. But both his right and his wrong came from Never-Never Land, where "compromise" is a word unknown and wars are fought in isolation from sordid political realities

A last example: Early in 1865, while the administration debated how best to liquidate most profitably the cotton Sherman's marchers were grabbing, he informed Stanton that the government "should assume a tone of perfect contempt for cotton and everything else in comparison with the great object of the war—the restoration of the Union." Perhaps the government should, but in a world of real Treasury Departments, war debts and cotton claims, it wouldn't.

Sherman seemed chronically baffled by the whole political cast of mind. That he chose to view politicians as slimy bugs is barely understandable; but that a man of his background viewed them as *incomprehensible* slimy bugs was both astonishing and unfortunate. As the war neared its end and the winning generals loomed as stars on the national stage, Sherman's perspective did not bode well for the future of the United States Army.

Had it not been for Grant's protection, John Sherman's clout and Lincoln's rare tolerance, W. T. Sherman's political obtuseness might have ruined his career many times over. At the close of the war, when Lincoln was no longer there to shield him, his innocence would come near destroying him.

Sherman at the head of his staff during the march through Georgia. The general had an intolerance for politicians and reporters and waged war with an uncanny determination. Still, he remained hopeful the North and South would easily reconcile their differences after the war ended.

Chapter 8

Goose Chase

It was now the important question to Sherman to decide what his adversary would do, for he did not mean to be led off upon a wild-goose chase if he could avoid it.
—General Jacob D. Cox

*D*espite shelves groaning with Civil War books, one of Sherman's campaigns has vanished. There are no books on it, and it's not mentioned in the latest Civil War encyclopedia.

It's a matter of classification. The events are no secret, but they have been filed most strangely. Historians treat them as an appendage—icing rather than cake. They group certain weeks as a sequel to the Atlanta campaign or, more often, as "background" to the March to the Sea. Even the *Official Records*, that Torah of Civil War research, is coy. The spines of three fat volumes read "Allatoona, Etc."

But "Allatoona, Etc." was a campaign. It lasted nearly as long as the March to the Sea and involved as much fighting and hiking. To confuse things further, its last stage was the true start of the famous campaign that followed: "Marching through Georgia" to the contrary, most of Sherman's force did not walk "From Atlanta to the sea." Though it makes for lousy lyrics, they marched from Gaylesville, Alabama.

When named at all, the unknown campaign is called "Sherman's Pursuit of Hood." I prefer to follow General Cox's hint and call it the "Goose Chase."

Broadly considered, the Goose Chase was the price Sherman paid for disobeying Grant's orders. As Sherman later put it, "I had not accomplished all, for Hood's army, the chief 'objective,' had escaped. Then began the real trouble."

After they parted company in Cincinnati, Grant did indeed "go for Lee." But Sherman did not often go for Joe Johnston or Hood, and particularly not when to do so meant sacrificing his men. Gradually, Atlanta itself became his target, rather than the Army of Tennessee. When he bothered to defend his course, Sherman used geography and his fragile railroad as excuses. Virginia's east-flowing rivers and the Atlantic gave Grant easy access to supplies and hospitals; but Sherman was deep in enemy territory, with only his railroad to help him.

His decision did not grieve his army. The men were devoted to him for the simple, perhaps selfish reason that he tried hard to save their skins. His troops did not mind that his casualties for the four-month Atlanta campaign were less than half of Grant's losses for six Virginia weeks.

When the blue army finally entered Atlanta, Sherman's stock kept climbing. Seen from within, the Rebel defenses were even more formidable than they had appeared from a distance—miles of gun emplacements, trenches, small forts; row upon row of stakes, with points bristling outward. Men gazed at Hood's defenses and saw their own dead bodies.

After he took Atlanta, part of Sherman's dilemma was that the antagonists had swapped sides of the board. Once he was inside, Atlanta changed from a prize to a cumbersome outpost: Now *he* had an army to feed there, while Hood was free to roam, with no supply base to rely on or to defend. Further, the Union army still depended on its railroad—120 miles of iron thread just to Chattanooga, and then hundreds of miles beyond that, through Nashville to the North.

In September there was little fighting. Sherman wanted to rest his army, and this was also the time of Atlanta's evacuation. Though the city was not fully depopulated, a great many people left. The ten-day truce lasted until September 20.

The day before it ended, Hood began moving west. By the evening of the 19th, much of his force had reached Palmetto, a few miles closer to Sherman's railroad.

But before Sherman knew what Hood might be up to, he faced problems elsewhere—from his old nemesis, Nathan B. Forrest. Starting in Mississippi on September 16, Forrest's latest escapade was a looping ride into Middle Tennessee, with Sherman's railroads around Chattanooga as his major target. The raid was pure Forrest: By the time he headed for safety, a trail of ruined blockhouses and bridges, crippled track, and flaming supplies marked his path. His captured horses pulled captured wagons, brimming with loot. Forrest took twenty-five hundred prisoners, and inflicted three times as many casualties as he suffered.

By late September, with every commander in Tennessee befuddled and Hood now almost certainly heading north, Sherman felt compelled to act. On the 29th he sent George Thomas to Nashville with two infantry divisions.

As things turned out, Thomas would operate from Nashville for the rest of the war. Officially, he remained under Sherman. Grant sometimes spoke teasingly to Cump of "your other army in Tennessee"; Sherman himself made sporadic efforts to convince his men that victories earned by Thomas were also "theirs," and vice versa. But in practice Thomas ran a quasi-independent command, made up of troops already in Tennessee, divisions Sherman sent north, and (at long last) the troops Banks had borrowed for a month back in March.

*   *   *

On September 26th, Sherman had dispatched General John M. Corse up to Rome, Georgia, with a division, in case Hood might have designs on that factory town. Full of fight and a hustler, Corse was an officer Sherman relied on and a man whose spirit he enjoyed.

By the time Thomas departed, three days later, Cump was nearly sure that Hood, or anyway part of Hood's army, was heading toward his railroad . . . or anyway somewhere near there. But not until October 1 was it finally clear that Hood's whole army was crossing the Chattahoochee. Sherman prepared to march north from Atlanta.

Actually, Hood was over the Chattahoochee on September 29. When Sherman got word of the crossing, Rebel cavalry were already on the Western & Atlantic, with infantry close behind. It's fitting that Sherman began the Goose Chase with two-day-old reports. He would never quite catch up.

Hood had been plotting strategy for weeks. He stated early in September that his next step must be to "place our army upon the communications of the enemy." With Atlanta fallen, he feared that Sherman might head for Mobile or some Atlantic port. Hood aimed to keep him too busy to seek new horizons.

Probably Hood had about thirty-five thousand men left. Sherman's ranks were depleted sorely by mustered-out troops and men enjoying their re-enlistment leaves; he had sent the two divisions off with Thomas and he left Slocum's corps behind to protect Atlanta. Still, his pursuing force probably numbered at least sixty-five thousand. In Hood's words: "Sherman is weaker now than he will be in future, and I as strong as I can expect to be."

The Confederate infantry reached Sherman's railroad on October 2nd, striking at Acworth and Big Shanty, a few miles north of Kennesaw. After capturing the garrisons, they got to work on the track. In two days, nine miles of it were gone.

While the Rebels toiled, Sherman's divisions were streaming out of Atlanta on several roads—still without knowing exactly where they were aiming. Wrote a general to Sherman on the evening of the 3rd:

> We cannot get the telegraph to work, and I send this via the office at Chattahoochee bridge. I arrived here at 2:30 p.m. . . . I have heard no firing nor have I heard anything from the cavalry. Have communicated with General Vandever at Marietta. He reports that he sent scouts out ten miles west of Marietta but they saw nothing . . . If Hood shows any disposition to turn east I will move to Lost Mountain in the morning.

Sherman replied in the same waffling spirit: "Tomorrow I will concentrate the whole army at Kennesaw and move upon the enemy wherever he may be."

On the 4th, he was still pushing his men toward Kennesaw when bad news reached him: Part of Hood's force had been seen marching north, toward Allatoona.

*   *   *

From the Victorian perspective, what befell on October 4th and 5th was heroic drama. Flamboyant accounts would tingle hearts throughout the North. To the modern taste, the dramatics are a trifle too dramatic; the tale reads like an opera libretto.

Allatoona Pass was a deep mountain cut. Along the bottom, where the track ran, warehouses held over a million rations that Hood coveted. Two small forts sat on the crest. Given reasonable odds, the pass was impregnable, which was why Sherman had declined to attack Johnston there in May. But the garrison under Colonel John Tourtellotte—nine hundred men—could be overwhelmed by a Rebel force of major size.

With his own armies still south of Kennesaw, Sherman himself could do nothing for the beleaguered garrison. Once his men reached Kennesaw, Allatoona would be another eighteen miles away by foot, or twelve as the crow flew—provided the marcher or the crow could bypass the Rebels now holding the intervening valley.

From Vining's Station, Sherman wrote a plea for help to Corse, up at Rome. His message was cabled to Kennesaw, then sent by signal flag—despite fog—over the heads of the gray army to Allatoona itself. From there, the wire to the north still functioned.

To Colonel Tourtellotte went another message: "General Sherman says hold fast. We are coming." Reporters would twist the phrase into "hold the fort," thus providing us all with another cliché. Later, an evangelist named P.P. Bliss made that line the basis of a hymn—"Hold the Fort, For We Are Coming."

Though Sherman didn't know it, Corse received his plea that afternoon. With no train at hand, Corse wired Kingston, ordering that an empty train be rushed to Rome. In Corse's words, "The train, in moving down to Rome, threw some fourteen or fifteen cars off the track, and threatened to delay us till the morning of the 5th instant, but the activity of the officers and railroad employees enabled me to secure a train of twenty cars about 7 p.m."

In an hour and a half, Corse loaded eleven hundred men and a mass of ammunition on board, and went dashing off at ten miles an hour toward Allatoona. When he arrived, at one in the morning, the skirmishing had already begun. (Corse sent the train back for the rest of his division, but it "unfortunately met with an accident." His re-inforcements finally arrived after the battle was over.) By dawn, when the Rebels began to bombard, Corse had pulled nearly all his troops and Tourtellotte's into the two forts.

Meanwhile, Sherman's army still hastened north. By morning, most of them were already past Kennesaw and heading for Allatoona. At their approach, Hood withdrew the bulk of his force to the west, toward the old battlefields around New

Hope. Remaining behind to take Allatoona was a division under General Samuel French.

Sherman reached the crest of Kennesaw about 8 a.m., to take his first view—

> The signal-officer . . . reported that since daylight he had failed to obtain any answer to his call for Allatoona; but while I was with him, he caught a faint glimpse of the tell-tale flag through an embrasure, and after much time he made out these letters— "C.," "R.," "S.," "E.," "H.," "E.," "R.," and translated the message—"Corse is here." It was a source of great relief, for it gave me the first assurance that General Corse had received his orders, and that the place was adequately garrisoned.

At 8:30, French ceased fire and sent in a message under white flag. He asked Corse to surrender, in order "to avoid a needless effusion of blood." Corse was not one to let Sherman do all the memorable phrase-making:

> Your communication demanding surrender of my command I acknowledge receipt of, and would respectfully reply that we are prepared for the "needless effusion of blood" whenever it is agreeable to you.

Of blood there was no shortage. Few of the war's smaller battles were as deadly as Allatoona. General Cox judged it "one of the most desperately contested actions of the war." French's shells and bullets came from three directions. Federal officers had to plead with their men to stand up when they returned fire. Lieutenants and captains who stood to set an example paid for it with their lives.

Corse's account reveals the drama, and a writer who made the most of it:

> The enemy kept up a constant and intense fire, gradually closing around us and rapidly filling our little fort with the dead and dying. About 1 p.m. I was wounded by a rifle-ball, which

rendered me insensible for some thirty or forty minutes, but managed to rally on hearing some person or persons cry, "Cease firing," which conveyed to me the impression they were trying to surrender the fort. Again I urged my staff, the few officers left unhurt, and the men around me to renewed exertion, assuring them that Sherman would soon be there with re-enforcements. . . .

All day, as Sherman watched from afar, he anxiously gauged the advance of his divisions by the barns they burned to mark their progress. In mid-afternoon, though his columns had not yet reached Allatoona, he finally saw the attack dwindle and then cease.

French gave up about 3 p.m. and withdrew to rejoin Hood; partly because of the approaching columns, but mostly because his three thousand could not wrest the forts from Corse's two thousand defenders. For such small forces, the casualties were appalling—around seven hundred dead and wounded for each side.

A few hours later came a message from Corse to Sherman: "I am short a cheek-bone and an ear, but am able to whip all hell yet." Later still, when the generals were re-united, Sherman counted Corse's ears, noted a bandage covering a scratch wound, and grinned—"Corse, they came damned near missing you, didn't they?"

Allatoona might be semi-grand opera; but the rest of the Goose Chase was a movie run backwards: everything going by in reverse, and too fast. Twisting and dodging around northern Georgia, Hood yanked Sherman here and there— over the same landscape where the armies had battled in the spring.

Even if Hood had lusted for combat, Sherman would not have ventured another battle in the New Hope-Pickett's Mill wilds, where the May fighting had been so dreadful. But that turned out to be no problem. Two days after Allatoona, Hood disappeared. None of Sherman's generals had a clue. "The only camp smoke seen is southeast from Dallas, about fifteen miles from here," wrote General Baird to Sherman that morning. Standing on Pine Mountain, where Polk had died, Sherman couldn't see a trace of Hood either. To General Cox he said:

> . . . I am satisfied the enemy is gone south. Please push ahead
> rapidly and observe the tracks on the Dallas and Acworth
> road. Burn a house or brush-pile every now and then, when I
> can tell where your head of column is. When you reach the
> road make a big smoke, a house or barn at least, and if you see
> the tracks pointing south, make three large smokes, 300 or 400
> yards, apart, so I may know.

He was far less certain than he claimed to be. Though he warned Slocum that Hood might pivot south for an attack on Atlanta, he didn't sound very convinced.

The next day Sherman issued new orders:

> . . . Should the enemy attempt our road about Kingston, or to
> invest Rome, the army must be prepared to leave at Allatoona
> the principal wagon trains and to march rapidly to the point
> threatened, but if the enemy simply move off toward Jackson-
> ville or Blue Mountain the army will remain, its right at Alla-
> toona and left at Kennesaw, until our roads are repaired.

"If the enemy does this . . . , but if they do that . . ." Throughout the Goose Chase, Hood, not Sherman, dictated the game. He bounced around Georgia like an agile boy dodging a clumsy one, shouting "Catch me if you can!"

Delayed by rain, Sherman moved north to Allatoona on October 9 (showing how little he believed that Hood had gone south). There he learned that the wires to Rome had gone dead. So the enemy had gone north. Probably. He sent worried messages to Corse, whose replies, when they finally got through, left things still muddled. Corse said that he could not yet decipher Hood's movements. He was hearing "the most extravagant reports" of a big Rebel advance on Rome, yet his patrols had stumbled on nothing but some gray cavalry. Sherman decided he had better support Rome. By now he was spluttering:

> ... I don't think Hood will attack Rome if we can reach Kingston by noon tomorrow, or if he does he must cross to this side north of the Etowah, and we would have him at great advantage. He may mean to go up to La Fayette, &c., but where he would get his grub is a question. His whole movement is inexplicable to any common sense theory.

He hastened to Rome in time to find nothing. Hood had skirmished around only long enough to pique Sherman's interest, then looped back east for an attempt on Resaca. There he demanded the garrison's surrender, warning that no prisoners would be taken if he were forced to assault. But in Resaca's commander he encountered another officer of Corse's stripe: "In my opinion I can hold this post. If you want it, come and take it."

Deciding that perhaps he didn't want Resaca after all, Hood again sallied forth. Once more he was gone before Federal re-inforcements came rushing in to rescue the tranquil garrison.

Up at Dalton, Hood had better luck. There the garrison did surrender. To celebrate, the Rebels destroyed twenty miles of track—the campaign's most extensive damage. The demolition ran north as far as Rocky Face Ridge—which is to say that Hood's spiral path had taken him, and his frustrated pursuers, clear back to where Johnston and Sherman first squared off in May. Hood was near the Tennessee line now, in spitting distance of Chickamauga and Chattanooga. As if to italicize the point, he made his next flight through Snake Creek Gap, reversing McPherson's old route.

October 17 found the Confederate army poised by a town

called La Fayette. Hood had taken a defensive posture and appeared, at last, ready to fight. Sherman eagerly approached, and Hood once more scooted away, to the west this time. By Hood's later account, he actually did wish to fight at La Fayette, but felt his subordinates would not sustain him. Perhaps so, but from Sherman's view, the departure seemed no less whimsical than any of Hood's other shenanigans—"I cannot guess his movements as I could those of Johnston, who was a sensible man and only did sensible things."

From the Rebel angle, Hood had done little but sensible things. His best hope lay in move and counter-move. It scarcely mattered where he headed, so long as his twisty path often crossed those frangible tracks and telegraph wires, and so long as Sherman came panting in his wake. Though Sherman had promised Slocum that he would "watch Mr. Hood close," that was exactly what he couldn't do. Hood's cool, controlled October performance was the one bright interlude in his otherwise dreadful handling of high command.

The Union army shared its leader's frustration. Back in Atlanta, soldiers griped because no mail was getting in and out. "For nearly a week Atlanta has been our world," complained Corporal Harvey Reid in a letter he couldn't send. With the railroad defunct, their ration of fresh beef had been cut in half, no salt beef remained, and forage was cruelly scarce. Reid consoled himself with bad jokes about the Hood that had been drawn over their trains.

Major Connolly was out on the chase, plodding down muddy roads in pursuit of invisible gray divisions, taking short cuts that turned into long cuts. In his growing sense of futility, Connolly spoke for thousands:

October 11
We were here at Kingston last May marching southward, with the enemy in our front, now we are here again marching northward, and still the enemy is in our front. This has been a funny

campaign from Atlanta north, the rebels have been using our breastworks of last Summer, and we have been using theirs.

On the 15th, Connolly's division marched all day, ending with a tough climb up a mountain, after dark. They went to sleep without supper or blankets. Then awoke to discover that "all this mountain march was useless; the enemy evacuated Snake Creek Gap in the afternoon and we might have gone through that."

October 16
I am well. We are reduced to parched corn and sweet potatoes, but we are close after the copperheads commanded by Hood. . . We may possibly force a fight out of them tomorrow
. . .

October 27
One thing is certain, there is no use of this Army of 70,000 "gallivanting" up and down through Georgia after Hood and his 40,000 any longer, for its like an elephant chasing a mouse; he wont let us catch him, and unless we can catch him so as to whip him soundly, his 40,000 are worth more to the rebels, than our 70,000 are to us, for it takes less to clothe, feed and pay them.

Hood's shortage of food and clothing annoyed Sherman. He took it as a nasty trick that Hood's army was woefully under-supplied or, as he put it, "little encumbered with trains." Thomas was no longer there to be blamed for his own mass of luggage, but other villains abounded:

I have labored hard to cut down wagons, but spite of all I can do officers surround me. All the [Atlanta] campaign I slept without a tent, and yet doctors and teamsters and clerks and staff officers on one pretext or another get tents and baggage, and now we can hardly move. I'll stop this or dispense with doctors, clerks and staff officers as "useless in war."

After the almost-battle at La Fayette, Hood kept going west, into Alabama. Eventually he halted at Gadsden. Sherman followed as far as Gaylesville, Alabama, thirty miles from Hood's camp. There both armies paused. Cump knew that Hood was awaiting his own next move—primed for another leap south, west or into the void as soon as the bluecoats took up the chase.

Meanwhile, the halt was fine with Hood. Closer now to his own sources of supply, he had no immediate wish to go anywhere. Insofar as his goal had been to smash Sherman's rails and wires, the campaign was over. But Hood knew that and Sherman didn't. It was several days before Cump felt fairly certain that Hood would not decide to jump back into Georgia or hop up into Tennessee.

By now Sherman was more than eager to call it quits. "To pursue Hood is folly," he told Thomas, "for he can twist and turn like a fox and wear out any army in pursuit." Gaylesville would suffice. He had toured far enough to suit him—every inch of it in the wrong direction. By one officer's measurements, the mouse had led the elephant about 140 or 150 miles; which would mean close to 300 by the time they footed it back to Atlanta.

*   *   *

Throughout this ramble, Sherman's attention had been divided and his feelings jumbled. All the time that Hood kept him flustered, another part of him was excitedly plotting his next campaign. That excitement in turn heightened his anger with Hood, who had him stymied when he yearned to be off and doing.

On October 1, two days before the chase began, Sherman had launched a very different attack. This battle he fought by cable, and against a general he understood far better—Ulysses Grant. If Hood should head north or west, said Sherman, "why would it not do for me to leave Tennessee to the force which Thomas has and the reserves soon to come to Nashville, and for me to destroy Atlanta, and then march across Georgia to Savannah or Charleston, breaking roads and doing irreparable damage?" Then a prophetic afterthought: "We cannot remain on the defensive."

Throughout October, Sherman kept pleading his case. More accurately, he wheedled and nagged. Under a thin facade of playing the dutiful subordinate who merely advanced a suggestion, he thrust Grant into a spot where only a peremptory "No" would keep Sherman from having his way. Even after Sherman got what he wanted, he kept arguing. He also pestered Halleck, and even Thomas—who would have to deal with Hood.

Sherman's body might be galloping from Kennesaw to Dalton, but his heart was in those cables—speeding off to Virginia whenever he could find an unbroken telegraph.

[Allatoona, October 9]
It will be a physical impossibility to protect the roads, now that Hood, Forrest, Wheeler, and the whole batch of devils, are turned loose without home or habitation. . . . Until we can re-populate Georgia, it is useless for us to occupy it; but the utter destruction of its roads, houses, and people, will cripple their military resources. By attempting to hold the roads, we will lose a thousand men each month, and will gain no result. I can make this march, and make Georgia howl!

Ever and anon, he hammered away on his main points— the need to stay on the offensive, and the impossibility of making Hood fight. He assured Grant that he would leave Thomas with enough men to whip Hood. Yet, when he thought it sounded better, he changed tactics, declaring that Hood would more likely follow him.

Above all, he expounded on the benefits of carrying the war to civilians. Many of Sherman's most famous remarks on terror warfare were penned that month:

—I would infinitely prefer to . . . send back all my wounded
and unserviceable men, and with my effective army move
through Georgia, smashing things to the sea.
—I am going into the very bowels of the Confederacy, and propose to leave a trail that will be recognized fifty years hence.
—I will then make the interior of Georgia feel the weight of
war.
—I propose . . . to sally forth and make a hole in Georgia and
Alabama that will be hard to mend.

Grant hesitated. Hadn't the point been to press the enemy
relentlessly?—"If there is any way of getting at Hood's army,
I would prefer that." If left alone, thought Grant, Hood would
probably advance toward Nashville. Could Thomas indeed
handle him? Grant also had qualms about the proposed
march: "If you were to cut loose, I do not believe you would
meet Hood's army, but would be bushwhacked by all the old
men, little boys, and such railroad guards as are still left at
home."

But on October 12 he consented—Sherman won the permission he craved. Characteristically, once Grant yielded, he
went the whole hog. He did his best to calm Lincoln, who had
demurred because of the dangers of the march. He arranged
for supplies to be shipped down the coast, to await Sherman's
arrival. On October 17th he gave Sherman approval to burn
"all of military value in Atlanta."

Grant loyally told Sherman that he was now convinced—it
was good strategy to march. But most likely Sherman got his
way for the same reason that you finally got your first bicycle:
Nagging works. The point came when it was easier for Grant
to agree than to jeopardize their friendship. Better Cump
eager than Cump petulant.

Knowing the ice had been thin, Sherman dutifully stuck
with the chase awhile longer. He did want the Rebels out of
Georgia; and after that he lingered awhile longer to ascertain
that Hood's eyes were more on Tennessee than on him. But

well before he halted at Gaylesville, he had mentally kissed Hood goodbye: "Damn him. If he will go to the Ohio River I will give him rations. . . My business is down South."

Speeding orders in ten directions, Sherman joyfully threw himself into the preparations. He reassigned Schofield's small army to Thomas. All the cavalry also went to Tennessee, save for one large division under Judson Kilpatrick. Thomas couldn't abide the cocky little powder keg whom the army called "Kill-Cavalry," but Sherman figured that his violent tendencies might be useful: "I know that Kilpatrick is a hell of a damned fool, but I want just that sort of a man to command my cavalry on this expedition."

Doctors examined every man slated to march with Sherman. The weak were shipped up to Tennessee, where those who could return to duty would augment Thomas's force. Sherman would benefit doubly from the medical check. He would lead one of the toughest armies in history; he would also lead men who viewed themselves as "select."

The rail damage was repaired with a speed that Sherman hoped the enemy would find demoralizing. Between Big Shanty and Acworth, a ten-thousand-man work crew fixed the roadbed and dropped crossties. Then Colonel Wright's specialists installed new track. The nine-mile job took about a week. Next, Wright got to work on the longer break above Dalton. By November 2 that job too was disposed of. Once the trains were running, Sherman returned to Kingston, Georgia, and did his supervising from there. He wanted a million and a half rations of bread, coffee, sugar and salt, plus half a million rations of salt meat shipped to Atlanta. For other food, he sent Slocum raiding. Monster foraging parties hauled in everything for miles around Atlanta that might be tasty to man or beast—two million pounds of corn, plus a mass of cattle, fodder, and other tidbits.

While Slocum stripped the country near Atlanta, those off chasing Hood had been doing their own gathering. During the time when the tracks were broken, Sherman sent out official foraging bands; and he did little to discourage informal looting or devastation. Major Connolly cheerily informed his wife that he was writing to her "by the light of a burning house." Another day, he mentioned a gentleman who had entertained them kindly and given up his bed—"but notwithstanding that we must have about 300 bushels of his wheat in the morning."

Sherman recounted a jolly story in his *Memoirs*—

> I remember well the appeal of a very respectable farmer
> against our men driving away his fine flock of sheep. I ex-
> plained to him that General Hood had broken our railroad;
> that we were a strong, hungry crowd, and needed plenty of
> food; that Uncle Sam was deeply interested in our continued
> health and would soon repair these roads, but meantime we
> must eat; we preferred Illinois beef, but mutton would have to
> answer. Poor fellow! I don't believe he was convinced by the
> wisdom of my explanation.

Months earlier, Jefferson Davis had prodded Southerners to sow food crops rather than cotton—a wretchedly timed action that now became a joke among Sherman's locusts. Sherman begged Stanton to "Convey to Jeff. Davis my personal and official thanks for abolishing cotton and substituting corn and sweet potatoes in the South. These facilitate our military plans much, for food and forage are abundant."

He had hoped to depart around November 1, but the track damage and heavy rains slowed him. Above all, he was delayed by the labor of moving a mountain of goods to Tennessee. On November 4, his frazzled chief quartermaster in Atlanta apologized for the delays. He had been able to receive "only seventy-seven cars in the last twenty-four hours, all of which have been promptly unloaded, reloaded, and started back." He was doing his damndest, but "They have accumulated more plunder in the last two months than I supposed could have been got here in six."

Sherman accepted the delays with remarkable calm. He even lingered a bit longer so that troops whose states permitted voting at the front could join in Lincoln's landslide over McClellan, on November 8. Months earlier, someone had asked him what he intended to do after Atlanta fell. He had replied: "Salt water!" That seemed to be about all he was thinking of now. In a note to a general in Missouri, his mood was exultant—"I will be off in a few days on a worse raid than our Meridian raid was, and you may look for a great howl against the brute Sherman."

Well before Sherman headed for salt water, Hood had moved west across Alabama, seeking a likely place to cross the Tennessee River. Said the general who had wheedled so hard to make it all happen: "It surely was a strange event— two hostile armies marching in opposite directions, each in the full belief that it was achieving a final and conclusive result in a great war."

According to the books, the March to the Sea began November 15. But for many a soldier, the trek started whenever his regiment hit the road for Georgia from Gaylesville. For the plundered farmer, it began on whatever day Sherman's or Slocum's looters struck his granaries and seized his cows. Symbolically, perhaps the march should be dated from November 10, when Corse destroyed all mills, shops and factories around Rome. That night his men began walking south. All along the route of the Atlanta campaign and the Goose Chase, blue divisions were streaming back toward Atlanta, destroying towns as they went, while freight trains bore the final shipments of loot the other direction. On November 12, Sherman left Kingston with what was by then the army's rear guard.

When the last train had steamed north, the marchers lingered to wreck, with their usual care, the track between the Etowah and Chattahoochee—twenty-two miles of it. By now Sherman and his flock were so used to picking up and putting down rails that nothing about this particular chore seemed odd. Who cared that a large chunk of what they demolished was the same Big-Shanty-to-Acworth stretch that Hood had so lately removed and they had replaced?

Nor did Sherman seem to find the pattern of his own year remarkable. In the spring he had perfected railroad warfare. Ever since, he had fought like a wildcat to keep his track open. But now he intended to feed sixty thousand men wholly on what they could carry and steal. The general who had best used the railroad would become the general most notorious for doing without it.

Early on the morning of November 12, he had a last brief telegraphic exchange with Thomas. Then someone somewhere cut a wire or chopped down a pole. Sherman was out of touch with the North—relieved to be beyond recall.

Sherman dispatches a final message to Major General George H. Thomas on November 12, 1864. He then cut communications and took his army in a destructive march across Georgia for the port of Savannah.

Sherman's infamous bummers wreak their trademark depredations on a Georgia plantation. A Southern newspaper said of such Yankees, "the cesspools of Northern infamy and corruption have been dredged to their foulest dregs in order to collect the infamous spawn of perdition sent out to despoil our country."

Chapter 9

The Man that Rules the World

*I*n late October, Sherman welcomed a new aide. A young St. Louis lawyer, Major Henry Hitchcock was the nephew of General Hitchcock; Sherman treated him like "real military," and trusted him from the start.

Like Major Connolly, Hitchcock wrote letters and kept a diary for his wife and himself. Though he apologized to her for sounding too much like Sherman's Boswell, his commander did intrigue him. A sharp observer, Hitchcock left the better account because he admired and liked Sherman without approving.

Hitchcock enjoyed it when his boss told him what was needed in a note to ladies who had sent a basket of fruit: "Somethin' sweet, you know, as the feller said—molasses and honey." Now and then, Cump warmed the major's heart, as he won affection all his life: "Gen. Sherman asks me this evening, if I happened to be writing to any of his old friends to give them his kindest remembrance—and added, 'when you write to your wife, give her my love—I never had the pleasure of knowing her but I have often heard of her.'"

Hitchcock was genteel, earnest and squeamish. In theory,

he agreed that the South must pay for treason. But theory was one thing and the homeless widow before his eyes was another. He agreed, but shuddered.

Riding through Marietta on their way back to Atlanta, commander and aide paused at a downtown hotel. Its furniture was gone. Several nearby buildings were aflame. They watched a company of soldiers fight a stubborn fire in the court house.

"'Twill burn down, Sir."

"Yes, can't be stopped."

"Was it your intention?"

"Can't save it—I've seen more of this sort of thing than you."

"Certainly, Sir."

They moved on, passing idle soldiers. Sherman said that men like them would sneak back and re-ignite the court house, no matter how well it was guarded. He guessed that the whole town would burn, or at least its commercial buildings—"I say *Jeff. Davis burnt them.*" The major said he feared that the general might be blamed unjustly. "Well, I suppose I'll have to bear it," said Tecumseh Sherman.

Hitchcock didn't smile at the Jeff Davis joke, but for awhile he continued to believe that Sherman was distressed by arson and pillage—trying to interpret as bad management what veterans (skilled at reading orders and officers) knew to be a deliberate hands-off policy.

Sherman had issued his marching orders a few days earlier, in Kingston.

Once gathered around Atlanta, the army would move in two wings, each including two corps; Howard's wing on the right and Slocum's on the left. Where possible, each corps would take its own road. The orders called for a fifteen-mile daily march; but Sherman soon dropped that to ten, to encourage more thorough despoiling.

Each corps hauled its own supplies and enough pontoons to build most of its own bridges. Regiments were limited to one ambulance each. Section IV began, "The army will forage liberally on the country during the march." Foraging parties. . .

> will gather, near the route traveled, corn or forage of any kind, meat of any kind, vegetables, corn-meal or whatever is needed by the command . . . . Soldiers must not enter the dwellings of the inhabitants, or commit any trespass, but during a halt or a camp they may be permitted to gather turnips, potatoes, and other vegetables, and to drive in stock in sight of their camp. To regular foraging parties must be intrusted the gathering of provisions and forage at any distance from the road traveled.

Foragers were told to use no threatening language, and to leave their victims some food.

Only army commanders were empowered to burn buildings. Where the march was unmolested, no destruction would occur; but if guerrillas or bushwhackers should try to thwart the march, "then army commanders should order and enforce a devastation more or less relentless according to the measure of such hostility." Later, when guerrillas did annoy them, he issued a second warning: "If the enemy burn forage and corn on our route, houses, barns and cotton gins must also be burned to keep them company."

Cavalry and artillerymen could seize whatever animals and wagons they liked, "discriminating, however, between the rich, who are usually hostile, and the poor or industrious, usually neutral or friendly."

Able-bodied Negroes might be taken along, but supplies were precious, and generals must look first to their soldiers' needs.

It was all very fine, and a great deal of it was strictly for the record.

Sherman made no systematic effort to restrain his men. His attempts to limit destruction were arbitrary, almost whimsical. Sometimes he guarded houses, sometimes not. Sometimes he extinguished fires. But he knew what would befall the mansion, or Marietta's court house, after the guards departed. When you lead hornets, it's needless to command stinging.

His orders were read so often that men learned key sentences by heart. Sherman wearied of meeting soldiers with hams on their bayonets and sides of bacon festooned over their shoulders, who grinned up at him and shouted, "Forage liberally!"

While Hitchcock worried over Marietta, other towns already smoldered behind them—Rome, Kingston, Acworth, Big Shanty—the first cracklings of a blaze that would burn for five months and stretch eight hundred miles. As they rode on toward Atlanta, Sherman foresaw the whole scorching arc. Recently, Howard had paid a visit while Cump was being massaged for a lame arm. As the rubdown continued, Sherman explained his plans in detail. Then he pulled over a map—"I hope to get there." His finger rested on Goldsboro, North Carolina.

When they reached Atlanta, Hitchcock was struck by the work of Captain Orlando Poe, Sherman's chief engineer. All over town, Poe's crews were hard at it. Most impressively, they were dismantling the stone-and-brick depot with a giant ram of Poe's invention. On the march, Poe would supervise the major demolition, as well as the bridge and road work. When a factory collapsed faster than seemed possible, Orlando Poe was generally lurking around.

That day, November 14, while Poe obliterated official targets, roaming bands of soldiers were doing volunteer work—burning whatever struck their fancy. They especially favored elegant homes whose owners had departed. Elsewhere, a soldier tossed a brand into the gas works "to see how it would burn." It would burn with enough smoke and vigor to be visible across the city.

Toward evening, one of Poe's rushed crews kindled a machine shop—discovering too late that it had served Hood as an arsenal and was crammed with forgotten ammunition. All night, Atlanta was shelled. Ten miles away, an army chaplain easily read his watch by the flames.

By the morning of the 15th, over a third of Atlanta had burned. All that day and much of the night, Poe's labors continued, as did the freelance destruction. Mid-November though it was, the city broiled from within. Shells still occasionally exploded. Before the army was gone, five thousand structures burned.

That day, the right wing and part of the left began marching away from Atlanta. Sherman and his staff departed early the following morning, riding out of town by way of Decatur. There Sherman paused:

> We stood upon the very ground whereon was fought the bloody battle of July 22d, and could see the copse of wood where McPherson fell. Behind us lay Atlanta, smouldering and in ruins, the black smoke rising high in air, and hanging like a pall over the ruined city. Away off in the distance, on the McDonough road, was the rear of Howard's column, the gun-barrels glistening in the sun, the white-topped wagons stretching away to the south; and right below us the Fourteenth Corps, marching steadily and rapidly, with a cheery look and swinging pace, that made light of the thousand miles that lay between us and Richmond. Some band, by accident, struck up the anthem of "John Brown's soul goes marching on"; the men caught up the strain, and never before or since have I heard the chorus of "Glory, glory, hallelujah!" done with more spirit, or in better harmony of time and place.
>
> Then we turned our horses' heads to the east . . . . Even the common soldiers caught the inspiration, and many a group called out to me as I worked my way past them, "Uncle Billy, I guess Grant is waiting for us at Richmond!"

* * *

The March to the Sea is not remembered for its battles. In a month-long campaign, until they reached the coast, there were but two significant fighting incidents.

On November 22, at Griswoldville, three thousand Georgia militia charged Walcutt's fifteen-hundred-man division, who were dug in atop a hill. The clumsy gray line came closer, then insanely close, before Walcutt's muskets sliced them apart. To the veterans' astonishment, the Rebels charged twice more before the survivors fled. Walcutt lost sixty-two men against enemy casualties ten times as high. When they came down to take a look, his troops were sickened. Many of the dead were old men and boys—the amateur dregs of Georgia, sent to face regiments with twenty battles sewn on their flags. Said an Indiana soldier, "We moved a few bodies, and there was a boy with a broken arm and leg—just a boy 14 years old, and beside him, cold in death, lay his father, two brothers and an uncle." Sherman believed that one hardened brigade from the days after Shiloh could have whipped both Bull Run armies together. No fight proved his point more terribly than Griswoldville.

On December 9, a few miles outside Savannah, two buried torpedoes exploded, killing a horse and wounding a few men. With Sherman, Major Hitchcock galloped up to see a lieutenant resting by the road—"*his right foot torn off* just at or rather just above ankle joint." Sherman ordered Confederate prisoners brought up, handed them picks and shovels, and made them test the road ahead: "They begged hard, but I reiterated the order, and could hardly help laughing at their stepping so gingerly along the road." One prisoner was sent to Savannah, to tell Hardee how Sherman dealt with such tricks.

With Hood off in Tennessee, the Confederacy had little to put in Sherman's path. The fighting on the march was mostly skirmishing, against Wheeler's lately returned cavalry. In Savannah, General Hardee was gathering militia and whatever troops he could catch. At Augusta sat a more imposing force: ten thousand infantry, under the resurrected Braxton **Bragg**. The crux of Sherman's strategy was to hold Bragg there, and to keep all Rebel generals unsure of where he was heading. While no available force could have halted the Federal army, even a lopsided big battle would have left more wounded than they could tend.

Thus, Sherman's left wing feinted toward Augusta and his right wing toward Macon. These feints were made as convincing as possible—once Kilpatrick's riders penetrated nearly to the outskirts of Augusta to suggest an imminent attack. The strategy worked admirably. Bragg's force stayed put while Sherman rampaged; and Savannah, his obvious target, remained less than obvious until he was nearly there.

* * *

The scale of the marches still remains hard to grasp. Sixty thousand men in four corps of fifteen thousand. Living in a town of twelve thousand, I struggle—and fail—to imagine Sherman moving five soldiers for every man, woman and child of us.

As an old man stood gaping at a corps treading by, a boy told him that he had seen just as many Yankees coming down the next road over. "Dar's millions of 'em, millions!" the old man shouted. Then he asked quietly, "Is there anybody lef' up North?"

"Sherman's army" is only necessary shorthand. No two of that multitude were alike or saw the same march. The burning of Atlanta? Some divisions bypassed the city. The slaughter at Griswoldville? A private in a distant corps might not hear of the battle for a week. Among that throng were brutes aplenty; and men who took orphans home to raise. Hundreds—perhaps thousands—were appalled by what they saw, finding secession no excuse for the havoc. Many guards ransacked the houses they were assigned to protect. There were also guards who rocked the baby or read to the children; some Georgia women stayed in touch for the rest of their lives with Union soldiers. Amid Sherman's host were fervent abolitionists, and many more whose idea of fun was shoving black women head first into molasses barrels. "Sherman's army" spent their nights gambling. And holding prayer meetings.

It's easy to forget the structure of the March to the Sea, for the mayhem and tumult obscure the pattern. Bruce Catton once called the march "a prolonged Halloween." True enough, God knows. But equally true that sixty thousand walked for a month and arrived at Savannah. We can picture their hell-raising so clearly that we ignore the most common scene of the march: men by the thousands, striding four abreast, in columns that took hours or days to pass a given point. It's easier to picture hogs being stolen than dinner for sixty thousand being cooked; easier to imagine the drunken looters, than the patrols that lingered to prod them along, lest Wheeler kill them.

For the entire campaign, the army suffered only 103 killed, 428 wounded, 278 missing.

The outermost corps sometimes marched fifty or sixty miles apart. Sherman didn't try to concentrate until he approached Savannah. A moving corps might stretch fifteen miles; its wagon train alone taking six. Day by day, every corps gathered runaway slaves, horses, cattle, and a mass of loot. By North Carolina, in some companies more men would be riding than walking.

Though random theft and destruction began at once, the army carried enough food to get well beyond the region Slocum had stripped. Then began official foraging.

Foraging parties left camp early. How long they were gone and how far they roamed varied mostly with what the district offered. "The troops now begin to live in a great measure upon sweet potatoes," noted a soldier in central Georgia. "And you ought to see these potatoes. It's no uncommon thing to find them as large as a child's head, and at every plantation we find from two to five hundred bushels." Men joked about yams so big you could sit on one end while you roasted the other. But when they neared the coast, sweet potatoes were a sweet memory, as the menu became rice and rice, with rice for dessert.

But even where the pickings were lush, Wheeler's cavalry sometimes got there first, and the blue foragers had to keep looking. (Many householders swore the Yankees scavenged less relentlessly.) When foragers struck a likely farm, they demanded a lavish dinner, and strengthened their appetites by loading the farm's bounty into its own wagons while the meal cooked. When they headed back, they tried to strike the road ahead of the army. As their regiment passed, food was dumped into wagons or distributed to the marchers, who toted it to their next camp.

By Howard's estimate, his wing raked in four and a half million pounds of corn and as much fodder. According to commissary reports, the army left Atlanta with thirty-five hundred head of cattle, slaughtered nearly ten thousand along the way, and reached Savannah with twice as many as they started with.

* * *

For most of the troops, the march *was* a month of Halloween. This was war with minimal risk—war transformed into picnic, drinking bout, roughhouse and treasure hunt. There was something phantasmagorical about the looting and destruction. On cold nights, miles of fences and barns vanished into campfires. Masses of goods and piles of food were stolen for the sheer hell of it, then discarded for no better reason. A looter would haul a stack of featherbeds into camp, sleep aloft for one sybaritic night, then rip them with his bayonet and toss them into a field or creek. Even silver became a nuisance to carry—forks and knives were strewn along ditch banks. Men nailed antique silver plate to trees for target practice. A woman saw her dead dog exhumed four times by treasure seekers.

Foragers stood by Georgia and Carolina roads, awaiting their regiments, garbed in whatever the attics and wardrobes had yielded—Revolutionary War uniforms, old-fashioned formal garb, women's fancy dresses. From a Columbia mansion, a soldier took only one prize—someone's Walter Raleigh costume left over from a costume ball.

Sherman's marauders seemed dazzled by chaises, fine carriages and other frilly vehicles. No sooner did Sherman order them discarded than a new assortment appeared. So too for horses of no military value. Kilpatrick's men once gathered five hundred of them from the columns, covered their heads with blankets, smashed them with axes, and left their carcasses to rot in someone's yard.

Old Abe, the mascot eagle of a Wisconsin regiment, rode proudly to the sea. He acquired plenty of company as regiments garnered raccoons, parrots, a peacock, lambs, and a plethora of dogs and cats. But fighting cocks were the marchers' darlings. After the nightly fights, losers were retrospectively christened Jeff Davis, Bobby Lee, Beauregard or Hood, then tossed into the supper pot. The winners—Grant, Johnny Logan, Sherman, Old Prayer Book [Howard]—lived to crow another day.

* * *

On November 23, Slocum's wing hit Milledgeville, then Georgia's capital. They had covered a hundred miles and were ripe for some town fun. A mob of officers took over the legislature's hall. Staggering drunk, General Kilpatrick belched a speech praising himself as a prince among vandals, and lauding his cavalry as men who could unearth silver or booze in any cellar. Someone called a point of order, and gave him another swig. Amid clinking bottles and off-key songs, the self-elected assembly repealed secession and voted Georgia back into the Union. Deposed but not forgotten, Governor Brown and President Davis were awarded official and plentiful kicks in the butt.

Meanwhile, soldiers had invaded the state treasury, where they paid themselves off in millions of Confederate dollars.

GEORGIA

SLOCUM'S
WING

Atlanta

SAVANNAH

SOUTH
CAROLINA

Augusta

RIVER

Milledgeville

Griswoldville

Macon

HOWARD'S WING

Savannah
Ft. M^c^Alister

ATLANTIC
OCEAN

Atlanta to the Sea

They played poker for thousand-dollar stakes, and expended more big bills to light their pipes. Next they struck the fine state library, where a horseman went prancing around on a heap of books and archives. Bibliophiles staggered away, laden with antique volumes. Major Connolly declined, knowing that the sight of purloined books on his shelves would embarrass him—"I don't object to stealing horses, mules, niggers and such *little things*, but I will not engage in plundering and destroying public libraries."

Two months later, when John Jackman, a Confederate soldier, passed through Milledgeville, the state house remained "all topsy-turvy. The desks overturned, the archives scattered over the floor—some places the papers being on the floor a foot deep."

* * *

The most infamous of the looters were not exactly the type who snitched law books. Sherman's bummers were a breed unique to the Georgia and Carolina marches. They were men who so took to theft that they went A.W.O.L.—some for occasional weeks; others for the duration of the two marches. Bummers roamed the countryside, dressed in whatever hodgepodge seemed worth stealing. After accruing a surplus of plunder, a party of bummers might drift back to camp long enough to peddle it.

A popular account of the march, written by another of Sherman's aides, Major George Nichols, includes a woodcut of the stereotypical bummer. With a self-satisfied grin, he rides his over-burdened mule away from a cabin, in front of which a woman waves her arms in despair. His gun is slung over his left shoulder; crooked in his right arm is a basket laden with invisible goodies. In front of the bummer droops a sack that might hold fifty pounds of flour. Behind him ride several unhappy ducks, while chickens dangle beneath the mule's belly. He drags a dead pig on a rope.

The bummers' reputation spread fast, adding its share to the general apprehension of Sherman's approach. As Sherman had anticipated, that fear became a weapon in its own right, stirring turmoil in districts his marchers never saw. In part, the story of the march is a tale of fears:

The fear of slave revolt had simmered throughout the war. From the earliest days, Mary Chesnut, in South Carolina, couldn't refrain from studying black faces. How much did her slaves know of the war? What might they do if the Union armies came close? As Sherman drew nearer, that dread increased throughout Georgia and the Carolinas.

There was also dread of rape. Here, even more than Sherman had anticipated, Southerners fell victim to their own mythology. Newspapers ran tales unlikely to leave the public tranquil. The *Macon Telegraph* told of women who had fallen prey "to the lustful appetites of the hell-hounds"; adding that "the cesspools of Northern infamy and corruption have been dredged to their foulest dregs in order to collect the infamous spawn of perdition sent out to despoil our country." In Milledgeville, according to a widespread fable, Sherman's officers had proven their depravity by staging an orgiastic ball with black women.

Other dreads did other damage. Union soldiers ignited cotton sheds only to discover from maternal screams that children lurked inside—hidden because Sherman killed babies. Many a forager risked his life, cursing and coughing the while, to save a toddler from a corncrib that the forager himself had torched. Some Georgians, better informed, knew that Sherman murdered only male children. A party of Kilpatrick's men, loitering in a farmhouse, watched a nicely dressed little girl swoop down a bannister. Entering the room, her mother shouted, "Bessie, my son, come down from there!" One guffawing trooper said he had wondered why all the neighborhood brats were girls.

Of deliberate terror, there was an abundance. Victims were tied up, searched, taunted and harried in various ingenious ways. Foragers held pistols to the heads of those who would not tell where goods were hidden. Men who kept silent might be threatened with hanging; now and then, they draped nooses around men's necks and began to string them up.

Sherman said he knew of two rapes; and only two rapists were ever prosecuted by the army. In the Carolinas, two other assaults were avenged by Wheeler's cavalry, who ran down bands of foragers and slit their throats. Taken together, trustworthy accounts seem to suggest fewer than half a dozen rapes for the Georgia and Carolina marches combined.

Here I think the record lies. Five or six incidents in five months for an army in enemy country seems absurd, unless we declare Sherman's the gentlest invasion in history. The Victorian preoccupation with female purity would alone have kept many victims silent. As well, there abides that tendency to equate "Southern women" with the higher classes. What of poor farm wives on their hardscrabble acres, living twenty miles off the line of march and visited by foragers or bummers?

No one bothered to count the assaults on black women, and there's little evidence that either side viewed such attacks as true rape. But by any name, accounts of rape and gang rape of slaves come down from both the army and civilians. There may have been hundreds of victims.

* * *

Clear across Georgia, Sherman's army passed through a corridor lined with dark faces. On the first night out of Atlanta, in a house where slaves had gathered, Sherman spoke at length with an old man whose intelligence impressed him—

> I then explained to him that we wanted the slaves to remain where they were, and not to load us down with useless mouths, which would eat up the food needed for our fighting-men; that our success was their assured freedom; that we could receive a few of their young, hearty men as pioneers [manual laborers]; but that, if they followed us in swarms of old and young, feeble and helpless, it would simply load us down and cripple us in our great task.

Cump felt convinced that his listener sent the word ahead through the grapevine, and that it reduced the numbers of refugees. To blacks everywhere, he repeated his message:

Stay home, don't assault your masters, wait. He explained that "freedom" would still mean work.

Louise Reese Cornwell of Hillsboro, one of the scores of farm and plantation women who left reminiscences, made frank, brief mention of neighborhood slaves who proved untrustworthy. But on her estate, things were different:

> Our slaves, be it said to their credit, did not turn against us, as many did, for they were closely questioned as to what money, watches, jewelry we had, but they did not betray us. Uncle Peter as we called him, was very kind and faithful. He secured for us some flour, meal, and butter and during the stay of the Yankee wounded, though nearly, or quite all of the negroes went to see them, Uncle Peter never did.

That, quite literally, is the stuff of legends. The slaves who "betrayed" or vanished generally stay anonymous, while Louise celebrates the loyal retainer. Thanks to a hundred such accounts, Uncle Peter waxed heroic in post-war memory.

Uncle Peter was real enough, but scarce. Across Georgia, slaves told looters where to dig for silver plate, and led them to the swamp where the horses were hidden. When bummers were lost or foragers strayed too far, slaves guided, hid and fed them. Some blacks gave their only shoes to barefoot soldiers.

To Sherman himself, the black response was ecstatic, religious:

> Whenever they heard my name, they clustered about my horse, shouted and prayed in their peculiar style, which had a natural eloquence that would have moved a stone. I have witnessed hundreds, if not thousand, of such scenes; and can now see a poor girl in the very ecstasy of the Methodist "shout," hugging the banner of one of the regiments, and jumping up to the "feet of Jesus."

To Halleck, he confided: "They gather round me in crowds,

and I can't find out whether I am Moses or Aaron, or which of the prophets; but surely I am rated as one of the congregation."

Hitchcock savored his commander's encounters with blacks, noting the contrast between Sherman's theoretical bigotry and the gentleness and patience he showed to those who came miles for a look at him. There was the man who begged a glimpse of Sherman, and afterward walked away saying, "He's got the Linkum head, the Linkum head, he's got the Linkum head." And the woman who served Hitchcock lunch one day—"Smart as a steel trap. She hid and fed three of our men, escaped prisoners: knew about Burnside, McClellan, and Sherman, also the fall of Atlanta ... They pointed out Gen. S. to her in the door of the house ... 'Dar's de man dat rules de world!' she exclaimed."

Cump was most tickled by the visitor who asked if he were truly Mr. Sherman. The general said he was. Walking around him, the old man kept murmuring, "Well, well. So this is Mr. Sherman. This is Mr. Sherman!" Then, as he departed— "They'll be no sleep for this nigger tonight!"

Despite Sherman's pleas, perhaps twenty-five thousand escaped slaves joined his columns. Nearly seven thousand were still with the army when it reached Savannah. The others had endured for a while, and then drifted away; ten miles a day was no joke for the elderly, or for women with babies. The refugees tended soldiers' clothes, carried their guns, and cooked. Soldiers complained of children underfoot. Mules clomped along with babies sticking their heads out of the packs. A mother who couldn't keep up the pace might hide her baby in a wagon, hoping that the child would reach freedom.

Many women slept willingly with their liberators. David Conyngham, the best of the dozen correspondents who marched, noted that the most attractive women

led luxurious lives, stowed away in baggage wagons ... and

feted at the servants' mess at night. It would be vexatious to the Grand Turk or Brigham Young if they could only see how many of the dark houris were in the employment of officers' servants and teamsters. I have seen officers themselves very attentive to the wants of pretty octoroon girls, and provide them with horses to ride.

At Ebenezer Creek, thirty-five miles from Savannah, came tragedy. Leading Slocum's rear corps was an officer with the improbable name of Jefferson Davis. (Usually called "Jeff. C. Davis"; the Confederacy's president was Jefferson F.) General Davis was the most bristly of Sherman's top echelon. Back in 1862, he had killed another Federal general in a quarrel, but had not deemed such a trifle worth resigning over. Davis made no secret of his pro-slavery views.

Like Sherman and other commanders, Davis was annoyed by the thousands of refugees, particularly now that Savannah was near and there was growing risk of battle. When his columns reached Ebenezer Creek, swollen with flood water and spanned with a pontoon bridge, Davis rushed them across, as guards pushed the refugees back. He then quickly removed the bridge. A throng of refugees were stranded, with others crowding them from behind as they too approached the creek.

Panic set in, and then multiplied when someone shouted that Rebel cavalry were coming. Hundreds leapt or were pushed into the surging water, including many who couldn't swim.

Hearing the screams, soldiers rushed back to pull people out. A few blacks slapped together a flimsy raft and ferried as many as they could. But dozens died at the crossing, or were swept downstream to drown.

And then Wheeler's cavalry did appear. They rounded up helpless people, and may also have killed a few.

Miles away, Sherman heard nothing of the disaster for awhile. But he would hear all he wanted before the repercussions died. Among the many outraged officers was Major Connolly, who was certain that Davis had acted with malicious intent. Connolly and others saw to it that the matter reached Stanton's attention.

* * *

In the second week of December, as they neared Savannah, the weather was unseasonably fine. But the roads were appalling. "All the creeks seem to spread into swamps," said Major Hitchcock:

> Peculiarity of this soil that it has a sort of upper crust or layer, from four or five to twelve inches thick, beneath which when wagons have worked and cut through it, it is very deep, bad mud, quite like quicksand. The train of one division may get along pretty well over one of these places, but those of the next may (and probably will) cut through the "crust" and go in to the wheel hubs.

Immediately before the city, the country was all marsh and canals, with roads and railroads crossing on long causeways. These straight-line causeways made the approach particularly risky: For Hardee's gunners, blue columns were pins in a bowling alley. Sherman was reconnoitering along a railroad when he noticed a gray cannoneer about to fire. He and his party skipped aside; but their shouts came too late for a black man crossing the track—decapitated by the ball's first bounce.

Savannah's defenses, like Atlanta's, were formidable; but here, beside the forts and earthworks, were floodgates that gave Hardee control of the canals. Sherman was never tempted to see what the Rebels could do with those gates against a direct assault.

After a good deal of mud-wallowing, he established a semi-circular line that blocked Savannah from the west. Next, he sent General William Hazen's division marching south—

toward Fort McAllister, fourteen miles below town. McAllister stood guard against naval attack, and Sherman suspected that its defenses on the land side might be weak.

On the afternoon of December 13, while Hazen wormed his way close to the fort, Sherman and Howard stood watching from a rice mill across the Ogeechee River, where Howard had erected a signal station. As the sun dropped low, and the generals fidgeted, yearning for the charge to commence, a steamer came up the river. "Soon the flag of the United States was plainly visible," said Sherman,

> and our attention was divided between this approaching steamer and the expected assault. When the sun was about an hour high, another signal-message came from General Hazen that he was all ready, and I replied to go ahead, as a friendly steamer was approaching from below. Soon we made out a group of officers on the deck of this vessel, signaling with a flag, "Who are you?" The answer went back promptly, "General Sherman." Then followed the question. "Is Fort McAllister taken?" "Not yet, but it will be in a minute!"

So it was, in one swift burst—a near-perfect assault with low casualties for both sides. The generals hurrahed and Cump shouted—"This nigger will have no sleep this night!" To Slocum, miles away on the siege line, went an easy order: "Take a good big drink, a long breath and then yell like the devil. The fort was taken at 4:30 p.m., the assault lasting but fifteen minutes."

McAllister's capture doomed Savannah. If necessary, Sherman could sustain his army with shipped-in food while spreading around to squeeze Hardee into surrender.

That night and the next day he turned sailor, rowing over to congratulate the victors and heading downstream to meet with Admiral Dahlgren of the navy. It was two days before he returned to the rice mill to pick up his horse. By then, he had caught up on the news: Grant still besieged Petersburg. Some part of Thomas's army had whipped Hood at Franklin, but Hood was still in Tennessee.

Sherman had scarcely returned to his own lines when he ran into his postal officer, Colonel Markland, who had just arrived from the coast, bringing sacks of mail. Markland approached with arm outstretched—"Before leaving Washington, I was directed by the president to take you by the hand wherever I met you and say to you for him, 'God bless you and the army under your command. Since cutting loose from Atlanta, my prayers and those of the nation have been for your success.'"

"I thank the president," said Sherman. "Say my army is all right."

The waterfront of the Georgia port city of Savannah. Sherman reported to Lincoln the day after he took the town on December 22: "I beg to present you as a Christmas-gift the city of Savannah, with one hundred and fifty heavy guns and plenty of ammunition, also about twenty-five thousand bales of cotton."

Chapter 10

Savannah Interlude

Sixty thousand men had marched off the earth—their path traceable only through rumors in Southern papers. "You all will hear we've been killed," a soldier had warned his family.

Not even Lincoln had been told where Sherman was aiming—"I know the hole he went in at, but not the hole he'll come out at." At a reception, the president shook hands with a friend without seeing him. When teased, he apologized: "I was thinking of a man down South." When the army finally popped out of their hole, church bells pealed throughout the Union.

The North's anxiety shows how quickly a feeling for new technology had spread. From ancient times, every marching army had vanished—often for years. So had every long-distance traveler; when Thomas Jefferson went to Europe, it was six months before his friends knew he had made it. But by Sherman's day, though the telegraph was not yet three decades old, steam, rails and wires had so altered perceptions that his move seemed wildly daring. Telegrams already felt natural, just as electricity now feels natural and a power failure seems an anomaly.

In Colonel Markland's bag was a letter from Grant that made Sherman wish he were still remote from mail and telegrams. Grant had been thinking that after taking Savannah, Sherman's best course would be to leave enough troops there to hold it, and then "with the balance of your command come here by water with all dispatch." Unless Sherman saw any objections, Grant would send every available ship to carry the western army to Virginia.

Sherman saw only one objection—he wouldn't do any such thing. His heart was set on more marching; Georgia had been only a warm-up. But almost before he could start protesting, Grant had second thoughts. He had found, he said, that it would take awhile to gather enough ships. Perhaps he had also been doing some thinking about Cump Sherman. On the very day that Sherman mailed his first wheedle, Grant informed him that "this whole matter of your future actions should be entirely left to your discretion."

So much for that. But meanwhile, there remained the little matter of Savannah to take care of.

Sherman began to stretch his lines farther around the city. Then, on the 17th, he asked Hardee to surrender: "I have already received guns that can cast heavy and destructive shot as far as the heart of your city; also, I have for some days held and controlled every avenue by which the people and garrison of Savannah can be supplied." If Hardee gave up, Sherman promised liberal terms. "But should I be forced to resort to assault, or the slower and surer process of starvation, I shall then feel justified in resorting to the harshest measures, and shall make little effort to restrain my army— burning to avenge the national wrong."

Lest Hardee feel Sherman was crueler than others, he enclosed the note that Hood had sent Resaca's commander during the Goose Chase, when Hood threatened dire things if there were no surrender.

William Hardee was not impressed. He replied that Sherman had made a few errors: The Union army was still far from town, and Hardee was far from being surrounded. As for Sherman's threats, he responded that he had always observed the rules of civilized warfare, and "should deeply regret the adoption of any course by you that may force me to deviate from them in future."

Hardee was bluffing. He was squeezed tighter than he admitted. But there remained a stretch of the Savannah River that Sherman didn't yet control. In a move worthy of his old commander, Joe Johnston, Hardee lay down a ramshackle floating bridge of rice flats, and ran it from island to island over to the South Carolina bank. On the night of December 20, he withdrew his whole command—by then about fifteen thousand men—and got all of his wagons across to boot.

As Hardee may have guessed, Sherman too had been bluffing. Savannah was far too valuable as a port and as a potential supply center to destroy. Should the war drag on, it would become the jumping off point for future Union operations in the Southeast. Hence, Sherman would avoid bombardment if at all possible. But it was due more to Hardee's talents than to Sherman's that the lovely colonial city changed hands without being shelled.

Sherman was up the coast at a conference on the morning of the 21st, already plotting his next campaign, when his men waltzed into Savannah. As at Atlanta, he had missed the actual capture. Though chagrined to learn of Hardee's escape, he found ample cause to rejoice. On the 22nd, Sherman sent Lincoln his most famous message of the war: "I beg to present you as a Christmas-gift the city of Savannah, with one hundred and fifty heavy guns and plenty of ammunition, also about twenty-five thousand bales of cotton."

* * *

The month-long occupation was peaceful for both the army and its unwilling hosts. Sherman chose the city's ruler well. General John W. Geary, who had governed Kansas and been mayor of San Francisco in its wild days, maintained domestic tranquillity. The army was tightly controlled, and there was very little vandalism. Many troops never saw Savannah or came in only on passes.

For the private, the interlude brought rest, new clothes and the first chance in his life to revel in fresh oysters. But beyond that, he had little cause to rejoice over his long, rainy Christmas break, particularly if he were camped out near the marshes or in a leaky hut in Savannah's slums. Officers lodged with local families fared much better, especially if they met young ladies who would stoop to consort with Yankees. Sherman and his generals, ensconced in the city's most elegant homes, had themselves a fine, festive Christmas.

Cump found Savannah long on refugees and very short on food and medical supplies. He handed out army rations, then arranged the sale of local rice in the North. Northern charities pitched in generously, and soon relief ships arrived. As well as proving that Sherman's cracker-sharing talk was candid, Savannah's occupation hints at what Reconstruction might have been like, had generals been given more say and politicians less.

Though citizens were free to depart for the Confederate lines, only two hundred did so. By December 1864, it took no prophet to see the end. Back in '62, Sherman had stood in church to add the presidential prayer; but now when a clergyman asked leave to pray for Davis, he smiled: "Hell, yes. Jeff Davis and the Confederate government need all the prayer they can get."

Cump gave himself as much of a rest as he was capable of enjoying. There was little military activity, apart from snagging a blockade runner who came proudly sailing into what he thought to be a Rebel port. Sherman caught up on his mail, answering all the letters of praise and thanks for his Christmas gift. For Ellen, he abridged the Georgia campaign: "We came right along living on turkeys, chickens, pigs, bringing along our wagons loaded as we started with bread, etc. I suppose Jeff Davis will now have to feed the people of Georgia instead of collecting provisions of them to feed his armies. We have destroyed nearly two hundred miles of railroad and are not done."

As soon as Fort McAllister fell, Dahlgren had cleared the channels of torpedoes. Since then, goods had been arriving. Part of Sherman's work time went to resupplying his raggedy army.

Weeks earlier, Quartermaster General Meigs had sent a shipment to Port Royal to await Sherman, wherever he might turn up. One of the most implausible Civil War orders is Meigs's request that the shipment be made "in such a manner as to attract as little attention as possible." The discreet stash that now came on to Savannah included—among a great deal else—30,000 coats, 30,000 pair of trousers, 60,000 each of shirts, drawers and socks, 100,000 pairs of shoes and boots and 30,000 blankets. There were 10,000 shelter tents and 100 hospital tents, 30,000 knapsacks and haversacks, 10,000 canteens. For the packers and horsemen, Meigs tucked in 2 tons of rope, 15,000 pounds of iron and steel, 200 horse rasps, 15,000 bushels of blacksmiths' coal, 50 tons of shoes, and—lest the battle be lost—5 tons of horseshoe nails.

*   *   *

The only December news big enough to match Sherman's own triumph came filtering slowly to Savannah from distant Tennessee. Hood's invasion had turned into one of the South's greatest disasters. After he and Sherman parted company in northern Alabama, Hood had been slow to cross the Tennessee River, giving Thomas more time to consolidate. Then came a race toward Nashville against Schofield, whose force was moving north to become part of Thomas's. At Spring Hill, Hood muffed a chance to attack the Federals from several sides at once. Marching by night, under Hood's nose, Schofield escaped to Franklin, where his bone-tired men spent the morning of November 30 digging in.

Hood pursued and, that afternoon, staged a frontal attack. He did so against his generals' advice and without waiting for his whole army to arrive. Six Confederate generals perished at Franklin, including Patrick Cleburne. Hood's losses came to over six thousand; Schofield's were under twenty-five hundred. After his victory, Schofield again marched by night, to reach safety within Thomas's lines.

Desperate, perhaps almost mad, Hood surveyed his wretched options and chose the worst. He came on toward Nashville and camped his shattered army in the hills south of town. It could hardly be called a siege, since thirty thousand can't besiege seventy thousand who have open railroads behind them. For two weeks, Hood sat there, exposing his hungry men to the December cold, inviting attack.

Pap methodically drew up his textbook battle plan, nearly getting himself fired for ignoring Grant's orders to attack at once. On December 15, two days after Sherman took Fort McAllister, Thomas was ready. Losses were low for a two-day battle—around three thousand for Thomas against roughly twice that many for Hood. But in conjunction with Franklin, Nashville all but disposed of Hood's force as an army. Pursued and harried by Thomas, Hood's survivors retreated back to Alabama.

Nashville was the last big battle in the West. Later in the winter, after Hood resigned, the remnants of the Army of Tennessee would march to the Carolinas, where they joined the final struggle against Sherman.

* * *

On January 11, Sherman got a little surprise. The secretary of war arrived for a four-day visit. Edwin Stanton announced that he came to settle the on-going fuss over cotton between Sherman and the Treasury Department and to catch some ocean air for his health. In truth, he had come to look into the matter of General Sherman and the Negroes, and to see what he could turn up regarding the disaster at Ebenezer Creek.

Sherman had begun to dig a pit for himself at least as early as July, when Congress authorized the governors to recruit freedmen to fill state draft quotas. Recruiting agents hastened south to sign up blacks as soon as the armies liberated them.

Sherman refused to co-operate, threatening to arrest any agents caught hanging around his brigades. Lincoln finally had to order him to co-operate.

Like the whole army, Cump despised any scheme that enabled healthy white men to dodge or buy their way out of serving. He found black troops tolerable—barely—for guard duty well behind the lines; and he was glad to let blacks dig his trenches. But that was about all. In September, he had spoken his bigoted mind to Halleck: "I am honest in my belief that it is not fair to our men to count negroes as equals. Cannot we at this day drop theories, and be reasonable men?" It was fine to seize slaves, but—

> We want the best young white men of the land, and they should be inspired with the pride of freemen to fight for their country. If Mr. Lincoln or Stanton could walk through the camps of this army and hear the soldiers talk they would hear new ideas. I have had the question put to me often: "Is not a negro as good as a white man to stop a bullet?" Yes, and a sandbag is better; but can a negro do our skirmishing and picket duty? Can they improvise roads, bridges, sorties, flank movements, &c., like the white man? I say no. Soldiers must and do many things without orders, from their own sense, as in sentinels. Negroes are not equal to this.

Later in the fall, Sherman had reminded Stanton that if the black fought, he would expect a higher status after the war. But "I much prefer to keep negroes yet for some time to come in a subordinate state, for our prejudices, yours as well as mine, are not yet schooled for absolute equality."

On December 30, before Stanton's visit, the circumspect Halleck went well out on a limb to give his friend a warning:

> I take the liberty of calling your attention, in this private and friendly way, to a matter which may possibly hereafter be of more importance to you than either of us may now anticipate. While almost every one is praising your great march through

Georgia and the capture of Savannah, there is a certain class, having now great influence with the president, and very probably anticipating still more on a change of Cabinet, who are decidedly disposed to make a point against you—I mean in regard to "Inevitable Sambo." They say that you have manifested an almost *criminal* dislike to the negro, and that you are not willing to carry out the wishes of the Government in regard to him, but repulse him with contempt. They say you might have brought with you to Savannah more than 50,000, thus stripping Georgia of that number of laborers and opening a road by which as many more could have escaped from their masters; but that instead of this you drove them from your ranks, prevented them from following you by cutting the bridges in your rear, and thus caused the massacre of large numbers by Wheeler's cavalry.

Where Halleck mentioned "a certain class," he trusted Sherman to include a certain Stanton, who was allied with radical Republicans in Congress.

What Sherman failed to realize—far from Washington and deaf as ever to political whisperings—was that the black had become more than a man. As Halleck tried to tell him, "Inevitable Sambo" had grown into a cause for those bent on a harsh Reconstruction. In asking, "Cannot we at this day drop theories, and be reasonable men?" Cump sounded roughly like someone of our day asking, "Abortion is a simple procedure—what's the fuss?"

The day Stanton arrived, he said that he wished to meet with Negro leaders. During that gathering, he asked the general to leave the room while he questioned the men. The minister who acted as spokesman praised Sherman without reservation, lauding his just and kindly treatment of Negroes. But to Cump that was beside the point. He was bitterly offended that, after all he had done for the country, Stanton should deem it necessary to go to anyone—let alone *niggers!*—to verify his character.

Otherwise the visit seemed to go well enough. Stanton

passed long hours in Sherman's office, bemoaning his health and chattering of this and that. He grilled Sherman on General Davis and the Ebenezer Creek disaster; but seemed to give Sherman a fair hearing and, overall, to take his views seriously. One evening, while they dined on Stanton's ship, the secretary requested his thoughts on how the freedmen should be provided for. Their talk developed into Sherman's Special Field Order 15, which appropriated coastal lands as settlement districts where blacks could control their own destiny.

To Ellen he wrote:

> Mr. Stanton has been here and is cured of that Negro nonsense which arises, not from a love of the Negro but a desire to dodge service. Mr. Chase and others have written to me to modify my opinions, but you know I cannot, for if I attempt the part of a hypocrite it would break out at each sentence. I want soldiers made of the best bone and muscle in the land, and won't attempt military feats with doubtful materials.

* * *

The New Year had hardly begun before Sherman itched to be moving. His staff were once more hearing all they cared to in praise of good old army hardtack, which Cump insisted was better for a man than any other nutriment. (Henry Hitchcock noted that Sherman did somehow force down soft bread whenever he got the chance.) The general apologized to Stanton because his Savannah table bore such dainties as canned fruit. "This is the consequence of coming into houses and cities. The only place to live, Mr. Secretary, is out of doors in the woods!"

In one of their exchanges that month, Grant finally acknowledged what both he and Sherman had long guessed: "My own opinion is that Lee is averse to going out of Virginia, and if the cause of the South is lost he wants Richmond to be the last place surrendered. If he has such views it may be well to indulge him until everything else is in our hands." So Grant would continue to hold the bear's leg while Sherman kept on skinning.

He met often that month with army and navy commanders, to plan and co-ordinate. His broad strategy called for smaller army and naval forces to "gather the apples" along the coast, as his big army shook Carolina's trunk. He felt sure that Rebel coastal defenses must collapse once he destroyed the interior railroads behind them.

On January 15th, a big load of fruit rattled down before Sherman started shaking, when Admiral Porter and General Alfred Terry captured Fort Fisher on the North Carolina coast. The capture sealed off Wilmington—the South's last harbor—which sat thirty miles up the Cape Fear River from the fort. Terry would next assail Wilmington itself. If he succeeded, Sherman would have a channel to the coast whenever his army crossed the Cape Fear.

In a more elaborate scheme, he ordered Schofield to bring his army from Tennessee, by train and ship, to the Carolina coast. Schofield would try to penetrate to the interior and link with Sherman.

Like Uncle Billy, many of his troops were eager to be moving. Anger was building within the army; not all of it directed toward the enemy.

The glad news from Tennessee intensified a conviction that had needed no boosting—the war was nearly won, and western armies had done most of the winning.

Tensions between East and West had grown throughout the war. By the time Sherman's men reached Savannah, their shoulders bore large western chips. As they saw it, they had whipped shit out of the Johnnies, pushing them back through half a dozen states, while the Army of the Potomac—the "paper collar soldiers"—doodled away four years, playing tag with Lee over the same corner of Virginia. Yet who hogged the supplies and the glory? If Easterners could fight, how come Sherman's army had to walk clear around to the Carolinas?

At heart, the strains were pure Americana. They dated back to the Whiskey Rebellion or before, and they still flourish in snide jokes about New Yorkers and Californians. Western troops delighted to watch Sherman get his hands dirty, or to see Logan caked in mud as he wrestled a wagon. One soldier boasted to the folks at home that the general commanding his division "is a more common man than a Potomic Lieut in both dress and deportment."

As they looked north, men joked about making fast work of the Rebs, and then thrashing the paper collar boys.

But most of the troops found that joke only mildly funny. Their disgust with the Army of the Potomac was adoration compared with how they felt about the state across the water.

No one had forgotten where secession started. Soldiers recalled their dead buddies, and then thought of the fire-eaters in Charleston—screaming until they drove the whole South out of the Union. Said an Iowa man, "South Carolina cried out the first for war and she shall have it to her heart's content. She sowed the Wind. She will soon reap the Whirlwind." In full accord was Major Connolly: "I don't care how soon we get over into South Carolina, for I want to see the long deferred chastisement begin. If we don't purify South Carolina it will be because we *can't get a light*."

Cump promised Halleck that the state would "not be quite so tempestuous" when his men were through with her. "The truth is, the whole army is burning with an insatiable desire to wreak vengeance upon South Carolina. I almost tremble for her fate."

The ruins of the capital of South Carolina, Columbia, after Sherman's army took the town. The burning of Columbia inspires debate even today; Southerners blame drunken Northern soldiers for the destructive blazes while Northerners claim they were started by retreating Confederates.

Chapter 11

A Visit from the West

I saw and felt that we would not be able longer to restrain our men as we had done in Georgia.

—Sherman, *Memoirs*

*T*he Carolina march began less dramatically than its predecessor. Rain and floods got things off to a slow, jerky start. Howard's wing began moving, by boat, over to Beaufort, South Carolina, on January 17; a few days later they started inland. But on the left, where Slocum was to cross the Savannah River, the rains held up the march a good while. The whole army wasn't out of touch with Savannah until February 1.

Sherman had spread rumors about destroying Charleston. But then he headed inland, ignoring that obvious coastal target. He aimed first for Columbia, after which he would point for eastern North Carolina. At the start, the right wing feinted toward Charleston, while the left again threatened Augusta. Then both converged toward Columbia. Viewed together, Sherman's Georgia march and the start of his Carolina march traced a semicircle around Augusta—constantly threatened, but never attacked. In February as in late autumn, Bragg abided with his ten thousand useless troops, polishing his cannon.

"Each regiment as it entered South Carolina gave three cheers," recalled Slocum. "The men seemed to realize that at last they had set foot on the state which had done more than all others to bring upon the country the horrors of Civil War." One soldier's voice boomed, "Boys, this is old South Carolina, let's give her hell."

Among the first towns hit was Barnwell, looted and torched by Kilpatrick's cavalry. Kilpatrick said that now the village should be called "Burnwell." Another gag had it that when they left Savannah, Little Kil's troopers stuffed their saddlebags with matches.

The army needed all their rage to keep them going those first two weeks. In Georgia, the weather had been good and the late-autumn granaries ripe for the ravaging. But this was winter and a less fertile, poorer country. Foragers often roamed thirty miles from the line of march.

It was the wettest winter in memory. Rain fell 28 of the first 45 days, and mostly fell hard.

For Howard's troops, with whom Sherman rode, the first treat was the Salkehatchie. Its smaller fork alone—the Little Salkehatchie—split into nine streams that required bridging. Pickets sometimes covered their beats in rowboats. The men laughed about Sherman's knack for hitting every river "endwise."

"We must all turn amphibious," wrote Cump to Slocum on February 9, "for the country is half under water. Mower had to fight at the Salkehatchie with his men up to their armpits, he setting the example."

Slocum wasn't awed. Throughout the swamp march, Sherman raged and fretted because the left wing never kept up. What he didn't know and probably wouldn't have credited was that he and Howard had taken the easy route. Striking Carolina farther south, Slocum's wing had to tackle a mon-

strosity called the Coosawatchie Swamp before they even
reached the Salk.

"I can give you but a faint idea of the devilish nature of the
country through which we passed," wrote General Williams
to his daughter:

> The streams . . . were generally in six to ten channels with the
> worst entangled swamps between, often three miles wide. Be-
> hind these the Rebs. would entrench, and it took a good deal of
> skirmishing in water waist-deep to get them out. We lost a
> good many men in these affairs. . . The roads, mostly sandy
> loam with a quicksand substructure, would become so satu-
> rated that there was no bottom.

Alpheus Williams was a cheerful soul. Conyngham, the
correspondent, was mucking his way through a road late one
evening when a voice boomed down—"Hello, old fellow.
You'd better come up and get yourself a roost." Perched in a
tree were Williams and his staff. The general, age fifty-five
and not slender, was swathed in a blanket, enjoying his
cigar—"looking as quiet and serene as if he had been in his
tent on dry ground."

After the Salk came the Edisto. There, though the fighting
was lighter, the crossing was worse. The water was colder—
often skimmed with ice—and the walks through it were
longer. Men plodded for miles through knee-deep water,
with mud sucking down their feet. Those whose legs quit
from numbness had to be carried. Those who gave up were
cursed and teased back into line.

All this, of course, while moving their thousands of wagons, their refugees, their cannon. And with a cattle herd that
still grew. Said Major Nichols, "Our conscription is remorseless. Every species of four-footed beast that South Carolina
planters cherished among their live-stock is swept in by our
flanking foragers, and the music of the animal creation
mingles with the sound of the footfall of the army."

Horses sank to the knee; wagon wheels sank until the wagon box slid over the mud. A Massachusetts captain asked a sergeant why he was standing with one arm up to the elbow in mud. "He explained that he was trying to find his shoe."

Beside insanity, their secret was corduroy. Said Williams: "We became expert road-makers, first piling on all the fence rails and then cutting the young pines of which there was an abundance everywhere. For days we corduroyed every mile."

Poe's engineers put down four hundred miles of corduroy, struggling to keep some facsimile of a bottom on the roads. When the wagons thrust it out of sight, it was the troops' turn. Working in crews of five and six thousand, they dropped another four hundred miles of it, at least. Said a disgusted prisoner, "If your army goes to hell, it will corduroy the road."

Through the swamps they made ten and twelve miles a day, the same pace they had kept up across Georgia.

After the war, frustrated that the public lauded the March to the Sea while ignoring Carolina, Sherman insisted that the Georgia march had been "only a shift of base." Remembering those swamps, he called the Carolina foray "by far the most important in conception and execution of any act of my life."

He was astounded by the army's health, swearing that he rarely heard a cough. Men seemed to shake off injuries or wounds that once would have hospitalized them. Illness rates stayed as low that winter as they had been in Georgia.

More Civil War troops were disabled or killed by illness than gunpowder. Though better in the last years, the camps remained incubation pits throughout the war. A marching army stayed healthier, even in February swamps, than one steeping all winter in its own sewage. And from today's perspective, another word comes to mind: aerobics. Tough to start with, Sherman's men had been moving steadily since spring; then they finished their year with that three-hundred mile hike to Savannah. Cump once bragged that his soldiers had "splendid legs, splendid legs!" Surely they did, with lungs and hearts to match.

* * *

The men called it "The Smokey March." Small towns went up in flames, as did farmhouses, barns, bins of cottonseed, and vast stacks of railroad ties. At Hardeeville, they smashed up a fine church, shouting "There goes your damned old gospel shop!" Then they burned the town. On the few rainless days, smoke smudged the sky.

Some of the coarse fun of the March to the Sea continued. They called themselves "Old Sherman's Smokehouse Rangers" and joked about their "epidemic of good appetites." One soldier declared them a migratory Biblical tribe—the Shermanites. But the Smokey March was no Halloween. Most of the anecdotes of soldiers whooping it up, or standing by the road in party dresses, come from Georgia. South Carolina destruction was savage. There was more terrorizing for the joy of seeing people in terror.

Hatred ran deep and the novelty was wearing thin. Although still often a sadistic treat, pillaging had also become a job—one that Sherman's army of workers performed with deadly efficiency. Nothing was more hapless than the efforts of Carolina people to hide their treasures from looters who had served their Georgia apprenticeship. Wrote Conyngham: "As for wholesale burnings, pillage, devastation committed in South Carolina, magnify all I have said of Georgia some fifty fold, and then throw in an occasional murder, 'just to make an old, hard-fisted cuss come to his senses,' and you have a pretty good idea of the whole thing."

Equally brutal were the dealings between enemy commanders. On February 7, Joe Wheeler sent word that he would stop burning cotton if the Yankees stopped burning houses. Sherman answered: "I hope you will burn all cotton and save us the trouble. We don't want it, and it has proven a curse to our country. All you don't burn, I will." He added (with tongue far in cheek) that his orders were to leave peacefully occupied houses alone. As for vacant houses, if the owners didn't want them enough to stay put, why should Sherman preserve them?

Later in February, cavalry under Confederate General Wade Hampton killed eighteen of Sherman's Smokehouse Rangers, slitting throats and leaving signs reading "Death to foragers." Sherman told Kilpatrick to choose eighteen Rebel prisoners and kill man for man. Hampton threatened to keep on killing; but once again, Sherman's harshness had worked. Both sides desisted after one exchange of corpses.

* * *

By February 15, they had pulled out of the swamps and Howard's wing was bearing down on Columbia. There, until much too late, Sherman's arrival had remained an unexpected pleasure. Because of Charleston's notoriety, South Carolinians had convinced themselves that Columbia was safe. Her population and wealth had multiplied as well-to-do people fled the coast.

On February 16, Howard reached the bank of the Congaree, opposite the city. From there, his artillery chipped the beautiful, still unfinished capitol and drove away civilian looters from around the depot. Sherman then halted the firing. The next morning, as the last of Hampton's cavalry departed, Mayor Goodwyn rode out to surrender his city; Union soldiers were already moving in.

In later years, the burning of Columbia, on the night of February 17, became one of the war's premier horror stories. And ever since the war, the question of responsibility has been raised. To borrow the title of a nineteenth-century book—"Who burned Columbia?"

Sherman's view, and that of many high Union officers, was that Hampton's cavalry had ignited bales of cotton before they fled. The cotton still burned when the Federals arrived; white shreds covered the streets, blowing here and there the

Carolinas

whole gusty day. Though Howard extinguished the flames, the bales still burned within. Later, they again burst out in flame. Cavalry, cotton and wind, said Sherman, were the primary villains.

From the Southern angle, "Who burned Columbia?" has never been a tough question. Disputes have revolved around the details, and around the question of whether Sherman ordered the conflagration.

In a post-war cotton-claims suit, where Sherman and many others gave testimony, an international board of arbitration decreed that neither Confederate nor Union officers had been responsible. That settled nothing beyond the claims. In his *Memoirs*, Sherman still blamed Hampton, while Hampton, the Columbia novelist William Gilmore Simms, and a host of others continued to damn the army in general and Sherman in particular.

The whole antique controversy seems absurd, when the mass of evidence leads to an obvious judgment: Had there been no cotton, Columbia would still have burned, from numerous fires set by Sherman's troops. But neither Sherman, Howard, nor any other general instigated the fire, save in the important indirect sense that they led a multitude of arsonists into town.

At Columbia, the army's hatred of South Carolina boiled over. As the marchers neared town, several escaped prisoners of war reached them. Their tales of the vile conditions in Confederate camps, and of the treatment they had endured, won a sympathetic, outraged hearing. Some of the escapees were later heard begging troops for matches and turpentine. But well before the prisoners' appearance, Sherman's soldiers had been singing

> Hail Columbia, happy land!
> If I don't burn you, I'll be damned.

Had the road taken them to Charleston, they would have found a different tune. Columbia was the only big South Carolina city they passed through, and Columbia paid for it.

As they entered the city, some regiments were greeted by blacks, who stood along the streets, ladling whiskey and brandy from buckets—"Here, Master. Try some of dis!" Nor were thirsty soldiers who missed out on the reception shy about emptying the shelves of liquor stores or breaking into the sideboards of private homes. When Sherman rode into Columbia, about noon, he was offered the freedom of the city by a gloriously drunk soldier. Howard rushed some of the early drunks out of town; but by dusk, Columbia teemed with intoxicated men, some of whom were already being guided by slaves on looting tours, from mansion to mansion. During the day, many citizens were threatened by soldiers who bragged of the fires to come.

The cotton bales are irrelevant—maybe they started a few fires and maybe not. In any case, there was not *a* Columbia fire until long after dark, when flames converged. There were dozens of fires, almost all deliberately set by Union soldiers.

Sherman had ordered only standard military destruction. The day of the fire, he assured the mayor that Columbia would be safe, and made a similar pledge to the mother superior of a convent, who had once taught his daughter Minnie. In the afternoon he called on a woman whom he had known in his old Carolina days. She made him smile, telling how she had fended off foragers by showing a book Lieutenant Sherman had signed for her in 1845. He went to bed early and slept until the fire aroused him. As Liddell Hart put it, "Generals who plan to burn a city are unlikely to take up their quarters in the middle of it."

Said Sherman later, "Though I never ordered it and never wished it, I have never shed many tears over the event, because I believe it hastened what we all fought for, the end of the war." Badgered by a lawyer during the claims trial, he put it less tenderly: "If I had made up my mind to burn Columbia, I would have burnt it with no more feeling than I would a common prairie dog village, but I did not do it!"

Fires began around twilight, and soon raged everywhere, despite all efforts of Federal officers and local authorities. But while troops watched by officers battled the flames, other soldiers lit more fires and interfered with the fire fighting when they saw the chance. For David Conyngham, the scene was demonic—drunken soldiers stripping houses, and then firing them; streets full of white and black men carrying plunder; streets packed with half-naked people who came screaming out of burning buildings. The correspondent himself was shot at when he tried to save a civilian from being killed. A troop of Missouri cavalry were supposed to be patrolling—"but I did not once see them interfering with the groups that rushed about to fire and pillage the houses."

Simms, the novelist, watched soldiers carrying pots and vessels of "combustible liquids, composed probably of phosphorus and other similar agents, turpentine, etc." from house to house.

For a local girl, Emma LeConte, the flames had a dreadful splendor. She watched sweeping columns of smoke "glittering with sparks and flying embers. . . . A quivering molten ocean seemed to fill the air and sky."

The spectacle was less beautiful to the slave girls—dozens perhaps—who were raped that night. Nor was there much splendor for the Ursuline nuns, who lost their convent despite a general's promise, and whom soldiers pestered and taunted—"Now, what do you think of God? Ain't Sherman greater?"

Nearly two-thirds of Columbia burned. Around four in the morning the winds dropped, preventing total destruction.

The next day, as Columbia smoked and stank, and thousands of the homeless milled about, Sherman saw no cause to cancel his orders. After all, he still had a war to win. That day and the next, Captain Poe's workers went about their standard chores—destroying everything of conceivable military value, just as they had done in Atlanta and every town along the way: a thousand bales of cotton, nineteen locomotives, twenty-five powder mills, half a million rounds of ammunition, and so on. The explosion of the powder magazines shook the ground for miles.

When an accidental blast killed sixteen soldiers, there must have been many Columbians who believed that God was finally speaking.

Mayor Goodwyn approached Sherman for aid, and the general sent him down the line, remarking that "Howard runs the religion of this army." With Sherman's approval, Howard gave the mayor five hundred cows that the army

A Visit from the West

didn't need, and a few muskets for keeping public order. Goodwyn asked how on earth he could feed his city, and Howard taught him how to organize forage parties.

On February 20, the blue army departed through streets lined with hissing, cursing spectators.

Since Savannah, slaves had flocked to join the expedition. Fewer of them drifted away than in Georgia, for the army's winter-time destruction didn't give them much reason to go home: After her village was burned, a woman begged Major Nichols to take her slaves—"for I have nothing for them to do, and can not feed them." When Sherman marched out of Columbia, blacks joined by the thousands, as did eight hundred white refugees.

The two wings drew closer as the army headed straight north, destroying track as they went. On the best Carolina roads they had seen, they quickly covered the forty miles to Winnsboro.

Winnsboro's fate typified what a dozen South Carolina villages had already suffered. At Sherman's approach, nearly the whole population fled. The Episcopal rector rode out to the army to beg protection for his community. In his absence, the bummers struck. They ransacked houses and burned thirty or so. They made bonfires of food—smashing flour barrels, and sending cracker boxes floating down streams of molasses and vinegar. Returning home, the Reverend Lord found his church's organ in the street, where the visitors had dumped it so that they might play "the devil's tunes" while burning the church. Since not a living soul was there to enjoy the music and the flames, they dug up a recent churchyard burial, broke open the coffin, and propped up the body to get what pleasure he could from the festivities. Better late than never, if only marginally, the regulars arrived to save what was left of the town.

After Winnsboro, Sherman turned northeast toward Goldsboro. With the swamps now well behind, the walking should have stayed easy, but the rains still poured and the

Streams were torrents. On February 23, three corps made it over the Wateree on a buckling bridge. Then the bridge went, leaving Jeff C. Davis and his Fourteenth Corps behind.

In the slickest mud they had seen yet, the front of the army slid and cursed their way into Hanging Rock Post Office, taking four days to cover twenty miles. But there was no reason to hurry, since Davis had gone nowhere. That worthy was having, in Sherman's phrase, "infinite difficulty in reconstructing his bridge"—trying one string of pontoons after another, only to see them smashed by logs and current. About the time the rest of the army skidded into Hanging Rock, Davis finally got a bridge to stay put, and came glopping along behind.

While Cump seethed and waited, Rebel captives brought him good news. As he had predicted, his eradication of railroads had shaken the apple tree. While Columbia was burning, Hardee had abandoned Charleston. Though Sherman didn't know it, Hardee's men were now on their way to join the assemblage of Rebel forces gathering in North Carolina.

Shortly after Davis's mishap, it was the right wing's turn to be stopped—at Lynch's Creek. Naked troops, carrying their guns above their heads, crossed the throat-deep water to drive away skirmishers. Then it took four days to bridge a stream that a healthy man could spit half way across in a dry year.

Next came Cheraw, their last stop in South Carolina. Sherman entered the quiet village in time to accept a luncheon invitation from Blair, who had appropriated a house.

> We passed down into the basement dining-room where the regular family table was spread with an excellent meal; and during its progress I was asked to take some wine, which stood upon the table in venerable bottles. It was so very good that I inquired where it came from. General Blair simply asked, "Do you like it?" but I insisted upon knowing where he had got it;

he only replied by asking if I liked it, and wanted some. He afterward sent to my bivouac a case containing a dozen bottles of the finest madeira I ever tasted.

Following lunch, Blair inquired if Sherman could use some saddle blankets or perhaps a tent rug. He then led his commander to a room jam-packed with elegant carpets.

Wealthy Charlestonians, seeking a haven for their valuables, had struck upon Cheraw, a town so remote that there was no chance of the Yankees reaching it. The village was a trove of sumptuous furnishings. Blair's madeira came from "about eight wagon-loads of this wine, which he distributed to the army generally, in very fair proportions." The slashing of carpets, tapestries, paintings and the like can be left to the reader's imagination; as can the guzzling.

The next day the hungover army removed Cheraw's railroad. In her arsenal they turned up numerous old cannon, including one whose brass plate said it was the first gun fired at Fort Sumter. The date was March 4. Before destroying the guns, they fired a salute in honor of Lincoln's second term. Observed Major Nichols, "His first inaugural was not celebrated in South Carolina."

In Cheraw they found a recent New York paper, from which Sherman learned that Jefferson Davis, yielding to popular outcry, had returned Joseph Johnston to command. Old Joe now led all Confederate forces in the Carolinas.

On the 5th, as the procession marched away, looters dawdled behind and burned much of the town. The next day saw the army well launched on the sixty-mile pull to Fayetteville, and over the state line. A soldier remarked that he doubted if South Carolina would ever wish to secede again.

* * *

North Carolina had joined the Confederacy late and reluctantly. To reward her, Sherman ordered wanton devastation halted. Far more houses were saved, and pillaging tapered off. Still, sixty thousand mouths demanded food, and crossing an imaginary line did not alter bummer nature. At this distance, it's permissible to wonder if the contrast between the invasions of the two Carolinas was quite as dramatic as memoirs written years after the war insist. Perhaps the soldier who had rampaged all the way from Kingston, Georgia, did not say to himself, "Ah, we have entered Unionist North Carolina. I shall hereafter eschew the theft of silver watches and chickens."

Certainly they did not spare the forests. They had reached the longleaf pines—turpentine country. This was the Smokey March with a vengeance. Every stream had its turpentine factory, and every one was burned. Barrels of tar, resin and turpentine flared up to join the flaring trees. Jet-black smoke soared above clearings; where trees grew thick, the smoke hung low, unable to break through the canopy. Fires roared hotter than any these well-traveled pyromaniacs had seen before. The army tortured itself—clogging its own air and turning creeks so hot they scalded men's and horses' legs.

Rumor had it that General Terry had taken Wilmington. On March 8, Sherman sent scouts to tell Terry of his approach, and to ask that Schofield meet him near Goldsboro. Cump reported that he had all the supplies he needed, but would be grateful for bread, sugar and coffee.

On March 11, they crossed the Cape Fear and settled into Fayetteville. The next day came the happy blast of a whistle. The scouts had gotten through, and Terry had sent up a small steamer. The boat brought word that Schofield was already pushing toward Goldsboro.

They sat in Fayetteville four days, doing routine military damage, but otherwise taking a breather. A larger steamer brought food and carried letters out. Cump told his wife, "South Carolina has had a visit from the West that will cure her of her pride and boasting." To Grant, he wrote of the Confederate change in command. Sherman had little respect for Wade Hampton. But Johnston was a soldier. He assured Grant that he would draw his army tighter, expecting trouble.

With battle likely, he grabbed the opportunity to disencumber himself of refugees. The journalists and a few of the wealthy went out on the steamer. Everyone else departed afoot. In old age, General Howard could still see that procession:

> . . . a column of whites and negroes, with all their indescribable belongings, were organized in a military way and sent down the river road. From the numerous men going out of the service, I furnished them abundant guards and wagons sufficient to carry the small children, the sick, and the extra food. It was a singular spectacle . . . There were 4,500, mostly negroes, from my wing alone.

Who knows how many departed? If Howard's memory was good, then nine thousand, assuming Slocum contributed about the same number. But Major Nichols described the headaches of marching "with twenty-five thousand useless, helpless human beings, devouring food, and clogging every step onward"; and Sherman spoke of twenty to thirty thousand. Once, at a review, Lincoln gazed at the thousands of young men pacing by and asked what would become of them when the war ended. The same question bears asking for that throng of homeless, newly emancipated blacks.

On March 15 began the final sixty-mile leg, toward the rendezvous with Schofield, set for March 20. Slocum's wing started a few miles left of Howard's, feinting toward Raleigh while Howard moved directly toward Goldsboro. Sherman switched over to Slocum's wing. The next day he found that he had made the right choice.

* * *

The size of Johnston's force during those last pitiful weeks of the war is hard to gauge; perhaps he led twenty-five thousand. It was an army top-heavy with generals, and its very existence bespoke the end of the struggle. Old corps leaders like A. P. Stewart now led one or two thousand troops. Hardee had arrived from Charleston; most of the generals Hood had failed to kill had made it from Alabama. Stephen Lee was on hand, but inactive—recovering from a Nashville campaign wound. Beauregard was nearby. Braxton Bragg, a few miles east, was doing what little he could to annoy Schofield. Johnston told his government that with the forces available he could do no more than pester Sherman.

With Schofield and at least one of Sherman's wings making for Goldsboro, Johnston's best hope was to isolate part of Sherman's army, before he and Schofield could unite. He was seeking the same advantage Sherman, back in Georgia, had denied him so often.

On sodden roads, Slocum failed to keep his wing compact. From the time they left Fayetteville his divisions scattered for miles. In Slocum's dilemma, Johnston saw his thin chance.

Near Averasboro Slocum's lead divisions bumped into Hardee, blocking the road into town. The little battle developed along predictable Sherman lines: The blue column hit Hardee straight on, in fierce but inconclusive action; but then Sherman pulled up another brigade from Slocum's drawn-out column and sent them circling to strike the Rebel right. It was a mediocre assault. Far from driving the gray line back, the flankers were themselves soon pinned by Rebel fire. There they remained until darkness stopped the fighting.

It also stopped the battle. Where the odds were so lopsided, a poor flanking move sufficed. Sherman had established his threat of pressing from two sides, and nothing prevented him from bringing up more brigades in the morning. The Rebels withdrew by night.

Hardee's losses were slightly higher and he had abandoned the field. Still, if "victory" had any meaning for the Confederates by then, Hardee could claim one at Averasboro. By halting Slocum awhile, he forced Sherman to slow down

Howard's wing, lest the army become even more seriously divided. As well, Sherman's losses included five hundred wounded. Had such a battle come earlier, it might have stymied an army with no hospitals behind it. And even with Goldsboro so close, Sherman's loaded ambulances made his situation precarious.

The next day, Slocum turned toward Goldsboro, doing his best to hurry closer to Howard. Sherman and Slocum tried to compress the left wing, while still keeping it moving. But Slocum's two corps remained badly elongated—still stretched out for miles, with big gaps between divisions.

By the morning of the 19th, Sherman convinced himself that the danger was past. As Slocum plodded toward Bentonville, Cump departed for Howard's wing—wishing to be there for the next day's meeting with Schofield. As he rode, Sherman could hear cannonading behind him. Then came a messenger: Slocum wanted him to know that they had tangled with Johnston's horsemen and were driving them back "nicely." Sherman was relieved.

Late that afternoon, he was napping in Howard's tent when Slocum's second messenger arrived. The battle had turned serious; he needed immediate aid. Half awake and half dressed, Sherman sent back orders to fight defensively. Then he and Howard rushed the troops onto the road for a night hike of nearly twenty miles. His date with Schofield would have to wait.

Slocum's lead divisions, of Davis's corps, had indeed driven the Rebel horse nicely that morning, because they were being lured into a trap. Suddenly Davis struck a Confederate line and was thrown back hard. His men could only grab what shelter they could and try to hold on.

Johnston's strategy called for fine timing. He aimed to hold Davis long enough for flankers to hit the isolated divisions on their left, but not long enough for Slocum to bring up re-inforcements. But because of bad maps and worse roads, the Confederate flank assault came late and struck weakly.

By then Davis had thrown up breastworks, and Slocum had finally realized that he had a battle on his hands. He sent the second message to Sherman, and hurried his men up the road. When the fighting ceased, after dark, Davis was still resisting and other blue divisions were coming up.

That night, Johnston stayed on the field, but pulled back into a strong defensive position. He stayed because he needed time to evacuate his wounded over a bridge behind him. But he ran a great risk—that bridge was his single line of retreat.

Early the next morning, Howard's lead brigades finished their long march and moved into place on Johnston's left. All morning Howard kept coming. Slocum too had kept bringing men up. By midday on the 20th, Johnston's army faced nearly all of Sherman's—Slocum on their right and Howard on their left; the odds were nearly three to one. The Rebel line reshaped into a "V"—one branch facing each Federal wing. For all the movement, there was little fighting that day.

On the 21st, Sherman began a steady, inexorable advance. Then suddenly a blue division under General Joseph Mower slammed a hole through the Confederate left. Before either side could react, Mower was pushing deep behind the gray lines, threatening to take the bridge at Mill Creek. Mower called for help. With re-inforcements, he could take and hold the bridge. Their escape cut off, Johnston's army would be squeezed into surrender or annihilation. Sherman hesitated, then ordered Mower to retreat. Johnston soon made his own withdrawal, and the battle was over.

Sherman's decision has been called a failure of moral courage. By moving boldly he might have gained one of the war's stellar triumphs. In later years he too had doubts—"I think I made a mistake there, and should rapidly have followed Mower's lead with the whole of the right wing."

But that was hindsight. At the time, his great desire was to bring his men safely into Goldsboro and end the march. With his ambulances full, he would not turn an unwanted fight into a major battle. And possibly there was more: On every front, Union superiority was now overwhelming. In March 1865, it took little imagination to view a Rebel soldier as a young man who would make a better farmer than a corpse. It seems possible that Sherman was less bloodthirsty at Bentonville than his armchair critics have been.

Confederate dead, wounded and missing came to 2,606; Union, to 1,645. Bentonville was Sherman's last battle.

On the 23rd, he finally reached Goldsboro and shook hands with John Schofield. That day and the next, both wings settled into camp, and the campaign was over. On the 25th, the first locomotive reached town; the indefatigable Colonel Wright had been toiling along behind Schofield, readying the track. Supplies began to flow in and the wounded were removed to hospitals.

"Many men are shoeless and few have a decent pair of breeches," wrote General Williams to his daughters. "Every man's face is as black as a Negro's with the smoke of the pitch-pine fires. A more begrimed and war-worn looking army I fancy was never seen." Williams' pants had left Savannah tan but were now "burnt-black." He thought his coat would make a fine costume for the "Beggar's Opera."

While the army washed itself off, Sherman looked back with satisfaction. He had covered 425 miles in fifty days, despite crossing five navigable rivers. His army had grabbed every important place in their path and forced the evacuation of Charleston. They "had utterly broken up all the railroads of South Carolina, and had consumed a vast amount of food and forage, essential to the enemy." All this in mid-winter, at good average speed.

The marchers' highest tribute would come after the war ended, from one whose opinion Sherman valued. "There had been no such army since the days of Julius Caesar," said Joseph Johnston.

As at Savannah and Atlanta, congratulations came pouring. Grant took the long view, praising Sherman for everything that he had achieved "since leaving the Tennessee River less than one year ago." Among the pile of letters and cables was an outburst from Stanton: "My earnest prayer is that Divine Providence may watch over you, shield and protect you from every danger, and crown you with its choicest blessings."

A cloud of smoke rises from burning resin left by retreating Confederates after their defeat at Bentonville, North Carolina, on March 21, 1865.

Chapter 12

Flapdaddle

*A*s soon as there was a train to carry him, Sherman headed for the coast, saying, "I'm going up to see Grant for five minutes and have it all chalked out for me and then come back and pitch in." A steamer took him to City Point, where he arrived on March 27th—his first visit to Virginia since 1861 and his first chance to shake hands with Grant in a year.

Lincoln was visiting too, staying on the steamer *River Queen*. Grant took Sherman calling that evening and again the next morning.

Sherman was struck by Lincoln's yearning for a swift peace. When the generals told him there would probably be one more huge battle, "Mr. Lincoln exclaimed more than once, that there had been blood enough shed, and asked us if another battle could not be avoided." Sherman asked how the president wished Rebel troops to be treated after the surrender. Lincoln said he wished to get them "back to their homes, and at work on their farms and in their shops."

The president assured them, as Sherman later remembered it, that:

> he was all ready for the civil reorganization of affairs at the South as soon as the war was over; and he distinctly authorized me to assure Governor Vance and the people of North

Carolina that, as soon as the rebel armies laid down their arms,
and resumed their civil pursuits, they would at once be guaranteed all their rights as citizens of a common country . . .

Sherman said goodbye at the gangway of the steamer: "I
never saw him again. Of all the men I ever met, he seemed to
possess more of the elements of greatness, combined with
goodness, than any other." By evening, he and Grant had
sketched the coming campaigns. Sherman hastened back to
Goldsboro.

To Ellen, he extolled Grant's friendship and dwelled on
Lincoln's kindness to him. Moreover, "Since Mr. Stanton
visited me at Savannah he too has become the warmest
possible friend." In Virginia, he had received another cable in
which the secretary heaped a second helping of God's beni-
sons on his russet head. Cump prided himself on the way he
had been handling politicians lately; he assured his father-in-
law, "You need not fear my committing a political mistake."

Grant told Sherman to take his time at Goldsboro, giving
his army a rest. To Lincoln, Grant spoke more frankly. If
possible, he wished to halt Sherman so that the Army of the
Potomac could whip Lee unaided; it would be better, he
thought, for the future of the country.

On April 5, Sherman's spruced-up force was leisurely
preparing to move out of Goldsboro, when the news reached
them—Grant had taken Petersburg and then Richmond. Both
Lee and the Rebel government were on the run, and Grant
was chasing Lee hard.

On April 10, Sherman's army—now eighty-nine thousand
strong, with Schofield sandwiched between the two old
wings—headed toward Smithfield, where Johnston was
camped. By the time they got there, Johnston had withdrawn
toward Raleigh, destroying the bridges behind him. On the
evening of April 11, while the army sat awaiting bridge
repair, messengers galloped into camp, shouting that Lee had
surrendered at Appomattox. The veterans went insane—

screaming, parading, turning somersaults, getting as drunk as they could manage. Someone shouted after one of the riders, "You're the sonofabitch we've been looking for all these four years!"

Two days later, Sherman took Raleigh, his cavalry entering town just as the last of the Rebels were departing. That night he moved into the abandoned executive mansion. Wrote the jubilant Hitchcock: "This is the fourth State Capitol he has walked into. It's a way he has."

Meanwhile, in Greensboro, North Carolina, the Confederate government had halted its flight south long enough to agree that General Johnston could negotiate peace with Sherman. On April 14, Sherman received Johnston's message. In the light of the Virginia news, Johnston hoped that further damage and bloodshed could be prevented in North Carolina. He asked Sherman to request that Grant halt all other Federal armies. Apparently, Johnston already had more than a truce in mind; despite a perfunctory reference to leaving the details to "civil authorities," he was playing peacemaker.

Sherman replied at once, naming the spot where he would halt and agreeing to ask Grant to stop other troops. He offered to make peace under the terms Grant had given Lee. In closing he said—"I really desire to save the people of North Carolina the damage they would sustain by the march of this army through the central or western parts of the State."

They arranged to meet between the lines on the morning of the 17th. Sherman was on his way, just entering the railroad car, when he heard that a cable was being decoded. He halted the train, read the message, and ordered the telegraph operator to keep silent. On the ride to Durham Station, he spoke little. From there, Sherman and his staff rode horseback about five miles before Johnston's party approached. The two commanders had never met. After handshakes and introductions, Sherman asked if there were a convenient private place. Johnston said he had passed a farmhouse. They rode there side by side, and together asked Mr. Bennett if they might borrow his parlor.

When they were alone, Sherman reached into his jacket pocket:

> I showed him the dispatch announcing Mr. Lincoln's assassination, and watched him closely. The perspiration came out in large drops on his forehead, and he did not attempt to conceal his distress. He denounced the act as a disgrace to the age, and hoped I did not charge it to the Confederate Government. I told him I could not believe that he or General Lee or the officers of the Confederate army, could possibly be privy to acts of assassination . . .

After discussing the murder and its implications, they got to work on peace terms. But Sherman was anxious to return to Raleigh, before word of the assassination reached his men. They cut it short, agreeing to meet at Bennett's farm again the next day.

Thanks to a night of hard work and soothing words by Sherman's officers, North Carolina escaped havoc. Raleigh should erect a monument to John Logan, commander of the occupying Fifteenth Corps, who spent the night shouting down mobs of arsonists, using all his influence over men who idolized him to prevent them from obliterating the city.

At their second meeting, Johnston won Sherman's permission for John C. Breckinridge to join them—arguing that they needed a skilled lawyer. Formerly vice president under Buchanan, Breckinridge now served the Confederacy as secretary of war. Sherman could not meet him in that capacity (without admitting that there was such a government), but agreed to including *General* Breckinridge.

No doubt Breckinridge influenced the document signed that day. But its major inspiration was the rapport between Johnston and Sherman. Old Joe sought a broad peace. Cump had always wanted a gentle one, and now he was touched deeply by what he believed to be Lincoln's wishes. Hence, the memo that Sherman wrote: a document by a political toddler that attempted more than any general had power to negotiate or that the canny Lincoln would have approved.

Sherman's memorandum not only halted fighting between Johnston and Sherman, but declared the end of war between all armies. There would be "a general amnesty, so far as the Executive of the United States can command." Rebel troops would be "conducted to their several State capitals, there to deposit their arms and public property in the State Arsenals." All Southerners were guaranteed full Constitutional rights. The document's close admitted that the signers were not "fully empowered by our respective principals to fulfill these terms" and pledged them to seek proper authority.

There was no mention at all of slavery. Later, Sherman explained that it would have been improper for him—merely a general—to appear to be ratifying the Emancipation Proclamation.

Guessing the scarcity of Confederate stores, Sherman had brought a bottle of whiskey. He offered a preliminary drink; then, as he wrestled with his phrasings, took a second swig without thinking to pass the bottle. As the Confederates rode back to camp, Johnston asked Breckinridge what he thought of Sherman. Breckinridge owned that Sherman was "a bright man and a man of great force"; but then began shouting: "General Johnston, General Sherman is a hog! Yes, sir, a hog! Did you see him take that drink by himself?" Johnston protested that Cump was a good fellow, only very absent-minded. But Breckinridge would not be dissuaded: "Ah, no Kentucky gentleman would ever have taken away that bottle. He knew we needed it."

Years later, when he heard the story, Sherman laughed ruefully: "I don't remember it, but if Joe Johnston told it, it's so. Those fellows hustled me that day; I was sorry for the drink I did give them."

* * *

In grudging fairness to Edwin Stanton, it is necessary to recall that Lincoln's murder, along with the attempted slaying of Andrew Johnson and William H. Seward, had driven many people to the edge. Stanton became virtual dictator for awhile, living on emotional turmoil and catnaps.

Sherman, known to hold improper views on race, was being mentioned as the next Democratic presidential candidate. There were also whispers that he meant to march on Washington and set himself up as dictator. In Raleigh, a group of his officers organized what would become a veterans' group, the Society of the Army of the Tennessee. Garbled accounts of their meetings may have reached a few Washington ears as further proof of a plot.

Stanton's motives, and what he really believed, can only be guessed. Broadly viewed, his clash with Sherman was but one example of a sad truth we were taught in high school American History: Lincoln's murder fueled and released a spirit of vindictiveness that Lincoln would have deplored.

Events moved swiftly.

Sherman wrote to Grant and Halleck, defending his peace and asking them to urge the new president's approval. His terms should be accepted without change, "for I have considered everything." To Ellen, he said: "I can hardly realize it, but I can see no slip. The terms are all on our side." Major Hitchcock left for Washington, carrying the memo and letters.

Privately, several of Sherman's generals decided that his memo would receive no kindly reception.

On the evening of April 21st, after Hitchcock made his delivery, Stanton called a Cabinet meeting. Johnson and the entire Cabinet rejected the provisions. Led by Stanton, several secretaries denounced Sherman. Grant was ordered to cable Sherman to end the truce; later that evening, Stanton (or perhaps Johnson) changed the order: Grant would go to Carolina and deliver the message personally—presumably, so that he could take charge if necessary. Grant left for Raleigh.

The next day, Halleck (temporarily moved to Richmond) wired Stanton that Jefferson Davis was said to be fleeing with millions in gold—to be used, perhaps, for making terms with Sherman. Halleck's cable ended, "Would it not be well to put Sherman and all other commanding generals on their guard in this respect?"

Stanton issued a release to the New York press, sharply criticizing Sherman's peace terms. He damned Sherman for ignoring a memo from Lincoln that told generals to shun political matters when making peace—a memo Sherman had never seen. Stanton also gave out Halleck's cable; but he deleted the final sentence, thus making it seem Halleck mistrusted Sherman.

Soon, Stanton also let it be known that Sherman had moved troops out of Jefferson Davis's path to ease his escape.

En route to Carolina, Grant wired Halleck that the truce might end. Halleck notified several prominent generals to "disregard any truce or orders from Sherman."

Early on April 23, Grant arrived quietly at Sherman's headquarters. (Said Slocum, "All is well. Grant is here. He has come to save his friend Sherman from himself.") Grant told Cump that his peace had been rejected, but did not mention the personal attacks on him. Sherman agreed to offer Johnston the same terms Grant had given Lee.

The next day Grant cabled Stanton, saying that Sherman had graciously accepted the rejection. He explained that Sherman had acted on what he thought were Lincoln's wishes.

To the Cabinet, Stanton read an abridged version of Grant's cable, deleting his defense of Cump and making it seem that Grant had gone to Raleigh to hold Sherman under control. There was Cabinet talk of Sherman's treason, and fear that he might arrest Grant.

Still ignorant of what was happening, Sherman wrote to

Stanton: "I admit my folly in embracing in a military convention any civic matters but unfortunately such is the nature of
our situation that they seem inextricably united."

On the 26th, Sherman and Johnston signed a new paper,
ending their war. Keeping his presence as quiet as possible,
Grant declined to attend the ceremony. Johnston may not
even have known that Grant was in Raleigh. After approving
the new peace terms, Grant departed. His tactful handling of
Sherman and his steady effort to salvage what he could of
Sherman's authority were high points of their friendship.

In the next few days, Sherman continued to feed Southern
soldiers, as he had been doing since the truce. He urged his
army to befriend their former opponents, and allowed Southern men to take farm animals home.

Then New York papers reached Raleigh carrying the stories Stanton had inspired. Pacing a room full of generals,
Sherman spoke (said General Carl Schurz) "with a furious
invective which made us all stare. He lashed Stanton as a
mean, scheming, vindictive politician who made it his business to rob military men of their credit earned by exposing
their lives." Cump tossed in a few predictable reflections on
that "engine of vilification," the American press.

He wrote Grant an angry rebuttal and demanded that it be
published. In other letters, he vowed to be revenged on
Stanton. That night, after the news reached the army, Sherman's men indulged themselves for the last time in arson.
Amid howls, boos and hisses, big stacks of New York papers
went up in smoke.

Yet even before that inflammatory matter had reached
Carolina, the worst of the outcry against Sherman had begun
to pass. Around the country, editors who had at first followed
the lead of New York papers began to have second thoughts.
Radical Republican editors continued to crucify Sherman,
dealing heavily in words like "traitor," "treasonable" and
"betrayal," and voicing the inevitable suggestion that the
general had reverted to insanity. But other papers, both

Democratic and Republican, were soon defending him, apologizing for him, or demanding that he be given a fair hearing. That most prominent of journalists, Horace Greeley of the *New York Tribune*, hooted at the idea that Sherman yearned to be a dictator. His peace terms, declared Greeley, had been "unwise but not treasonable." And the notion that General Sherman was in cahoots with Jeff Davis? All that, said Greeley, was "flapdaddle."

Late in April, plans were shaping up for a Washington gala. Grant would hold a "Grand Review" of his two largest armies—Meade's and Sherman's—before the troops went home.

Once he had issued his orders for the march north, Sherman sailed to Savannah for a couple of days, among other reasons, to arrange a continued supply of provisions to the city. En route back north to catch up with his army, he had reached Hilton Head when he saw his next batch of newspapers. Besides learning that in some circles he was still a traitor, he read for the first time of Halleck's cables, telling George Thomas and others to ignore orders from Sherman.

A storm that halted his boat along the Carolina coast may have kept him in the army. By chance, the new chief justice, Salmon Chase, had sought haven in the same port. Sherman had drafted a sulfuric proclamation to his armies regarding the whole mess. If issued, it might have forced his resignation. But he showed Chase his draft and, during the many hours they passed together, Chase got him calmed down. Sherman destroyed his draft.

For the next few weeks, through the Grand Review and beyond, Cump both suffered and nourished his griefs. He acted like a child who has been smacked unfairly—genuinely hurt, and bent on making the most of it.

On May 8, he docked at Fortress Monroe. Awaiting him was an invitation from Halleck to share his headquarters. Sherman answered, "I cannot have any friendly intercourse with you." He preferred that they not meet.

Halleck had forbidden the western troops to enter Richmond. Some troops barged into town anyway, daring anyone to stop them. They greeted Halleck's city guards—men from the Army of the Potomac—with insults and rocks. Others in Sherman's ranks suggested that they ought to shoot their way into Richmond—it wouldn't take *them* four years. Hoping to ease things, Halleck invited the Fourteenth Corps to enter the city and be reviewed. Sherman rescinded the order. His men would march only by his command or Grant's. And when they did pass through Richmond, he begged Halleck "to keep slightly perdu"—so enraged was the army over Halleck's "insult to a brother officer."

Thus ended a friendship going back to West Point days. When Sherman's army marched through town, some of the men stopped by Halleck's headquarters, where they stood around making choice remarks on the spiffy sentries. As a guard paced by, a Wisconsin soldier spat tobacco on his well-shined shoes.

Sherman was doing plenty of his own spitting. To Logan, he called the army's exclusion from Richmond "part of a grand game to insult us—who had marched 1,000 miles through a hostile country in mid-winter to help them." He told Ellen that "Washington is as corrupt as Hell. . . . I will avoid it as a pest house." But he assured her, "I am not dead yet, not by a long sight."

Sherman saw to it that his letter to a friend hit the papers about when his army reached camp outside Washington, on May 17:

> It is amusing to observe how brave and firm some men become when all danger is past. I have noticed on fields of battle brave men never insult the captured or mutilate the dead; but cowards and laggards always do. I cannot recall the act, but Shakespeare records how poor Falstaff, the prince of cowards and wits, rising from a [pretended] death, stabbed again the dead Percy, and carried the carcase aloft in triumph, to prove his

valor. So now, when the rebellion in our land is dead, many Falstaffs appear to brandish the evidence of their valor, and seek to win applause, and to appropriate honors for deeds that were never done. . . .

He hardly cared if readers took Falstaff to be radical congressmen or the desk-bound Halleck.

The parades were slated for the 23rd and 24th. Until then, eastern and western troops were kept apart. Few of Sherman's men crossed the Potomac until the day they were reviewed. Afterward, when they did come to town, things got so squally that Grant was obliged to say a word to Sherman. General Augur, in charge of keeping the local peace, was in a dither:

> He has purposely avoided arresting them for fear of leading to violence and the charge that it is a hostility on the part of the Secretary to them and yourself. Yesterday many of the officers were at Willard's, drinking and discussing violently the conduct of Mr. Stanton, and occasionally would jump on the counter and give three groans for Mr. Stanton, then get down and take another drink.

In the end, Sherman's army were shipped West and mustered out of service somewhat ahead of schedule.

But that was later. During the week before the Grand Review, the great task was to placate Sherman. Andrew Johnson and his Cabinet (with one notable exception) had him to Washington and fussed over him. The president wanted Sherman to know how badly he himself had been misled by news stories. John Sherman, though frank in telling Cump that his peace terms had been too generous, stood by him and tried to dampen his rage against Stanton. The Ewing clan, in town for the festivities, took their turn at unruffling him. Ellen came for the review, bringing nine-year-old Tommy, but arrived too late to join the pacifiers.

Coddled to his heart's content, Sherman gradually began to snarl less and smile more—to enjoy the party; but he rebuffed all attempts at a reconciliation with Stanton.

* * *

There has never been anything like the Grand Review. Only the close of a civil war leaves whole armies at home, on hand for a national thank-you and farewell. Around 150,000 men passed under Grant's eyes—Meade's army the first day and Sherman's the second. Each procession began at nine, and lasted far into the afternoon. Spectators came from all over the North. Families rejoicing that their sons had lived, statesmen, the diplomatic corps, tens of thousands who just wanted to be there. Washington was decked in flags, floral arches, banners and bunting, all of it intermingled with black decorations that still marked Lincoln's death. Regimental colorbearers would march with mourning ribbons trailing from their flagstaffs.

On Meade's triumphal day, Sherman stood on the big reviewing stand erected in front of the White House, along with Grant, Johnson and the Cabinet. Meade led his first regiments past, then mounted to the stand to be welcomed. As they stood together, Sherman told him, "I'm afraid my poor tatterdemalion corps will make a poor appearance tomorrow when contrasted with yours." Meade assured him that the public would understand.

Sherman noted that many Potomac soldiers, as they passed the White House, turned to gawk at the statesmen and generals. He was also not very taken with two big civilian bands. All those opera tunes made for pleasant listening, but were poor stuff to march by. Tomorrow, he decided, only his regimental bands would play. His competitive juices began to flow.

Back in Alexandria that evening, the word went out. The men were to do their best marching; they were to keep proper intervals and must keep their eyes to the front. All were to stay in line until they returned to camp—they would get their chance to see Washington later.

Sherman's best decision was to offer the crowd some notion of his army as they really were. Apart from the fancy marching, he discouraged elegance. It was already too late to show off their true ragged splendor. At Goldsboro had come new boots, barbers and fresh uniforms. And in Washington, proud officers had bought their men white gloves or other niceties for the parade. But, to Sherman's satisfaction, thousands still wore battered uniforms, stained with Carolina mud; and many still went barefoot.

He bustled around all evening, getting them into line and bedded down—much of the army still in Virginia, the lead brigades camped in Washington. He also arranged for a few float-like displays, such as pontoons cut open to show how they worked. His only harsh words went to someone who asked if Sherman could provide tomorrow's spectators with a program showing the order of march—"There's no damned printing press with this army!"

On the fine morning of May 24, Sherman was in his place early. To salve feelings, he had asked Howard to ride beside him, so that Logan could lead the Army of the Tennessee. Someone draped huge garlands on their horses' necks. Yesterday, the crowd had run out of flowers; but today they came better prepared. Every regiment would be pelted with blossoms.

The crowd was bigger than the seventy-five thousand who had greeted Meade. To Washington, the Army of the Potomac were old friends. Ever since the ancient days of McDowell, their brigades had been marching through town. But this was the army that went to the sea!

The signal gun boomed and off they rode, down under arches that welcomed the Western Heroes and spelled their battlefields in flowers. The crowd started roaring—anything but jaded after yesterday's orgy.

Sherman's great concern was that his men not disgrace

themselves by sloppy marching. Yet he hesitated to look back after making such an issue of eyes to the front. As he came up the rise by the Treasury, he could bear it no longer, and turned in his saddle—"The sight was simply magnificent. The column was compact, and the glittering muskets looked like a solid mass of steel, moving with the regularity of a pendulum." He would remember it as the happiest moment of his life.

Near Lafayette Square, someone told him to look up. At a window sat William Seward, still wrapped in bandages. Sherman rode over and tipped his hat, getting a feeble wave in return.

Then it was on past the White House, with the whole reviewing stand on its feet, and the crowd screaming. Sherman and Howard drew their swords and rode by saluting, Howard with his sword in his left hand and the reins wedged under the stump of his right arm. They pulled out of the line of march, dismounted, and made their way to the front of the reviewing stand. Just then, there was no more prominent spot on earth.

Sherman embraced Ellen, and started down the line. A hug for Tommy, and another for Thomas Ewing. A firm handshake for President Johnson. A warmer one for Grant. Next came Edwin M. Stanton. The secretary held out his hand, then began to withdraw it as he saw what was going to happen. Ignoring the hand, Sherman glared at him with contempt. A few slow, blistering seconds passed. Then he moved on.

Sherman stayed in his place for the whole six and a half hours, savoring his revenge and enjoying his little triumph over Meade. His men marched better than the Easterners. Their steps boomed down in unison, and they gazed forward so rigidly that to some onlookers it seemed eerie—they marched as if there were no audience. Their strides were longer than the Eastern pace, and they moved with more spring. Said an onlooker, "They march like the lords of the world!" One private stole a sideways glance as he marched and saw in his friends' eyes "*a glory look.*"

To a reporter, their faces seemed more intelligent, self-reliant and determined than Potomac faces. They were "hardier, knottier, weirder." To Carl Schurz's eye, their bodies were all skin, bone and muscle.

In front of the brigades came the black pioneers, bearing their picks and shovels like muskets. Behind came a sampling of refugees. Mother Bickerdyke was there, riding properly side-saddle. They drove along their cows, goats and pigs. In the wagons came the dogs, gamecocks, raccoons. Behind many regiments rolled their ambulances, the stretchers caked and stained with dried blood.

Sherman could usually glance at a regiment and tell Ellen and Tommy whether that bunch had been to Meridian, or walked up to Knoxville and back to watch Burnside eat his turkey. Most of the regiments had covered a thousand miles in the last year, and he saw plenty who had done fifteen hundred.

Some were tricked out with bright new regimental flags. But he noticed which flags drew the BIG cheers. Some were only rags now. The crowds had to strain to read the muddy letters. Ezra Church . . . Chattanooga . . . Shiloh . . . Bentonville . . . Atlanta.

Westerners of Sherman's army triumphantly parade down Pennsylvania Avenue during the Grand Review. Thousands came to watch the spectacle, one of whom said "They march like lords of the world!"

Epilogue

The Cosmopolitan

Your "Memoirs" are rich in incident, anecdote, fact, history. . . . its interest is unflagging and absorbing; it is a model narrative and will last as long as the language lasts. If I had read my own books half as many times as I have read those "Memoirs," I should be a wiser and better man than I am.

                     —Mark Twain to Sherman

*A*fter the Grand Review, Ellen sent Mrs. Stanton a bouquet and paid a conciliatory call. Her apology seems emblematic of Sherman's later army career. Like it or not, he would have to live with Washington. He and Stanton *had* to patch things up, for Stanton remained his boss.

We often view the Civil War in isolation, as if it were some heroic pageant whose actors took their bows and vanished backstage when the curtain fell. But the war—the great divide in our history—lasted only four years. Those who leapt the chasm had to get on with their lives.

Most Civil War scholarship would prefer otherwise. A book may admit parenthetically that Generals Grant, Hayes and Garfield, Colonel Benjamin Harrison and Private William McKinley did certain later things; Custer met with problems; Lew Wallace wrote a book. But beyond that, it's as if two million men were laid away in mothballs one spring morning at Appomattox Court House.

In my research, I struck a few passing references to one of Sherman's artillery officers. Despite an arm lost at Shiloh, he served with honor in the Vicksburg, Meridian, Atlanta and Nashville campaigns. But no military scholar seemed aware (or thought it worth mentioning) that Major John Wesley Powell went on to explore Grand Canyon. We pay a steep price for specialization.

No generation ever knew such changes as the Civil War veterans who reached old age:

—O.O. Howard lived till 1909. After heading the Freedman's Bureau and founding the university that bears his name, he served many years on the frontier. (Said Chief Joseph of the Nez Perce, "Tell General Howard that I shall fight no more forever.") Howard wrote numerous adult and children's books, many of them on Indians.

—Joe Wheeler, twenty-nine at the surrender, climaxed his career in the next war, leading a cavalry division at San Juan Hill. They made him a brigadier for that, in a blue uniform. It's said that during one action in Cuba, Fighting Joe stood up in his stirrups and shouted, "We've got those damn Yankees on the run now!" The old Rebel horseman died in 1906, in Brooklyn.

—Sherman's typical private was twenty-five or younger at the surrender. He would be only thirty-six when the telephone came, only sixty-three when the Wrights flew at Kittyhawk. If he reached eighty, he would see another armistice, and the start of the Roaring 20s.

Sherman was forty-five at Bennett's Farm. He lived to be seventy-one. For four years, he commanded on the western plains, with St. Louis as his headquarters. When Grant became president, in 1869, Sherman replaced him as head of the army, was promoted to full general, and moved to Washington. He led the army until 1883, then turned the job over to General Sheridan and retired to St. Louis. In 1886, he moved to New York, where he remained until his death on February 14, 1891.

* * *

Sherman savored his frontier command, despite having to struggle with the chronic woes of a tiny, under-funded army. As had been true in his dealings with blacks, his treatment of Indians was often kindlier than his theoretical view that the sooner a doomed people vanished, the better. He worked hard on peace commissions. There are photographs of him stolidly expounding federal policy to equally stolid Sioux and Arapahoe chiefs.

His dealings with the Navajo reveal Cump at his best. In 1864, the tribe had been forcibly moved from today's northern Arizona to a reservation on the Pecos called Bosque Redondo—scorching hot, and hundreds of miles from their homeland. For the Navajo, "the Long Walk" remains a memory of horror. In 1868, Sherman listened to tribal grievances, saw their wretched conditions, and agreed that the Navajo should go home. Whatever he thought of the attempt to turn nomads into farmers, he saw that the government had done little to *make* them farmers. To Ellen, he suggested that it might be useful to impeach Congress. Ignoring protests from New Mexicans who were profiting from the reservation, he pleaded the Navajos' case to Washington.

His western interlude was the only time in Sherman's post-war career when his profession and his pleasures overlapped. To travel the West—learning, investigating, seeing—was the cream of his job.

He loved to roam the open country, whether plains, mountains or the Southwestern deserts. By preference, he traveled with the smallest possible escort; between forts and settlements, he enjoyed camping out or dropping by to spend the night at isolated ranches. In a fine book on Sherman and the frontier army, Robert Athearn describes a typical moment: The general writhing through a dressy reception in Denver, then casting off his boiled shirt, and hurrying away to dusty Fort Garland, where he could slouch around in old clothes, sharing time and a bottle with Kit Carson.

When his duties called him to Washington (and particularly in 1868 during the maelstrom of Andrew Johnson's impeachment), he itched for the moment when he could hop a train, put all that foulness behind him, and head back to his canyons and Comanches.

Thrilled to see the transcontinental railroad become a reality, he acted as a doting godfather to the Union Pacific (whose first engine was named the "Major General Sherman"). The chief construction engineer was a close friend, the same Grenville Dodge whose men had returned in time to block Hardee the day McPherson was slain. Dodge's invitations to keep an eye on the road's progress brought Sherman often to the tracks. His inspection rides could be traced by the waved hats and shouts of work crews—men who called out the names of their old regiments and asked Uncle Billy how he liked seeing them *build* a railroad.

He knew that the tracks stretching so fast toward Promontory Point would mean the end of the open West; but what he knew he could never make himself believe. In later years, he came back to the West whenever he could find an excuse, only to be stunned each time by the growth of new towns. In 1878, Sherman said that the plains and Far West had changed more in a decade than any other spot on earth in half a century. Later, he voiced and embodied the paradox inseparable from his century's idea of Progress: He spoke proudly of what his frontier army had done to help make the West safe and modern; and yet, as he roamed Arizona or Idaho in the sleek new Pullmans, his soul yearned for the trail and wagon days.

When Grant's election made Cump's move to Washington unavoidable, he spoke of it as "my banishment."

* * *

When Sherman took command of the United States Army, his duties and his delights parted company.

Grant permitted the secretary of war—first John Rawlins and then W. W. Belknap—to deal directly with officers in the field, bypassing army headquarters. Sherman complained to the president, got nowhere, and finally gave up. His friendship with Grant was strained, and the breach never wholly mended. For most of Grant's two terms, Sherman deemed his own job an empty title, a farce.

In 1874 came one of those gestures that was pure Sherman. He relocated army headquarters out to St. Louis. Since he had no work in Washington, why should he stay? Besides, St. Louis was closer to the Indian wars, living was cheaper, and he liked it there. Two years later, Alphonso Taft became secretary of war and announced that army business would henceforth go through the commanding general's office. With that settled, Sherman brought the army back to Washington.

But no move could solve the other headache of his fourteen years as commander—the army's poverty. Following the surrender, the military and its budget shrank to ante-bellum size, despite the burdens of guarding the former Confederacy and the growing West. Had Sherman been politically deft, his troops would have fared much better; but even a prince of diplomats would have had to fight Congress for every dime of appropriation.

Here, a wartime decision came back to plague him. John Logan returned to Congress, rose to the Senate in 1871, and remained a leading senator for most of his life. Logan had never forgiven Sherman for choosing Howard. If Sherman thought Satan's middle name was Washington, Logan knew it was West Point. He made a fetish of "The Volunteer Soldier," even using the phrase to title his memoirs. In 1870, Logan sponsored a bill that cut the pygmy army by a third, plus taking a bite out of Sherman's salary. For decades, frontier soldiers suffered for a choice made on a hot July day in Georgia before many of them were born.

Such difficulties could only strengthen Sherman's loathing for politics. "Our country is bound to be governed by its meanest people and soon no honorable man will be tolerated," he confided to the distinguished senator who happened to be his brother.

Sherman's abhorrence of the presidency never wavered. Every four years he was mentioned, and each time he found fresh ways to say no. The Sherman boom thundered loudest in 1884, the year after he retired. That summer James G. Blaine told him that he could not honorably decline a nomination that came unsought. Sherman replied that he certainly could. Whatever he owed the nation he had paid in the war. To John's similar plea he answered, "I would not for a million of dollars subject myself and family to the ordeal of a political canvass and afterwards to four years' service in the White House." This was the same summer when word came from the convention that Sherman was the only candidate acceptable to all. According to his son Tom, Cump neither removed his cigar nor changed his expression while he scribbled his reply: "I will not accept if nominated and will not serve if elected."

James G. Blaine, John Sherman . . . Now and again he smiled to think of those political fellows salivating over the plum he kept thrusting off his plate.

* * *

The sense of fulfillment that Sherman's work denied him was hardly to be found on the home front. His marriage became badly strained in the 1870s. When Cump entered a mixed social gathering, the lady on his arm was usually one of his four daughters, or perhaps a niece. Ellen had little energy and less interest to waste on his pastimes; she almost never traveled with him. Every year, her church work seemed to absorb more of her.

Sherman cannot have been easy to live with; but then it was no joy to dwell with a wife who never saw her husband as a grownup, and whose gaze seemed fixed on a Better World. In pictures of their later years, Sherman looks markedly younger. Though his hair and beard turned white early, his face shed its wartime wrinkles. He stayed thin, elastic, tough, while Ellen grew more ethereal, fragile-looking.

For about a year they separated, partly because she found his social whirl intolerable. But what mainly drove her out of the house was Sherman's fury over his oldest son's decision to become a priest. Apart from Willy's death, nothing in his life hurt Cump so grievously. He broke off relations with Tom, railing against the church that had lured his boy to throw away his life. In time, they became cautious friends again, but Cump would never fathom Tom's decision. He made a point of being far away when Father Sherman was ordained.

Cump and Ellen apparently grew somewhat closer, more indulgent of each other's peculiarities, in their last years; but it was never an enviable marriage. When she died in 1888, he grieved intensely, withdrew into himself for awhile, then gradually resumed his activities.

* * *

With too little work to occupy him, and scant reason to stay home, Cump became one of the great gadabouts of his era. (Lloyd Lewis remarked that Sherman's post-war life was "one long chicken dinner.") Throughout the country, he attended a staggering array of annual reunions and veterans' galas, plus scores of other banquets and functions. The only office he ever desired was the presidency of the Society of the Army of the Tennessee, which he held from 1869 until his death; but that did not hinder him from gathering with the Army of the Ohio, the Army of the Cumberland, the Army of the Potomac, and on and on.

Sherman became a superb after-dinner speaker—one of

those men who could provide a few words on any occasion. (It was during an impromptu talk at a G.A.R. rally that he said "War is all hell"). As a toastmaster, he came to be ranked among the finest in the land, along with Chauncey Depew and Mark Twain. Audiences loved his terse idiom and no-nonsense manner as antidotes to flowery, long-winded oratory. Sherman never hesitated to cut in with, "Thank you, Colonel, we have all heard enough," or to tell an orchestra leader that a few bars between toasts would suffice.

To keep his calendar full, there was also the opera, the concert hall and, especially, the theater. In his Washington and St. Louis days, he seldom missed a play. In New York, he rented boxes in several theaters so that he could come and go at whim, catching an act here and there. He loved to invite friends to theater parties, and to hover around backstage. Together with Mark Twain and others, he helped Edwin Booth found the Players' Club—the first social club to admit actors as gentlemen.

Cump's social whirl seemed to nourish his intellectual vitality. Easy as it is to grin at all those reunions, a quarter century of roaming the nation did its share to keep the mind of an observant man flexible and growing. If anything, Sherman's sweeping vision grew still more sweeping as the years passed. He remained the opposite of provincial.

In 1875, he turned author. *Memoirs of General W. T. Sherman* was one of the year's top sellers. As always, his style was tough, muscular and often funny. The *Memoirs'* biggest defect was too much documentation and petty detail; he was wont to include minor military orders verbatim, or to name the captains of ships he had taken in the 1850s. Yet that too was Sherman—fascinated with facts and specifics, and eager to share.

Outspoken as ever, he scorned the maudlin sentimentality about the Old South that was becoming fashionable. He still called secession treason, and still knew that in 1861 the South had been a pack of befuddled idiots. He included much that a tactful man would have suppressed, such as a wartime letter stating that the South would never become civilized until all her cavaliers were put to honest work or killed.

Though his book stirred a fuss and wounded feelings (Sooy Smith's, for instance), Cump stood pat in his second, expanded edition. A new preface reminded the reader that "no three honest witnesses of a simple brawl can agree on all the details." This book voiced *his* opinions. Those who saw differently could write their own.

* * *

Lloyd Lewis suggested that "Neither self-satisfaction, patience, nor repose" ever came to Sherman. It's a shrewd perception; but is the self-satisfaction part criticism or praise?

Sherman never lacked things to holler about. But there are grouches and grouches. What makes many bristly people so unbearable *is* their self-satisfaction—that smug certitude that the world has gone to hell because we fools won't see things their way.

Sherman never soured, never shrank into a mere curmudgeon, never ossified.

He had fought a war against localism—choosing the side that rejected the right of any part to hold itself superior to the nation. At the end of the war, when he dismissed his armies, his proclamation of thanks reminded the men that America was so large, so diverse, "that every man may find a home and occupation suited to his taste."

Before he retired, his last undertaking was to treat himself to a three-month railroad tour around the West. He hungered to see it all one more time.

Despite his ties to St. Louis and his feeling for the Mississippi Valley, he found three years of retirement there enough. St. Louis was too poky for him. He needed to be where things were bubbling, and in the 1880s that meant New York.

Sherman was sixty-seven when he wrote his piece arguing that Grant was Lee's superior because Grant's sense of war was continental. The next year came his sweeping article on the grand strategy of the last year of the war.

That year, too, he published an essay called "Old Shady with a Moral"—a defense of the rights of blacks to vote. Sherman didn't care for what was happening to blacks in the South, and he'd been doing some thinking. Approaching seventy, he was less of a racist than he had been at forty.

* * *

For his seventieth birthday, February 8, 1890, congratulations poured in, and there were big public celebrations. On the day itself, Sherman hosted a small dinner. Senator Sherman and Tom Ewing, Jr., came. John Schofield was there, now leading the army after Sheridan's unexpected death. (Sherman had lately complained that too damn much of his time went to attending his friends' funerals. He had decided to go to no more, except his own.)

Howard sat on his right and Slocum on his left, in token of their places on the march. Though Cump had grown more frail since Ellen's death, and had lately been plagued by his asthma, he seemed particularly vigorous that day. Stirred by his energy and the occasion, Howard burst out with, "Sherman will never die!" Sherman said he was afraid he couldn't agree.

That summer, speaking to a veterans' group in Portland, Maine, he made comparisons with Portland, Oregon, remarking that he had never seen anything lovelier than Mount Hood. He told his audience they should be proud to have such a growing, prosperous namesake, three thousand miles away.

That evening, he heard that his comparisons had ruffled local sensibilities. So the next day he tried again—not apologizing much, but dwelling once more on national diversity: America's glory, he said, was that she could span two such cities and everything between—"Whether Portland, Oregon, or Portland, Maine, is the more beautiful city makes no difference, they both belong to us."

He put it more eloquently in a letter to a Southern journalist whose narrowness had distressed him:

> ... every American should be proud of his whole country rather than a part.
> How much more sublime the thought that you live at the root of a tree whose branches reach the beautiful fields of Western New York and the majestic cañons of the Yellowstone, and that with every draught of water you take the outflow of the pure lakes of Minnesota and the drippings of the dews of the Allegheny and the Rocky Mountains.

* * *

Sherman's funeral took place in New York, on February 19, 1891. Afterward, the body was taken to St. Louis, and placed in the tomb he shares with Ellen and Willy.

Generals Howard, Slocum and Dodge handled the funeral arrangements. President Harrison, ex-President Cleveland, and a host of dignitaries rode in the procession.

The day was cold and raw. An honorary pallbearer, eighty-four years old, stood bareheaded in the rain as the coffin moved by. Said a bystander, "General, please put on your hat; you might get sick."

The old gentleman turned—"If I were in his place and he were standing here in mine, he would not put on his hat."

The general went home with a cold that developed into pneumonia. Ten days after Sherman, Joe Johnston was dead.

Sherman as a full general in 1876. After Grant was elected president in 1869, Sherman took his place as general in chief of the army. When he retired, he turned down offers to run for the presidency.

Suggested Reading

The Civil War will consume as much of your life as you care to sacrifice. I know people who have toured a battlefield and call themselves "real Civil War nuts." I also know a man who has spent more years sleuthing one obscure Georgia battle than I have squandered on this book. There are pedants who dismiss Shelby Foote's three thousand pages as a superficial overview.

Assuming that your fascination with the war is controllable, a fine one-volume history is James M. McPherson's *Battle Cry of Freedom* (Oxford, 1988). Also good is the beautiful volume prepared to accompany the PBS Civil War series, Geoffrey C. Ward, *The Civil War: An Illustrated History* (Knopf, 1990).

For more detail, Shelby Foote's *The Civil War: A Narrative* (Random House, 1974, 3 vols.) is unsurpassed for style, grace and good sense.

There is no outstanding modern life of Sherman. New biographies keep being promised, but the best now available is an antique, Lloyd Lewis, *Sherman: Fighting Prophet* (Harcourt, Brace, 1931). More satisfactory on his personal life and marriage is James M. Merrill's *William Tecumseh Sherman* (Rand McNally, 1971), but Merrill is sketchy on military topics. When he or she arrives, the ideal biographer will be as enthralled with the West and with the late-Victorian social milieu as with the war. As yet, no biography is very good on Sherman's post-war decades.

Among campaign studies, *War So Terrible: Sherman and Atlanta* by James L. McDonough and James P. Jones (Norton, 1987), is first rate. Though sometimes annoying in its anti-Sherman bias, *Sherman's March*, by Burke Davis (Vintage paperback, 1988) is very readable on the Georgia and Carolina marches. I also greatly admire Joseph T. Glatthaar's *The March to the Sea and Beyond: Sherman's Troops in the Savannah and Carolinas Campaigns* (New York University, 1985). Glatthaar describes the men who did the marching, and quotes their words generously.

That brings us to the only real experts: Those who lived the war. The least polished letter collection or diary has an immediacy that no modern study can match. Such books began appearing shortly after the war, and they have been coming out ever since. The most famous is the diary of a South Carolina aristocrat, *Mary Chesnut's Civil War* (Yale, 1981). I have relied most on *Three Years in the Army of the Cumberland: The Letters and Diary of Major James A. Connolly* (Indiana, 1959), and on *Marching with Sherman: Passages from the Letters and Campaign Diaries of Henry Hitchcock* (Yale, 1927). But there are hundreds of such books, and even small libraries will offer a few—the words of the men and women, South and North, who were there.

The Library of America has issued both *Personal Memoirs of U. S. Grant* and *Memoirs of General W. T. Sherman*. Available separately or as a set, these superbly edited books are the best starting point for anyone who wishes to know their authors.

Index